OTHER NOVELS BY
DONNA JO NAPOLI

Stones in Water

Fire in the Hills

The Prince of the Pond

Jimmie, the Pickpocket of the Palace

Gracie, the Pixie of the Puddle

Soccer Shock

Shark Shock

Shelly Shock

The Magic Circle

The Bravest Thing

On Guard!

Changing Tunes

Spinners

Three Days

Zel

When the Water Closes Over My Head

The Smile

DONNA JO NAPOLI

The Smile

DUTTON CHILDREN'S BOOKS

DUTTON CHILDREN'S BOOKS
A division of Penguin Young Readers Group

Published by the Penguin Group
Penguin Group (USA) Inc., 375 Hudson Street, New York, New York 10014, U.S.A. |
Penguin Group (Canada), 90 Eglinton Avenue East, Suite 700, Toronto, Ontario, Canada M4P
2Y3 (a division of Pearson Penguin Canada Inc.) | Penguin Books Ltd, 80 Strand, London
WC2R 0RL, England | Penguin Ireland, 25 St Stephen's Green, Dublin 2, Ireland (a division of
Penguin Books Ltd) | Penguin Group (Australia), 250 Camberwell Road, Camberwell, Victoria
3124, Australia (a division of Pearson Australia Group Pty Ltd) | Penguin Books India Pvt Ltd,
11 Community Centre, Panchsheel Park, New Delhi - 110 017, India | Penguin Group (NZ),
67 Apollo Drive, Rosedale, North Shore 0632, New Zealand (a division of Pearson New Zealand
Ltd) | Penguin Books (South Africa) (Pty) Ltd, 24 Sturdee Avenue, Rosebank, Johannesburg
2196, South Africa | Penguin Books Ltd, Registered Offices: 80 Strand, London WC2R 0RL,
England

CIP Data is available.

Published in the United States by Dutton Children's Books,
a member of Penguin Young Readers Group
345 Hudson Street, New York, New York 10014
www.penguin.com/youngreaders

Designed by IRENE VANDERVOORT
Printed in the USA
First Edition
10 9 8 7 6 5 4 3 2 1
ISBN 978-0-525-47999-4

Thanks to Barry, Eva, and Robert Furrow, to Libby Crissey,
Aimee Friedman, Annette and Jack Hoeksema, Samara Leist,
Anders Lindgren, Luciano Pezzolo, Andrea Pinkney, Mimi Svenning,
Richard Tchen, and my superb and exacting editor, Lucia Monfried.
But most of all, my gratitude is to Nick Furrow, whose initial and
constant suggestions sustained me.

For Hayden Headley,
my newest joy

The Smile

PART One

CHAPTER *One*

"ELISABETTA, where are you going?"

Oh, and I was so close to the door. Ah, well. I descend from tiptoe and walk from the corridor into the kitchen. On the cutting counter in front of her lie a skinned hare, raisins, pine nuts. "The garden is lovely this morning, Mamma." I lean around her shoulder from behind and kiss her cheek. "But if you want help, of course I'll stay."

"Ha! My sweet delight, do you think you fool me?" Mamma gives me just the briefest twinkle of her eye and returns her attention to mincing. "I know how you feel about cooking." She makes three little *tsks* of the tongue.

Many women of the noble class don't cook, but Mamma takes pride in it. Under her quick blade, the bright green pile of parsley and rucola turns to a deep forest green mash. I move to stand beside her. The aroma bathes us. I can almost taste it.

"This is your father's favorite dish; I must be the one to prepare it. Alone. A good wife takes pride in her husband's hums of pleasure at the dining table. You should mend your ways and learn the culinary skills. It will bring you joy." She smiles contentedly, though she doesn't look up. "False offers of aid—who taught you that?"

I pick up a loose leaf and chew it. The bitterness makes me

suck in my breath. "A good wife does so many things. You're always adding to the list. I wager a good wife needs to know how to make false offers, too."

"Watch that tongue." But she laughs. She wipes her hands on her apron, then turns to me. Her palms cup my cheeks lovingly. "You're clever, Elisabetta, but you'll be thirteen in just two months. In many ways you seem older than your years—yet in some ways, you're far too young. Think about what needs your attention rather than running off to the woods."

"I said the garden."

"You meant the woods." Mamma tilts her head. "Are you becoming deceptive?"

"If I am, I might as well give it up. I'm clearly no good at it." I peek under the cloth covering the basket on the table. The rolls are still warm. Old Sandra has been busy. She does her work before dawn, then goes home to care for her ailing husband. "You can't understand anything these days, Mamma. When I woke, I threw the shutters wide and the scent of jasmine snaked into the room." I snatch a roll and twirl around the table. "It twined up my arms, up my neck. It pulled me almost flying out the window."

"Oh, my." Mamma makes a pretend show of alarm. "Beware that sharp nose. We mustn't have flights of fancy turn you into an angel. By all means, use the stairs to descend, like the rest of us mere mortals." She protrudes her lips in thought. "It's best you put charcoal to paper today and think about the dress we need to have made."

I swallow the last of the roll and bounce on the balls of my feet in triumph. "I've already thought about it."

"Do you have to bounce in that undignified fashion?"

"Yes."

"Sassy girl." But then she takes a deep breath. "Desist in the presence of others, at least. That's better. Now tell me these thoughts of yours."

"I can show you. I drew it last night."

"Well, then." Mamma appears so surprised, she's at a loss for what to say next.

"We'll look at it later," I say, taking control before Mamma recovers. "After Papà has eaten and hummed up a storm. In the meantime . . ." I let my eyes plead.

"There are so many things that need to be planned." Mamma speaks very slowly. Her eyes hold mine. "But I suppose there's time for the woods, too."

"Hurrah." I grab a few pine nuts and make for the door.

"But if you want to be the belle of your own ball, Elisabetta, cover those arms with something other than the serpentine odor of jasmine vines. A man of noble birth notices a girl of noble birth. And a girl of noble birth does not allow the sun to color her arms like those of a peasant."

"Country nobles know the sun isn't picky about who it shines on, Mamma."

"Who's fishing for a country noble? You'll get betrothed to a city man. From one of Florence's best families, I'll wager. The Rucellai, perhaps, or the Pazzi, or the Acciaiuoli, or the Martelli, or the Ginori, or . . ." She pauses for effect, her index finger poised in the center of her cheek. ". . . the Medici."

I press my lips together hard. Mamma's counting on this party, on me. I'm an only child; who else can she put her hopes on? But it's still unfair. I speak as gently as I can manage. "Your dreams are too lofty."

"Don't be silly! This party is exactly what the males of those families need to remind them of you."

"They never noticed me in the first place, so how can one remind them?"

"Of course they noticed you. You're Papà's beauty."

"Papà's. Exactly. No one else thinks I'm a beauty, not even you."

Mamma's face looks stricken. "Don't be difficult, Elisabetta. You've played with their sisters and daughters every time we've visited Florence your whole life."

"Daughters?" My cheeks go slack. "I don't want to marry an old man."

"Widowers make attentive husbands."

I'm pressing my knees together so hard, they ache. "I can't," I say through clenched teeth. "I can't marry one of them. And you can't make me."

Mamma's eyes go liquid. "I didn't make the rules. This is the way the world is."

"I won't. I simply won't."

She reaches out and her fingertips lightly brush my throat. The look on her face is of such tenderness, I want to cry. "Then you'll have to be at your best, Elisabetta," she says softly. "Cover those arms well. Don a hat, too."

I nod, unable to speak.

"Now . . ." She flicks the back of her hand at me. "Off to the woods with you." And she returns to her meal preparations as though the moment has passed and we can both immediately put it out of our minds. Another good-wife trick.

I remain immobile, weighted by her words—but only momentarily. She's released me for now and, oh, the woods are calling. I race up the stairs, popping pine nuts in my mouth. I pull a light waistcoat from my closet. Then I close the heavy doors.

This is a very fine closet. It stands on four carved eagle claws that curl over gilded balls. The doors hold large mirrors. I can't stop myself from looking.

My dark brown hair hangs just below my shoulders. It's never been cut, not once in my whole life. For some reason, it doesn't grow to the same length as other girls' hair. Still, it's long enough to make elaborate hairdos, which is what Mamma will do for my party. And it's thick and wavy, forming a fine frame for my face.

My eyes match my hair. There isn't much else to say about them.

My nose is straight. My cheeks are high and round. My chin comes to what Mamma calls a sweetheart point.

And since my monthly bleeding started, my body has become womanly.

That's the sum of it, I guess.

I look down at my arms. I haven't been outside without long sleeves yet this spring. It's only early April. My skin is still the color of the underside of olive leaves. I slip on the waistcoat. How strange to think my skin must stay light until after the party— in June. Mamma says my birthday month is as good a time as any for such a party. That means two whole months denying my skin the sun, when I so much like turning brown. Papà calls me his little nut, his almond.

Two months till the big party. A shiver shoots through my shoulders and neck. I walk to my table. The dress design I finished yesterday stares up at me in all its coarseness. Drawing is a boy's activity, yet it annoys me that I'm so poor at it. Still, Valeria's mother is a good tailor. She'll see what I was trying to get at.

Can Valeria's mother make a ball dress that transforms me into a noble girl? Well, I am a noble girl, of course. But can she make me appear dignified, so that I'm worthy of the grand men of Florence? The grand young men, that is.

We are neither city folk nor rich. And this year Papà's silk business is only limping along. Nonetheless, he wants a lavish party. It will be an announcement of my active participation in real society. He's absolutely sure it will lead to marriage offers.

Many fathers arrange for a betrothal entirely on their own, father to father, as if it were a business arrangement, for economic sense. But Mamma wants me to marry better than money alone would determine. So Papà came up with the idea of this party. He truly believes men's hearts will pound, for he truly believes I'm beautiful.

I'm glad for that. Every girl needs someone to believe she's beautiful, after all. I love being Papà's prize.

And I'm glad for the party, too. This way I can see the men and veto some and encourage others. I lift my jaw in defiance. I will not be married off to an old man with a bulging purse. I want passion before comfort. The passion I learned about when my tutor struggled to teach me to read Ovid's poetry.

In two months, I'll be betrothed. And when I am fifteen, my marriage will pull our family up the rungs of the social ladder. I press my hands on my chest to hold in my banging heart. Fifteen. That's so soon to leave home.

But I'm not leaving yet. Now I'm going to my belovèd woods, where I can wander. Where I can be the Lord's smallest sparrow and no one needs me for anything.

I slap on a broad-rimmed hat. I'm actually grateful for both hat and waistcoat, now that I think of it. They'll keep the insects off. I race down the stairs.

"Elisabetta," calls Mamma.

I stand with the door open. "I'm listening."

"Gather truffles, will you?"

"I'm not a dog, Mamma, despite my love of smells."

Mamma comes into the corridor and looks at me with her hands folded behind her back. "The moon has almost finished waxing. They'll give off the strongest odor now. And if we don't get some soon, we'll go without till June—for there aren't any in May."

I don't want to dig and find nothing, and dig and find nothing, and wind up dirty and empty-handed, having lost all my time for wandering. But she's looking at me as though I can do anything. She always looks at me that way. "I can try."

Her face softens into a slight smile. For an instant I want to grab her skirts and hide there, small again, roll back the years, smooth her skin.

"We still have a black one," she says. "So look for the little white ones. Your father's going hunting soon, and we can stuff pheasants and make a truffle cream sauce."

"All right, Mamma." I step outside.

"And, Elisabetta?"

I hold the outer door handle now. This feels like an escape. "Yes, Mamma?"

She extends her right hand. "A substantial first meal never hurts." It's another roll, with a thick slice of salami inside. The moist kind with fennel that I love so much.

"Thank you." And I'm already eating. "I didn't realize I was still hungry."

She's smiling but almost sadly. "There are things I can understand."

"I know that, Mamma. I was just talking. I didn't mean anything by it."

"You have a lot of energy, Elisabetta. You dance around the

kitchen and you eat heartily." She hesitates. "But you worry me lately."

As you worry me, I think.

"Your eyes are solemn. I miss the sound of your laughter. Where has my cheerful daughter gone?"

I close the door.

CHAPTER *Two*

OUR GARDEN STRETCHES OUT in brilliance. A rosemary border breaks the sweep of wind off the hills. Within this aromatic hedge, gravel walks weave through sun-warmed flower beds. Spikes of white lilies and purple callas perch high. Lilacs perfume blankets of blue delphiniums and yellow chrysanthemums. And roses hide in tight buds, soon to dazzle the eye with pinks and reds. April is a showy month.

I rub my face in blooming lavender, then circle the statues of the muses out of habit. Once I reach the vegetable terraces, I run. A breeze skims the leaves of the olive grove. They flutter: silver, green, silver, green. The immature fruit shimmer. Our oil is the best in the Chianti area. That's what Papà says. Every autumn landowners bring olives to Greve to be pressed, but there are many landowners and few presses. So it takes months. Papà pays the miller a tip, and just like that our olives get pressed right away, while they are fresh and the taste is robust. I love to dip bread in our oil, all thick golden green.

Now I'm running in the meadow beyond the grove. A herd of cows grazes. Most hills close to Florence are too steep for cows, but the ones around here slope gently. That's why Mamma can make dishes with cream and why we can have many cheeses and not just pecorino all the time.

This is, indeed, a perfect place to live. When I marry, I will make my husband buy a country home here, and I'll visit often. For weeks at a time. Maybe months.

A cow lows. A calf wobbles beside her. It's new! I gape. Oh, I'd love to pet it. The bull raises his enormous head at me. "All right, grumpy," I call, and run on by.

Orange poppies shake their blank faces at the world. They're so dumb and guileless, they make me grateful. And now I enter the cool shade of the woods and breathe the heady lemon scent of citronella and watch the light dapple on the beech trunks. I'm leaping and playing the role of fawn, when Oh! "You startled me."

Cristiano shakes his head. "You're the one running." He smiles, and there's a gap on the top, where a tooth is missing. Not many brawls go on among the boys in this area without Cristiano taking part. Twigs stick out of his hair, as though he's been crawling under bushes. He carries a large crate.

His dog, Paco, bounds out from the woods behind him and zips past without a hint of greeting. A big brown thing that galumphs. I don't know how Cristiano trained Paco, but that dog behaves as though Cristiano's the only human worth acknowledging, and this is strange, because he's a Spinone and that's a friendly breed. We used to have one.

When I was little, Paco's indifference made me so mad, I wanted to tackle him. Nothing's more fun than romping with a dog at your heels.

My nose twitches. I lean toward Cristiano's crate. "What have you got in there?" His eyes grow guarded. "You've got truffles, don't you? I can smell them."

"Ain't no law against digging truffles in open woods."

"Indeed. Mamma asked me to bring home white ones for her."

"And you expect me to give you some?" Cristiano frowns. "Blackmail, is it?"

What would I be blackmailing him for? But a glance tells all. I walk around him and point. "Bee stings on both arms."

"Pah! I knew it." Cristiano lowers his crate to the ground gingerly, as though it's full of eggs. He reaches in, carefully not exposing the contents, and takes out two white truffles. "Here, you scoundrel."

Scoundrel? "Keep them. Who wants your dirty truffles? I'll dig my own."

"And soil your fancy waistcoat?" Cristiano's lip curls in disgust.

Why on earth? I've never done him wrong. His father works for Papà. And in the past few years, Cristiano has, too. We used to be friends. I'm still best friends with his sister, Silvia. But lately he's been standoffish. And right now, he's positively rude. "I only put the waistcoat on because Mamma said. I'll slip it off when I dig."

"Rubbish. Take the truffles and hold your tongue."

So that's it. "Don't worry, I won't tell. I'm not a scoundrel. Besides, whoever's raising honeybees in a woodland meadow is doing it secretly. He probably doesn't have land of his own, so he's not paying his taxes, though he's taking from the earth. It's not my business if you stole honeycombs that shouldn't be there in the first place."

Cristiano is all smiles again. He drops a truffle back in his crate, then stretches out his hand to offer the other. "Here, take this one, anyways. As a present."

"I meant it when I said I'd dig my own, thank you very much. The beekeeper is in the wrong, but those who steal from him are, too. You've got some explaining to do."

"Not to you, Monna Nobility."

My cheeks burn. "Of course not. To the Lord." I walk past his hand.

He puts the truffle on top of the crate, picks the whole thing up, and walks beside me. "If I confess the honey, will you take the truffle?"

"Why should you want me to?"

"For peace. Between you and me." He looks sincerely and surprisingly contrite.

I blink. "You did rather hurt my feelings."

"I know. It showed."

"Thank you." I take the truffle. "I didn't really want to dig for them. I could have looked for hours and not found any. Thank you, Cristiano."

Paco dashes between us and zips ahead, lost to the eye again.

"Your crate isn't full of just honeycombs and truffles, not with how large it is."

"Nosy Elisabetta." Cristiano laughs. "My crate—oh ho, wouldn't you like to know." He walks backward, swinging the crate slowly in front of my eyes with such ease, I'm sure it's quite light. Then he hugs it and turns to walk forward again.

I wait. He says no more. We walk in silence, past oaks and yellow broom bushes. I glance up at his face. "I want to pinch you when you do that."

"Do what?" he asks innocently.

"Wear that maddeningly self-satisfied smile."

He laughs again. "All you have to do is ask. Nice. Can you stoop that low?"

"And just why is asking stooping?"

"A noble lady. A country bumpkin. Can a lady ask a bumpkin about his crate?"

"A lady can grab his crate and dump the contents on the ground."

"Try." He tosses his head back and waits. "No? You got some sense, anyways."

"All right, Cristiano, may I see what's in your crate? Please, sir?"

"Now that was nice." He settles the crate on the ground. Then he lifts the lid and, with both hands cradling it, takes out an orchid. It stands stiff on a tall stem. The large petals are red inside and purple on the underside. The two smaller petals are darkly stained, almost black. They fall from the center, like blood falling from an open heart.

"It's beautiful."

"I got more. Lots of types. But this one's best. What you think? Ain't it the bestest flower you ever set eyes on?"

I put my face close to the tiny speckles of yellow near the center. Every mark on one side is matched by another across the center of the petal, as though the two halves of the petal are mirrors of each other. Every petal is balanced by another identical one across the center of the flower. A pattern within a pattern. "Yes."

"Right. And that's what they'll think at Foiano della Chiana."

"Oh, you're going to the flower fair in two weeks? But that's over near Arezzo. Why travel all that way when Greve will have its own flower show in a month?"

"Foiano's is a real fair, not a show. It's huge."

"I didn't even know you liked flowers."

"They give a purse to the winner, and I aim to win. Let them others have their fancy garden flowers. I have my wild beauties."

"So you're doing it for money?"

His lip curls again. "People like you, you act like money don't matter. Let me tell you something, Monna Elisabetta. To them that don't have it, it matters."

"We're not rich, Cristiano."

"To me you are. And you're aiming to get richer."

"What do you mean?"

"Silvia told me about your party. You invited her, at least."

I haven't invited Cristiano, of course. It doesn't make sense to. But I refuse to be forced to explain that to him. "The orchid is a marvel. I hope you win."

He shrugs one shoulder as though he couldn't care less what I hope. "Silvia's going to make money, too."

"How?"

"Raising silkworms. Like your family. She already tried once. But last time her mouser got into the shed. He knocked over the tray and that was the end of the worms."

"Worms and cats don't mix well," I say agreeably.

"This time, she'll fasten the doors and shutters tight."

"Good for her. I hope her business thrives." I fight off a heavy feeling. Their shed is small; there's no room for much there. "You better get those orchids home before they suffer too long in the crate."

"Yup. Delicate, they are, wildflowers. But I'll gather more tomorrow and the next day, just in case. Then I'll get them growing steady and strong in pots." Cristiano places the orchid back in the crate. He straightens up and looks at me with an expression I can't read. "Did you speak true? You really think that one's the bestest in the world?"

"I told you I did."

"Want to know where I found it?"

Something sly in his tone warns me off. I cross my arms. "It can stay your secret."

"Ah, but near those orchids there's something you'll want to see, Monna Elisabetta. Something furry . . . and warm . . . and cuddly."

I drop my arms in surrender. "All right, you win. What's there?"

"A den with eight—eight!—hare kits. Want to know now?"

"Yes," I breathe.

"What will you give me if I tell you?"

"What do you want?"

"A kiss."

I stare, dumbfounded. Then I turn and walk up the slope.

"I knew you'd be too stuck-up. Monna Nobility, that's your true name, all right."

When I look back, Paco's the only one left. The dog regards me expectantly, his tail held straight and horizontal. He gives a single quick wag, then disappears after Cristiano. That's the most attention that dog has ever given me.

Tears roll down my cheeks. I didn't mean to hurt Cristiano. I've just never thought of him that way. He's right; I never could think of him that way. He is a country bumpkin. I wouldn't have put it in those crude words, but that's how he put it, and he's right. My coming party has made it obvious—to everyone but me.

My life is about to change. Radically. It's Mamma's wish. And Cristiano has no right to try to make me feel bad about it.

Monna Nobility—what a nasty thing to call me. Here Mamma thinks I don't act noble enough, and Cristiano thinks I act it too much. I can't please anyone.

I move quickly through the woods now. I have half a mind to toss the white truffle away. Instead, I tuck it into the tie at my waist. I might not be lucky enough to find another.

But I can find orchids on my own. And if Cristiano wasn't lying about those hare kits, my nose will lead me from the orchids to them. I head uphill. What I need is a ravine between peaks. That's where peat bogs lie; that's where orchids grow. I march.

CHAPTER Three

WHO, THEN?" comes Papà's voice, in clear agitation.

Are they fighting? My stomach clenches. I hurry into the kitchen.

Mamma takes a seat on the bench. "Please sit, both of you."

Papà doesn't budge. He picks up a piece of bread and smears it with pork lard.

I blink. "Have you forgotten it's Sunday? If you eat, you can't take communion."

"Your father has decided to ignore the Lord's day." Mamma makes a *tsk*. "He's determined to get to the stables before the men so he can direct their every move."

"Do you fault my behavior?" Papà plunks onto the bench and stuffs the entire piece of bread in his mouth. "You can't trust a single one to do it right. Besides, Giacomo and his son, Cristiano, are shifty. They'll make off with supplies."

They're talking about the rebuilding of the stable roof. That day I spent in the woods searching fruitlessly for orchids and hare kits, a wind rose. By evening the heavens unleashed a fury of hail. In the morning, we found a chestnut tree had dropped on the stables. For the two days since, every man available has been working on the repair.

"You wouldn't have to watch over them if you gave them the Lord's day off."

"We can't afford a rest day now. I have to go to Florence in two days. The stable must be finished before I leave. And the worms have been neglected too long. If someone doesn't feed them today, they'll die." He slams a fist on the table. "There's no choice. I'll have to take one of the men off the stable job."

"Is that all you're arguing about?" Relief loosens my whole body. I take a cup and pour myself some hot mint brew.

Mamma stays my arm. "You can't drink before the holy Mass."

"I'm not going to Mass. I'm feeding the worms."

"A lady always attends the Mass, even if a gentleman can skip. Sit down, Elisabetta, and don't be ridiculous."

I grab an almond cake from the basket and sit. "It's not ridiculous."

"Not at all!" Papà stands as I sit. Our eyes meet. "First you . . ."

"I've watched it done thousands of times. I know every step, Papà."

Papà smiles. "Of course you do. It's settled then."

"Don't let her do this, Antonio. Please. It's not proper for a noble girl."

"Silk is our business. And business right now is bad. The Lord understands I revere Him. Anyone else who doesn't . . . you know where they can go." He kisses the top of my head. "I'm counting on you, Betta." He takes more bread and leaves.

Mamma turns to me with frightened eyes. "What if someone finds out?"

"About skipping church?"

She shudders. "About the nasty worms." Her shoulders rise as she hugs herself.

She's sincere. I almost laugh. I take her hands in mine. "You always speak of piety and purity, Mamma. There's nothing impious or impure about decent work." I go to the drawer where she stored the dress design and place the drawing on the table in front of her. "Those nasty worms will make this dress."

Mamma lets out a noisy breath of concession. "We had plans for after church, if you'll remember. Shall I select the music for your party without you?"

"Please." I grab a burlap bag and walk out the door in my shift, arms bare. It doesn't matter; I won't be outside long. And my arms should be bare for this work.

The brash morning sun promises a hot day. Blue haze rises off the hills as though it's summer rather than spring. The weather is so variable, and its effects are so dear. Poor Cristiano, repairing a stable instead of searching for orchids, as he'd planned. And Papà, I don't know what his plans were, but they got tossed away, too. I'm the only lucky one. I don't mind missing Mass. Latin peeves me. And, while I like music, I'm tone-deaf and sing like a crow. Let Mamma select the music. I'd rather work.

I go to a spreading mulberry tree and stuff leaves into the bag and sour berries into my mouth. Then I head for the silking building. It takes my eyes a few minutes to adjust to the dimmer light inside the large room. Little Valeria enters behind me. She sneaks, thinking I haven't seen her. I walk to the closest tray, stick both hands down into slippery worms, and quickly turn, lifting them toward the girl. "Want a taste?"

"Aaaaa!" She runs out the door and I stifle a laugh.

Valeria is five, the youngest child in her family and the only girl. Her father works for Papà, so it isn't right that I tease her. And I don't want to anger her mother; she's going to make my party dress. But everything scares the girl; and with her big brothers coddling her, she'll wind up a spoiled coward if I don't teach her to develop pluck. That's what Mamma would call a poor excuse for bad behavior. I should be ashamed of myself. And I should have sympathy; I run from spiders, after all. Still, any girl who lives here should learn to appreciate silkworms. They're our livelihood.

"Need a hand?" Silvia appears out of nowhere.

"There's no pay in it for you."

Silvia shrugs. "And who heard me ask for money?"

"Aren't you going to church?"

"I see you making the sacrifice of skipping Mass." She grins and I know she's thinking about how we squirmed through last Sunday's service. "I'll just tell Mamma the master's daughter required my assistance."

"But I haven't required anything."

"You always need me."

Her tone is ordinary, but the words needle me. "Do I?"

"Friends do. And that's the truth."

Indeed. "All right. I haven't started yet. I was just tormenting Valeria."

Silvia laughs. "That little rabbit."

Oh, I am glad Silvia's here; *rabbit* is exactly the word for Valeria. Papà would chase Silvia away —he doesn't trust her any more than he trusts Cristiano. But the job will be more fun together. "Let's pretend we're sisters, like when we were little." Of course, that would make Cristiano my brother. Well, that's good. Then he couldn't stay sweet on me. "We're working to save the family business."

"Is this truly pretend? Not the sister part. One look and anyone can see we ain't. But the other part? About saving the family business?"

Has Silvia's father caught wind of Papà's problems? Well, I won't confirm it. This is more than a master's daughter can con-

23

fide in a worker's daughter, regardless of friendship. "Dreaming of hardship makes the game more exciting."

"Right. Let's get to work, sis. If not, them brothers of ours, the little snot noses, will starve. And starving's a cruel death."

We rub olive oil over the trays so nothing sticks and it's easy to move the worms after they've fed. We move in harmony, spreading mulberry leaves a thumb deep. Then we gather the mess that covers most of the old tray where the worms squiggle—the frass. It's worm excrement and it smells, but not bad. Mamma uses it for flower fertilizer. We drop it in jars. My mind jumps ahead two months: I want flowers at my party. Lots.

The thought of flowers brings Cristiano back to mind. Does Silvia bubble inside with the same resentments as he does? I look at her sideways. She works with a contented face. And nothing she's said today, nothing in her tone or manner, rings false.

"Dinner, little gluttons," I croon as we transfer the worms to the clean tray. They tickle our hands. These were the size of pinheads when they hatched ten days ago. Now they're half as long as a finger. In another ten days they'll be double this length. Papà says no creature in the world increases its mass as fast as silkworms.

I look away when Silvia sneaks some into her hair. Who cares about a few dozen worms? Each moth lays hundreds of eggs. We have thousands and thousands of worms in this room. And it's not stealing, because she's working. So the worms are payment.

Silvia's smart. It's hard to transport moths; they die easy. But she can carry these worms home in her hair with no problem. I wish I could tell her how clever I think she is. But if I said anything now, she'd feel caught. Mortified.

The worms munch noisily, and Silvia and I fall silent in response. The sound is like a hillside stream cascading over rocks. I could fall asleep to it.

"Look, these are starting to make silk." Silvia stands by a tray of older worms.

I rush over. She's right; they're ready to form cocoons. If they're left in the leaves and frass, the silk will adhere to the trays and be ruined. "Quick!" We oil fresh trays and set little wooden cylinders upright on them, packed close. We drop three fat worms into each cylinder. In a few days, they'll spin cocoons, hanging on the insides.

Silvia moves her shoulders in a funny, stiff way. How does it feel to have worms in your hair? "I can finish up alone now." I nudge her with my elbow. "You go on."

A worm drops down her forehead. She bites her bottom lip.

I look away. "Thanks for helping."

"See. You needed me." And she's gone.

I wonder if she knows everything about our money troubles. She could have been pretending ignorance to spare me—like I pretended not to see the worms in her hair.

I finish and wander around the room. It's warm in here. The worms need it that way.

Papà appears. "I came to check on you. Thanks for taking over, my little Betta." He walks up and down the aisles of tables, inspecting the work. "You're fast. I'm amazed you've done it all already. I expected half this."

I could tell him Silvia helped. But he'd get annoyed. He'd suspect theft.

"What's this?" He's looking at a shelf of trays by the far wall. "These cocoons are complete. Who knows how long they've been here." He rubs the back of his neck, and his face contorts. "We're going to lose this batch."

And then maybe I'll lose my party. "No we won't. Let's get busy."

"It's a day's work for two people. And the day's more than half gone."

"We can do it." I light the fire under the big pot. There's clean water in it, at least. Someone must have been planning on doing this when they got interrupted.

"We have to bake them first, to kill the chrysalises."

"They'll die in the boiling water anyway." I drop cocoons into the water as I talk.

Papà has been looking at me circumspect, but now he blinks as though waking to the idea. "The men can work alone. This is more important." He rubs oil over the metal hoop on the pulley mounted above the pot. Now he cleans the reel beside the pot.

The gummy stuff that holds each cocoon together dissolves in the boiling water. I hope the chrysalises died quickly. I hope it wasn't cruel of me to skip the baking stage.

A cocoon turns fuzzy; the silk loosens. I take the hand broom and whisk around it. I whisk around a second and a third. They look fuzzier every minute. The filaments are so fine, they're hard to see. I pluck the end of one from each of the three cocoons. The steam burns my fingers. But it only took a second; I'm quick. I twist three filaments together and thread them through the hoop and over the pulley. Papà takes the end from me and wraps it around the reel. He pumps. The reel spins with a high-pitched creak.

This is the best part: the cocoons jump on the water. They're dangling from the filaments, of course, but the filaments disappear in the steam, so the cocoons seem alive. I suck on the tips of my burning fingers and watch, mesmerized.

Papà pumps hard. The threads are enormously long—one giant thread per cocoon. But already the cocoons turn transparent, showing the brown inside. "Stop!" Papà blinks at me. But he nods and stops pumping. I scoop out the thin shells with a wooden spoon, crack them open, and drop the little brown nuggets, all that remain of the chrysalises, into a jar. Papà pumps again and reels in the rest of the silk thread.

We begin over again with three more cocoons. We work all afternoon. All evening. All night. Mamma brings food and tries to feed us as we work, but we have no appetite. I feel distilled; in this moment I am a silk spinner—nothing more, nothing less. My hands and arms move on their own.

Long after dawn the last pristine white reel is finished. My fingers blister. My eyes smart. My neck and shoulders ache. And I'm young. Papà must feel half dead.

The chrysalises already stink. I leave the jar lid off so Valeria will discover them by the smell and tell her father, who will fry them. He considers them delicacies.

Papà throws his arm across my shoulders. "Home to eat, my amazing daughter."

I yawn and shake my head. "Sleep first. I'm almost asleep right now."

We go out to Papà's horse. The poor forgotten thing has been standing all night with her bridle on. I'll have to bring her a bucket of oats to make it up—but tomorrow. Right now I can barely manage to pet her. We mount, Papà in front, me behind. My shift rides up, exposing my legs. Mamma would blanch. My legs should always be covered and I should go only sidesaddle now. But who's to tell?

"We did it," says Papà. He gives a little laugh. "You're going to make someone the best wife in the world. Did you know that, my little Betta?"

I rest my cheek happily on his wide back.

That's when we hear hoof beats at a gallop. The messenger pulls up alongside us. "Il Magnifico is dead."

Papà shakes his head. "What? What are you saying?"

"Lorenzo de' Medici. Il Magnifico—he died!"

The leader of the most important noble family of Florence. And Papà's friend. One of his best customers.

Papà twists around to look at me. "This is awful." His eyes glitter with fright.

My chest goes cold.

CHAPTER *Four*

WE STAND JAMMED TOGETHER in the street in front of the Medici family palace. Everyone's talking confidently.

"I knew it would happen. I saw a comet that night."

"I heard wolves howl. Did you hear it? Wolves."

"The lions in the enclosure by the Palazzo Vecchio—they fought for no reason. Vicious attacks. One actually died."

"The most beautiful one. I saw him myself."

"And that thunderbolt! It destroyed the cupola lantern in the Santa Reparata church. Huge stones fell in the direction of the Medici palace. Exactly this direction."

I hold Mamma's arm tighter. An eerie sensation goes around my ears, up my temples. Nothing feels familiar. Florence has changed from the bustling, happy city I've visited before to a town with secret ways that make my skin crawl. Faces contort in fear and grief. I nestle against Mamma. She reaches her hand across her chest to caress my cheek. "Everyone saw signs," she whispers. "Everyone knew Lorenzo was dying—it's so easy to know . . ." She lowers her voice, till I can barely hear. ". . . after the fact."

Ah. Thank heavens for a sensible mother, who can dismiss specters with the briefest words. Maybe nothing phantomlike happened. I straighten up and look around.

I was last here for the Christmas festivities. A visit of four thrilling days—not nearly long enough. Musicians, storytellers, and preachers posted themselves in the center of every piazza. The greatest spectacle was the nativity play that Lorenzo de' Medici himself wrote. His children acted in it. The costumes took my breath away.

And now he's dead. Lorenzo Il Magnifico—the magnificent one. Many people are called magnificent. But Lorenzo was truly worthy of the title. Papà keeps saying that as people exchange condolences. He died in his villa in Careggi—to the northeast. But the funeral is here, and all Florence has turned out. Most of the countryside, too.

A man climbs onto a box and recites a poem in Latin. His voice drags. Much of the crowd disperses. The rest of us do our best to look attentive.

I'm terrible at Latin. I used to have lessons from a visiting tutor, and I learned to read the tongue I speak. But Latin is tedious, with its case endings and strange verb forms. And Greek! My tutor once gave me a hint of the Greek lessons that were to follow when I would turn fourteen—enough to convince me that Greek is nothing short of cruel. I was glad when my tutor finally quit, declaring that students like me were the reason education is optional for noble girls.

Still, I recognize this Latin poem now, because I've heard it before. Another man delivered it at noon in the Medici Chapel of the church of San Lorenzo, where the great Lorenzo is buried beside his brother Giuliano, who was assassinated before I was born.

It's a lament. The famous Poliziano wrote it. A Flemish composer made the music for it. It's being recited all day long. And not just here. Funeral orations will be given throughout Italy all week, as the news of his death spreads—in the republics and kingdoms and princedoms, even in the papal states—Lorenzo was so important.

Papà explained to me what this ode says: poetry and music have fallen silent now that the fine poet Lorenzo, the greatest patron of the arts ever, is dead. The claim is patently false, given that the ode itself is an example of both poetry and music.

I abandon pretense and look around for anyone I know. Everyone is decked out, on display. Tables line the streets; feasting is part of the lamenting. And tournaments tomorrow, I've heard. This whole thing is like a party.

Oh, I know the people sincerely mourn Lorenzo. He held theatrical performances and circuses in the streets. He fed the crowds at long banquet tables, sometimes days in a row. Because of him, Florence is known as the city where people can come to enjoy themselves in peace and prosperity and stay to make a wonderful life. So the city truly grieves. But right now it just feels like a lot of people are showing off.

Mamma takes my hand. She always knows when I'm restless. It's ironic that only a few days ago I said she didn't understand anything.

The ode ends and now the young painter Michelangelo reads a poem he wrote. He's squat-nosed and surly, a thoroughly unappealing person.

"What an ugly boy," I whisper to Papà.

"They say his paintings are marvelous," Papà whispers back. "And his sculptures, they're even better. He's only seventeen and already he's a master."

My cheeks burn in shame. After all, the artist can't help his appearance.

"Ser Antonio, it's you." A middle-aged man appears at Papà's side. He pulls Papà out behind the crowd, far from the orator's box. Mamma and I follow.

The man tips back his hat and I see his face. Oh! Could it really be him?

"Ser Leonardo," says Papà with joy.

I was right: It's Leonardo da Vinci, the son of the notary Ser Piero, one of Papà's important customers. Papà admires Leonardo in the most ferocious way, for the man makes inventions that amaze. I haven't seen his face since he moved to Milan a couple of years ago, but it's impossible to forget: straight nose, bold eyes, full lips, thick beard. He's fun; I remember how he used to make me laugh. I bounce on the balls of my feet in excitement.

Mamma flashes me a look of reproval. I stand still and try to appear composed. Papà and Leonardo hug, and Leonardo winks at me behind Papà's shoulder.

"But I thought you were far away, in Milan," says Papà.

"I was visiting in Pisa when the news came." Leonardo kisses Mamma's hand, then he gasps and pretends he's just seen me. He kisses my hand, as though I'm a grown-up. "Little Monna Betta, isn't that what your father calls you? What a stunning woman you're becoming." He glances at Mamma. "Exactly what anyone should have expected, given your beautiful mother."

Mamma looks down demurely.

"We should call you by the full title—Madonna Elisabetta—for you rival the Madonna."

I'm blushing. I'm not foolish enough to believe such nonsense; men go to absurd lengths in flattering women. I blush only because this behavior is new to me. I've always been just a girl. I won't look down, though. I keep my eyes on this illustrious man, to let him know I'm not taken in, though I do appreciate his words.

"What do you make of it?" says Leonardo, turning to Papà.

"Only forty-three years old. Brothers of the Medici family seem ill fated. But he wasn't assassinated, at least."

"He was sick for months," says Papà. "Everyone expected it. Especially after that Dominican monk predicted it."

"Girolamo Savonarola." Leonardo shakes his head in disgust. "I heard he said Lorenzo led Florence into debauchery. Such sanctimony."

"He even criticized the Pope for his worldliness. He's a renegade, that one. He's predicted trouble ahead for Florence."

They go on talking, and I'm confused. Papà speaks as though he discounts Savonarola. But last night he told Mamma that Savonarola's predictions worry him. He said Lorenzo called his three sons "the fool," "the wise one," and "the good one." And the oldest, the heir to his father's position, is the fool. Trouble ahead, all right—that's what Papà said, though now he's guarding his opinion. That puts me on edge. What harm could there be in speaking plainly? Especially to Leonardo, a man we've known forever?

I recognize all three Medici sons by sight. Anyone in Florence does. When I was ten, I was actually introduced to the youngest. It was a chance meeting of our fathers in the street, with each of us in tow. Papà does business with them, after all. And a few times, when I was little, I played with the youngest Medici daughter. She's only a year and a half older than me, but she's been going to balls for a long time already. My own party, after my birthday, would have been the first real social event of my life. And now I don't even know whether we'll have it. Papà said you don't talk about celebrations in the middle of mourning.

"Madonna Elisabetta," says Leonardo with a crisp nod to me.

I'm pulled from my reverie. I have no sense of what they've been talking about. My eyes question him.

"Let me take you as my companion for the rest of the day." He turns to Papà. "With your permission, of course. I promise to keep her out of harm's way."

"How could I refuse?" says Papà.

Mamma's eyes shine with hope and determination. I know why. Leonardo is the talk of the town. He was born the illegitimate son of a peasant mother and noble father in Anchiano, near Vinci. His family moved to Florence and his father—a champion of intellectual and artistic freedom himself—insisted the boy study with the best tutors. He was apprenticed to Verrocchio, the leading sculptor and painter, who, in turn, had been the student of the great Donatello. But Leonardo soon surpassed both. No one commands higher fees than him. I've heard Mamma say it's because his artistic talent is undeniable—she swoons over his drawings, while Papà admires his inventions. The man has something for everyone. But his physical self has to be part of his allure; he's handsome. With a wonderful physique. And he sings well, on top of everything else. He might be the finest artist, scientist, philosopher, anatomist, astronomer, engineer, inventor, who knows what all—like people say. But he's a man first—and even at forty, most women consider him one of the best bachelors Florence has to offer.

He paints for the wealthy, though he has a reputation for working years on a project and never finishing. He did a portrait of Ginevra de' Benci that everyone calls marvelous. And one of Cecilia Gallerani, the Duke's mistress. Every noblewoman wants him to paint her. That's why Mamma lets me go with him—so I can hobnob with the wealthy. His invitation rescues her plans to find me a noble husband soon.

Leonardo offers his arm. A fish swims in my belly—an anxious spirit. What do I say to him? But I won't be a scared rabbit, like little Valeria. With a swallow, I accept his arm and we're off, weaving in and out of horses, mules, wagons. I don't see Mamma and Papà anymore. I'm not even sure where I am. Florence is not entirely known to me.

I look down a side street by chance. A man defecates there. His shirt is rags, his breeches filthy. I turn away, praying that Leonardo has not seen or, if he has, is not aware that I have. There is misery all over. Everyone knows that. Even in Florence. The district of town where Papà brings our silk to be dyed is a hellhole. I heard Valeria's father say that. But why doesn't that man go over to the Franciscan church for help?

Fortunately, I'm not allowed to dwell on his plight. For Leonardo stops and introduces me again. And again. I nod to everyone, grateful that he repeats my name loudly and keeps exclaiming upon what a fine young lady I've become. Most of these people know my parents; the nobility of Florence is not so large a group. But it's good to impress my name into their minds beside the image of Leonardo.

The older men wear heavy, rich brocade; the young men, elegantly slim, wear tight hose and velvet overcoats trimmed with fur. The women's clothing rivals the men's in colors. We pass horses decked out as extravagantly as their owners. Gilded spurs. Gold thread interwoven into the silken sashes across their backs. Pride swells my chest. "Papà's responsible for the gaiety of much of the finery here," I say to Leonardo.

"Indeed? And how is that?"

"Linen resists dye. Wool takes it grudgingly. But silk welcomes it." And, because he stops and questions me, I talk at length about our business. Leonardo seems to want to know the process from start to finish. He listens attentively.

A woman catches my eye. "Look at the pearls in that woman's

hair," I say, clapping. "So marvelous and refined. Pearls like that make anyone beautiful."

"Do I detect a wistful note?" Leonardo holds me out at arm's length, and looks me up and down. My dress is yellow silk, dyed with marigolds. It's a year old and tight in the bodice. It can't compare to the finery around us. I suddenly want to run away, back to Mamma. "You are a golden, flickering point of light. You scintillate. Especially when you bounce on the balls of your feet." His eyes tease. "But there's something else in you. A practicality that gives you substance. Mysteries promise in those limpid eyes, as though you're watching and waiting. As though nothing will really surprise you. It's unsettling. Mark my words, Madonna Elisabetta, someday, when the right blend of experiences adds the final touch of perfection, I will be honored to paint your portrait."

My hands rush to my throat and press, as if to hold me from falling forward. I feel tipsy at such strange talk. Leonardo takes my hand and tucks it through his elbow and we're off again. Everything shines. Laughter dots the air. Or is it just my eyes, my ears, that filter out funeral mourning?

CHAPTER *Five*

DECADENCE," comes the booming voice. "Dissipation. Moral decay. It will be the downfall of Florence! Beware!"

I turn to look, but a man hooks Leonardo's other elbow with his own and pulls us along. He's dressed in red velvet and white lace with so many long feathers trailing from his hat that he rivals the showiest bird. Who is this fantastic creature?

He jerks his chin toward the preaching voice. "Scrofulous Savonarola. He kept civil for the church ceremony, at least, but he can't control himself any longer. My father made a mistake to let him stay in Florence."

I turn for a full view of this man's face. Why, it's Piero, the oldest son of Lorenzo de' Medici, and now the wealthiest man of all Florence. My heart skips a beat.

He notices me now. I realize I'm gaping. I shut my mouth. Piero smiles and his eyes linger on me in a shocking way. I stop dead in my tracks.

"Let me move to a better spot." Piero inserts himself between Leonardo and me. He grabs my hand and puts it in the crook of his elbow, holding it in place with his other hand. He acts oblivious to the insult he's just inflicted on me. "We'll make introductions once we have privacy." He turns to Leonardo. "So how is life in Milan? I hear you're Duke Sforza's principal engineer for bridges and ships and, most fascinating of all, armaments. Tell me,

Ser Leonardo, does he plan to use them to invade Florence?"

"I'm not privy to the duke's plans," says Leonardo. "I merely design things."

"And do you 'merely' paint still, as well?"

"I wouldn't be me if I didn't paint."

Piero sweeps us along the road and up steps into the Medici palace! I can't believe it. Once inside, Piero spins on his heel and I almost fall against his chest. He kisses my hand. Then up my arm. I cry out and pull away.

"Behave." Leonardo steps in front of me. "Monna Elisabetta is a lady."

Piero crosses his arms and tucks his hands into his armpits. "Hands off, eh?" He moves around Leonardo and bows. "Is that truly the lady's wishes?"

This man is the oldest Medici son. Disgust must not show on my face. I search for the least offensive answer. "You're a married man, Ser Piero." And a father, but I don't add that. I look up at Leonardo, who's eyeing a painting on the wall.

"And do you know Alfonsina, my lovely bride?" Piero gives a lopsided smile.

I shake my head.

"Do you know what my wife thinks about? Forks, sheets, tablecloths." Piero counts off on his fingers. "Towels, linen shirts, crisp cakes, puff pastry, Trebbiano wine, salad, pickles, boiled chicken and kid, roast pigeons, almond paste, boxes of sweets." He drops his hands and sighs. "Guests seem to need these things." I smell his breath. But he isn't drunk. "Shall I go on? Want me to name clothing? Or jewelry? Or maybe . . ."

"Please, stop."

"Stop? Do you realize you're telling a genius to stop? A bona fide genius! Have you no respect?" He sticks his tongue out, like a spoiled child. "Tell me, what office did my father hold?"

I can't remember anyone saying. I blink fast. This is shameful. My head is hot.

"Don't know, do you? Well, don't fret, little monna. There's a reason for your silence. My father was a genius, like his father before him, and his father before him. It runs in the family. Lorenzo Il Magnifico ruled the Republic of Florence by owning the banks and playing the big peacemaker with the other Italian states . . ." Piero pauses with a triumphant smirk. ". . . and all without holding office. So he was never under the thumb of elections that could oust him. We rule—and no one can stop us. Don't you agree that's genius?"

I stare at him.

"Well, don't you?" he barks.

I flinch.

"Is that a tear?" Piero shakes his head. "You feel sorry for yourself. You think you're a babe compared to me, don't you?"

I pluck on Leonardo's sleeve, but he takes no notice.

"I'm twenty-one," Piero says. "The age my father was when his father died. What do you make of that?" He gives a mirthless smile. "Maybe I was born to take on heavy responsibilities before my time. But, between you and me, don't you think I deserve more fun before I grow old? Wouldn't you like to be part of that fun?"

I step backward quickly and my bottom and shoulders meet the wall behind me.

"We haven't eaten yet. I invite you to dine. I'll stuff myself with parsley, rucola, anise, mint—greens that enhance amorous prowess. Imagine me enhanced." He laughs.

"Who are you harassing now, brother?" A priest comes in.

Oh, Lord, thank you. And, no, this isn't a simple priest, he's a cardinal, wearing the red hat. A boy follows.

"Ah, pious Giovanni," calls Piero, with an expansive sweep of the hand. "Do you know little Monna Elisabetta? Let me introduce you. And, yummy little monna, this is my brother, the youngest cardinal ever. He managed to get that red hat at fourteen."

Cardinal Giovanni puts an arm around Piero and bows his head briefly to me. "A pleasure. And this is our little brother, Giuliano." He nods toward the boy.

The fool, the wise one, and the good one. It should be a delight to stand before the three Medici brothers. And one of them a cardinal! There are but seventy cardinals in the world, and here is one before me—round belly and round cheeks and red hat. But not even relief and awe at the cardinal's presence can quell the need to distance myself from Piero. Still, I must find a way to do it kindly; they are mourning, after all. I nod to the two younger brothers and take Leonardo's arm, this time tugging insistently.

"Is this by Sandro Filipepi?" asks Leonardo. His hand moves in the air as though under a spell that makes him paint the picture himself.

I glance at the canvas. It's six women in gauzy clothing with a half-dressed man at one side, a baby angel at the top, and a flying blue man on the other side. Remarkable. I would look closely, only I can't risk diverting my attention from unpredictable Piero.

"He goes by the name Botticelli," says Piero, his eyes still on me. "His work isn't evocative and atmospheric, like yours, Ser Leonardo. It's erotic." He closes and opens his eyes slowly. "Tell me, little monna, do you like my brothers more than me? Admit it; I see it in your movements. But I have news for you. All we Medici have our gifts. Besides the men being geniuses, that is.

Lucrezia, the eldest, sings and reads at the same time. She was Father's favorite, not counting Giovanni. Who can beat a cardinal, after all? But, oh, how could I have forgotten Michelangelo, Father's chosen boy, better than any blood son?"

Cardinal Giovanni looks quickly at Piero. Is that jealousy on his face?

"The second child," says Piero, "is Maddalena, who knocks her head against the wall without getting hurt. That's a talent. She was Mother's favorite. Back when Mother was alive. Aha!" He points at me. "Was that a twitch of sympathy in your otherwise placid face? Do you pity us orphans?"

Mamma's parents died in a boat accident when she was ten. A spinster aunt raised her. Oh, I do feel sorry for the Medici brothers. Especially Giuliano, standing there so silent. He's my age.

"Father called Maddalena 'the eye of her mother's head.' Pretty strange. And then there's Luigia, whose gift is talk. Nonstop talk. She's no one's favorite. But then, I guess, none of the rest of us is. Then we have Contessina, who screams loud enough to scare the lions. That's the girls. Now the boys—the sum total before you, if we discount the dead. Giovanni thinks only of the Lord. Giuliano thinks only of laughing."

I feel breathless, though Piero's the one who's been speaking at a fever pitch. I'm unsteady on my feet. Piero's energy has sapped my own.

"A pretty speech." Cardinal Giovanni keeps his arm around Piero's shoulder and leads him away.

"But I haven't yet explained to the little monna what my talent is," Piero says over his shoulder as Cardinal Giovanni ushers him out a door with a nod of apology to us.

Gratitude spreads warm in my chest. My shoulders relax.

Leonardo is still studying the painting. And Giuliano appears to be studying me.

"Any questions?" asks Giuliano. His eyes twinkle as though he's laughing at me. And to think just a moment ago I felt sorry for him! How rotten, to tease after his beast of a brother tormented me. Well, I'm not scared anymore. I let loose of Leonardo's arm and sniff loudly. "Does Maddalena really bang her head against the wall?" I ask pointedly, for if I were in this family, I might.

"Not all the time." His voice is gentle and low. I have to strain to hear it. "And Contessina's screams don't always scare the lions, either."

Did he guess that was what I really wanted to ask? Contessina is the only sister I know—the one I played with a few times. I can imagine her screaming.

"Want to see them?" asks Giuliano.

"Who?"

"The lions, of course."

I start in spite of myself. "I've walked by the enclosure on the east side of the Palazzo Vecchio," I say, adopting a formal tone. I may live in the country year-round, but I am not without sophistication. "I've seen them a number of times."

"Those belong to the Republic." Giuliano smiles. "We have our own in the palace. You can get much closer to them." He touches Leonardo's sleeve. "Ser Leonardo, may I borrow your companion?"

Leonardo is pressing his temples with his fingertips. He looks at us now as though disturbed from a trance. "You're the only one I'd really trust her with. If she wants to go, of course." He raises an eyebrow at me.

Lions up close. And this is the good brother. Even Piero said all he thinks about is laughter. So his teasing is harmless. I should be plucky enough to put up with that. "Yes."

We walk halls lined with tooled leather chairs and mirrors in blown glass frames. I peek into a room and stop, letting Giuliano walk on. A dining table is covered with a cloth embroidered not just at the edges, but everywhere. There are silver settings and china plates holding silk napkins folded in swan shapes. Beside each sits a delicate white bowl of water. Ah, for cleaning fingers. My family passes around a bowl before the meal. But here everyone has their own.

White lilies cluster in vases of swirling red and gold glass, surely from Venice. Their scent saturates the air. The white candles are not yet lit in the enormous red glass chandelier, but I imagine they give off a dazzling light. And heat.

The aroma of spiced fresh bread comes from a basket covered with red silk. Everything's red and white. There's even a fine white sculpture of an angel in the center, a meter tall. And with a flash, I realize that Piero must have ordered the color scheme just for the occasion; it matches his outfit.

"Are you already hungry?" Giuliano has returned to my side in the doorway.

"The angel glitters," I say. "I've never seen marble glitter so."

He laughs. "That's sugar."

Sugar? Someone went through all the hours of sculpting a block of sugar, which will last only . . . what? . . . a week at most.

"Here, let me break you off a wing tip."

"No! You mustn't ruin it. Not after someone worked so hard."

"Then something simpler." He goes into the room, reaches his hand under the red silk and comes back with a bread in the shape of an angel. He puts it on a velvet-cushioned bench outside the door. "You can take it when you leave. Come on. No more stopping. Unless you prefer tables to lions." His tone teases again.

"I love animals," I announce firmly. "Take me to see the lions."

"As you wish." Giuliano leads me down a flight of stairs.

The smell is what I notice first. The hair at the nape of my neck stiffens. I suppress the urge to run. The lions look at us, turning their massive heads. Three of them, behind thick bars. A female yawns. Her jaws are enormous. She rises and paces.

I step back.

"They're fed often and a lot," Giuliano says quickly. He looks at me kindly. "I bet if they got out, they'd be too lazy to chase anyone. I wanted to impress you, but, really, it's nothing impressive. They're just wild animals, pathetically locked up."

I stare at the pacing lioness. Suddenly she seems tragic. This is her prison, probably for life. I look back at Giuliano. He's changed. His face is as sad as I feel. And then I remember: "I'm sorry about your father."

"Thank you." He turns his head away.

Is he crying? Oh, I wish I hadn't said anything. It is a funeral, though. It's what you're supposed to say. What do we do now? "Do you have other animals?"

He nods and smiles again. "But your face tells me you don't want to see them. At least, not the ones in cages. The giraffe, now, you would have wanted to see her."

"I did," I say, happy at both the memory and the turn in the conversation. "We came to town just for that. I was seven, or maybe eight. But I remember."

"So you liked her?"

"Oh, yes. A beautiful creature. Graceful. And quiet. She

didn't make a sound. Papà fed her from his hand. I wanted to, too, but Mamma wouldn't allow me."

"That's a pity. Her lips tickled. Put out your palm. I'll show you."

I go suddenly shy. But this is the good brother. I offer my palm.

He makes a fist and rubs his knuckles ever so lightly all over my hand.

I hold in a laugh. "It does tickle."

"The giraffe lived free," says Giuliano. "She wandered the streets. People would be a flight up, eating their evening meal, and her head would pass the window." He laughs. "She was the most popular character of Florence. A present from the Sultan of Egypt." He leads me back out the corridor and upstairs, and he points. "See that beam?"

The ceiling has an architrave, intricately carved, though it's hard to make out the details from the floor.

"That's how she died."

"Who?"

"The giraffe. She smacked her head." He laughs. His fingers play above his upper lip hesitantly. "You never seem to know what I'm talking about. But I'm just trying to have an ordinary conversation, Monna Lisa."

I smile in surprise at the way he shortens my name. "Papà calls me Monna Betta. But no one calls me Monna Lisa."

"Meet No One, then." Giuliano bows.

I make the deepest curtsy ever and tuck my hair behind my ears and then feel immediately silly for acting this way. Whatever possessed me?

"I finally got you to smile. And now that I've found the key to the treasure box, I'll always call you by that name. It suits you. You have too beautiful a smile to be called anything but Lisa."

I don't know why I haven't been smiling, but I know it's true. Like Mamma said. I hold in laughter; I hold in smiles.

And now I hold in my breath. Giuliano has used the word *beautiful* about me. Or, well, about my smile, but that's enough. It feels good in an uncomplicated way. Nothing hinges on it. I don't care anything about his family. He himself is a decent sort; I'm sure of that now. The way he talks about the animals. His quiet manner and quick laughter. He's the good one. And he admires me, in a clean, free, easy way that makes me happy, and I don't want to breathe because I don't want this moment to pass too fast.

CHAPTER *Six*

I STAND IN FRONT OF my closet mirror in the light of earliest dawn and look at my reflection. I'm wearing an ordinary nightdress—not the beautiful party dress Valeria's mother was supposed to make for me. It's been a month since the great Lorenzo died and neither Mamma nor Papà has mentioned the party, though they talk together all the time, hushing when I come close. Who knows when I'll ever have that party?

It's ridiculous, especially after I was so anxious about the whole thing, but I feel cheated in a way.

What would I look like in that dress? I hold my nightdress from the rear and pull it tight, so the form of my body is exposed. I turn sideways and blush in satisfaction.

I know how men talk about women. When Silvia and I were little, we often played around Papà's workers, watching out of curiosity. Our presence was so natural and frequent, they rarely stopped their talk before us. And once we hid outside the small shed by Silvia's cottage and listened to Cristiano and some of his buddies talk about girls. We listened till they said something truly obscene. Then Silvia took me by the hand and pulled me away.

I wanted to stay. I want to know what boys think. But no matter how hard I pleaded, Silvia wouldn't hear of it. She said if anyone ever found out it was her who let me listen to such things, she'd get in trouble. But that was an excuse. Silvia didn't want to stay for her own reasons; I'm quite sure she's more put off by that kind of talk than I am. I believe it frightens her.

I wondered after that if maybe there was something wrong about me. Something wicked. I confessed before Easter, of course. And I said the penance the priest assigned me. But I knew I'd listen again if the chance ever came. I guess that makes it not a true confession, but, well, some things the Lord has to forgive, or we'd all wind up in hell.

Piero de' Medici did me a favor that afternoon at his palace: there is nothing wrong with me. The memory of his sleazy behavior brings nausea. I am a decent girl. But I'm still glad that my body's turning out the way it is. And I'm so very glad Giuliano said my smile is beautiful. I slip on a shift and run downstairs, armed with determination.

Old Sandra is busy in the kitchen. The body of a plucked and gutted goose lies before her on the cutting counter. She is rubbing salt into the prickled skin of the goose. Mamma will stuff it later. She likes Old Sandra to gather the ingredients and do messy preparations, then she takes over for what she calls the creative part. The creative part of cooking is at the top of her list of what a good wife does.

"Morning, Sandra." I press my cheek to hers.

"Ah, morning, Monna Elisabetta. Ain't you up early." It's not a question.

"Do you know where Mamma is?"

"In the bedroom still, I imagine." She flops the goose over and rubs the other side with salt, leaning her weight into the job. Her knobby fingers redden with the work.

"Where are the cucumbers?" I ask, for I recognize this dish.

"Ain't you heard? There's an outcry against cukes and melons these days. Them nobility of Florence. They got nothing better to do than make up cockamamie rules. And your mamma said we might as well be cautious."

It strikes me that Old Sandra talks as though we aren't part of the nobility of Florence. I suppose it's not disrespectful. After all, we don't live in the city, though we're still within the boundaries of the republic. So in the strictest sense, in the city sense, we're not part of the nobility of Florence. But what irritates me is the slightest suspicion that maybe she doesn't consider us nobility at all. She's our servant, so she has to see us as higher than her. But higher doesn't necessarily mean nobility. Maybe she even thinks Mamma puts on airs to ban cucumbers and melons.

She's old. And she takes good care in what she does. And, well, I like her too much to say anything now that might cause her distress. I go back upstairs and stand outside Mamma and Papà's door. I listen. Rustling sounds come. I put my hand on the door latch, then hesitate. Piero de' Medici's words come back to me; some herbs enhance amorous prowess. He listed parsley, rucola, mint, and anise. Papà's favorite dish has parsley and rucola. Mamma's favorite drink in the morning is mint brew.

A strange sensation runs from my belly up my chest. Like fast fingers touching with only the barest tips. I've never thought of my parents' activities in bed. And I don't want to, ever. I calm myself and knock primly.

"Betta?" comes Papà's voice. "Is that you?"

"Yes."

"Well, what's stopping you? Come on in, my little almond."

With relief, I rush in and climb onto the bed between them, like I used to do when I was small. We're squished, of course; I'm not small anymore. And both Mamma and Papà have widened in the past few years. But I like it. So I stay there.

49

"Is something on your mind?" asks Mamma.

"My party. I turn thirteen in a month."

"We've been talking about that," says Mamma. "Just now."

I swallow.

"Florence is behaving like mourning is over." Papà beams at me. "So why shouldn't we? Let's have that party, right on schedule."

"Oh, yes." I hug Papà. "Thank you so much."

"Which means we have to act quickly, Elisabetta." Mamma gets up and fetches a dress from her closet. "We must get the invitations out immediately, so everyone can save the day. We have to engage the musicians. Then there's the menu to settle. And getting the dress made. And, oh no, I haven't done anything about getting your *cassone* painted—that wedding chest must be vibrant. And the flowers. And . . ."

"I'll take care of the flowers, Mamma."

"By yourself?"

"Why not? I don't care about the rest—except for the dress, and I already did my part by designing it. But I do know flowers. The Greve flower show starts today, in fact." I jump off the bed, excited by the coincidence. "Isn't that perfect? Why, I can go and buy pots and pots of things to scatter all around the house and on both sides of the walk to the front door and, well, everywhere."

"But will they last till then?"

"I'll get plants with lots of buds. And kinds that bloom over and over."

Mamma smiles broadly. "That'll be lovely."

Papà claps and shakes his hands together. "I'll get Giacomo's son, that Cristiano, to drive you to the market in the big wagon."

I haven't seen Cristiano since that day in the woods, more than a month ago. I wonder if he ever entered his wildflowers in the fair at Foiano della Chiana. Maybe he's already planning on bringing some to Greve today, despite the fact that there's no purse to win. I could tell he really cared about the flowers for their own sake, no matter what he said.

So it's fine for Cristiano to drive me. It might even suit us both. But I don't want to be alone with him. "I'll bring Silvia, too," I say brightly. "She has a good eye."

"But a poor mouth," says Mamma. "I don't like you listening to her rough peasant talk."

"Cristiano talks the same way, and you didn't object when Papà proposed him."

"Cristiano is a boy. You won't be conversing with him. You'll just tell him which plants to pick up and put in the wagon. But with Silvia, I know how it is; the two of you chatter nonstop."

I pinch my lower lip. "How will it look for a noble girl to be in a wagon with a young man and no one else? Especially a young peasant man."

Mamma stops dressing and looks at me. "Clever again. You use my own worries against me." She shakes her head. "I miss your old direct ways, Elisabetta. All right, I can ask Sandra if she'll accompany you."

I look to Papà for help. He just watches Mamma and me with a half-amused expression. I could strangle him. He should be on my side, for I'm always on his. I'm his amazing daughter. Has he forgotten? Help me, my eyes plead.

But his don't change. This is my battle. All right, then. I shall be direct. "Old Sandra needs to stay with her ailing husband, Mamma. We both know that." I go to her and wrap my arms around her waist. "Talking with Silvia hasn't changed my talk. Listen to me, Mamma. Hear me. You understand me better than anyone. At times better than I wish you did. You know I obey you. I don't adopt Silvia's ways of speaking." Even when she makes fun of me, I think. But I don't tell Mamma that. Besides, Silvia hasn't said a peep about my language for a long time now.

Mamma takes a deep breath and strokes my hair. "I don't know why you're so set on her. You should have outgrown that friendship by now. It only happened because you're so isolated out here. The two of you have little in common. But all right, take her. As your helper, not your friend. And outfit yourself properly. A nice dress."

"A shift makes more sense, with all the dirt from the plants and everything."

"You won't touch the plants. Cristiano will. And Silvia will."

"But . . ."

Mamma puts her hand up in the halt signal. "What if someone should see you, Elisabetta? Aren't you the one who just brought that possibility to my attention?" Her face softens. "You know I want the best for you. Always."

I wonder if her idea of best might be at odds with mine. But I love her so much. I kiss her on both cheeks.

Soon I'm sitting on the wagon bench beside Cristiano. Mamma wouldn't hear of me sitting in the wagon bed with Silvia. Especially not in my dress. Arranged like this, it's hard to talk. So we're silent most of the way to Greve.

The main piazza of Greve overflows with flowers. My chest swells in happiness. Children run through the pots, pointing at the brightest ones, the biggest ones, the most unusual ones.

And there are some unusual ones, indeed. Black roses. I've never seen such a thing. As I approach, I realize they're not really black, but of such a deep, rich red, they appear black from a distance. Beyond them is a tall bush of shiny, thick green leaves all peppered with large pink buds that I'm sure will open before my party. "Good day, fine lady," I say to the vendor. "Can you tell me about your flowers?"

"They're not for sale, if that's what you want to know." The woman is dressed well. Not richly, but not in farm clothes. She has a city accent.

"What a pity. I'd love to have some for my party."

"These flowers are beyond the means of a girl like you."

I stiffen in offense. "Please state your price."

"I told you, they're not for sale. They're here only to allow the country folk to see what fine things grow in the Medici gardens at Careggi."

"Medici?"

"Those roses you had your eye on are from Spain. And these . . ." She points to large white flowers. "They're sea daffodils from Crete. They don't usually bloom till autumn, so that makes them even more special. And those ones over there . . ." She points at small blue buds. "They're also from Crete. Those irises bloom only in the second half of the day. At noon you can watch them open. We have Egyptian lotus. And African vines." She waves her hand expansively. "We have everything."

"And how much did you say the roses are?" Roses keep blooming. They'd be perfect.

"Persistent, eh?" One corner of the woman's mouth goes up reprovingly. "The Medici don't sell. They keep or give. Nothing in between. And I don't see my master about to give you anything."

Could this woman be any ruder? "Who might I ask is your master?"

"Giuliano de' Medici himself. He oversaw the selection of which flowers to bring."

My heart thumps like a fist. "Is he here?"

"He was. He insisted on coming with me, though we had to leave the city long before dawn. Just a while ago he left."

"Where did he go?"

"Why are you asking?"

"I know him."

"You know Ser Giuliano?" The woman frowns. I can't tell if she doesn't believe me or if she regrets having summed me up so wrong. "He brought his own horse, tied to the back of the coach. When we got here, he mounted and rode away. He said he wanted to see the countryside."

"When is he coming back?"

"He's not. He left me here with the coach driver. We have rooms for as long as the flower show lasts. But Ser Giuliano is returning to Florence on his own horse today."

"Do you think he might come back to Greve before leaving for Florence?"

"Do I look like a mind reader? He told me nothing."

I suddenly feel like crying.

The woman tilts her head. "Is something amiss?"

I can't understand why I'm acting like this. I'm too frustrated to talk.

"I wouldn't expect him to come back to Greve. People talk of the charm of the villages, but really it's much exaggerated. I should think Ser Giuliano will find his countryside ride boring."

I grit my teeth and curtsy good-bye. Then I spend the rest of the day choosing flowers. None rival the exotic ones from the Medici garden. And I didn't even learn the name of the tall bush with the pink buds. It would be humiliating to return to that supercilious woman and ask now.

I buy flowers and aromatic bushes till the wagon is full. But nothing overcomes my glumness. I stare at the wagon and realize there's no excuse for not returning home.

"What hurts?" asks Silvia. She stands beside me and takes my hand.

"What do you mean?"

"Don't talk rubbish. It's me. Something's biting you. And hard. If you tell me, it'll hurt less. And that's the truth."

I move closer to her and my eyes blur with tears I can't understand. It's been a beastly day. First Old Sandra, with her treating us as though we're not nobility. Then that servant of Giuliano's acting like anyone out here is a country bumpkin, no matter how they're dressed. Did she even see my fine clothes? I hate her. And then there's Giuliano himself. He was here. So close to where I am. And I didn't get to see him.

"Come on," says Silvia. "You can tell me."

But I can't. I can't talk about any of this to Silvia. She's not part of noble society. And she is part of country folk. If she doesn't already resent me, talking about these things now certainly would. My best friend, and I can't talk to her. It's maddening. I hate the world.

"Keeping secrets from me now, is that how it is?" Silvia's face shows hurt.

"No, no," I say quickly, "it's no secret. I'm just thinking about my party. Worrying."

"Worrying? What on earth for? Florence has dozens of middle-aged men on their own. And them fellows, oh, when they see you, just wait. One will snatch you straightaway. Then you're set. Sitting pretty. No cares for the rest of your life."

I pull away from her in shock. Middle-aged men? Sitting pretty? "How can you say that?"

"Don't you believe it?" She laughs. "You're good-enough looking. And you're sweet as can be. So when your daddy offers a dowry, someone will step forward. You're so lucky. I'd give anything to marry one of them men. But . . ." She laughs again. "I ain't got nothing to give." Her eyes fasten on me. "Elisabetta?"

"What?"

"Help me win one."

"What? How could I help?"

"There will be so many at your party. I'm smaller than you. Let me wear one of them dresses of yours from last year, so I look good. Then I can get a man to love me before he finds out I'm poor."

He'll realize she's poor the instant she opens her mouth and says her first word. I shake my head. "It won't work."

"Sure it will. I'm prettier than you, no matter what Cristiano says." Her face pinches in anger. "But you ain't never learned to share."

She is prettier than me. The sun bounces off her chestnut hair in red highlights. And she's lithe and graceful in a way I've never been. "Of course you can wear a dress of mine. You can take your pick."

"Really?" Silvia's hands fly up and form little fists of happiness beside her cheeks. "You are a good friend. The best. I'm sorry I said that nasty stuff. It ain't true—I was just being spiteful. Maybe we'll both find husbands at your party." She laughs. "We can get with child at the same time and grow fat and old together."

With child, fat, old. How is it that Silvia is so ready for all that? I feel foolish and childish beside her. She's grown up and left me behind.

But what's foolish about wanting love?

I must get betrothed to the right person. And that means having the right party.

The whole bumpy road home, I brood. And I arrive at a conclusion. We cannot have my party in Villa Vignamaggio. It is my belovèd home and it is truly glorious. But if Giuliano's servant woman is a just indicator, the nobility of Florence don't understand this kind of beauty. At best, people will condescend. At worst, they won't even come.

We have to find a more suitable place.

CHAPTER Seven

MAMMA IS WAITING FOR ME when I get home. She doesn't even look at the flowers in the wagon. She rushes me into the living room and sits me down. "We had a visitor while you were away." She licks her lips in excitement. "You'll never guess who."

"Giuliano de' Medici."

"How did you know!"

Nothing else could have made this terrible day even more wretched than to have missed Giuliano's visit. "What did he want?"

"Nothing, as it turned out. But your father was so pleased to see him, he came to sit with us. The Medici boy, though, well, he simply chatted agreeably about the surroundings. And he asked about you. He remembered your name. From years ago. Imagine that. You must have made quite an impression on him."

"Not at all, Mamma. He remembered from just a month ago. I saw him at his father's funeral. Leonardo da Vinci took me to his palace."

Mamma's hands go to her mouth. "And you didn't tell me?" She drops onto the bench.

"There wasn't anything to tell." Or, rather, there wasn't anything I could tell without upsetting Mamma. She'd have been mortified at how Piero treated me. "Anyway, Mamma, there's something I need to talk to you about."

Mamma lengthens her neck and leans toward me, alert as a mother bird.

"I want to have my party in the city."

"What? Villa Vignamaggio is enormous. It's built for entertaining." Mamma stands as the words stream out. Then she sits again. "I do want you to be happy, Elisabetta. More than anything. But this new desire . . ." She lifts her shoulders in confusion. "Why on earth?"

"I don't think city people will want to come all the way out here. It's a long ride, Mamma. And to make it twice in one day is too much."

"Nonsense. If we wait till late in June, the heat will already have driven the nobility from the city to their country homes."

"Which are scattered all over the hills, to the north and west of Florence, too, not just to the south, Mamma. Besides, the men will be in the city doing business still, and it's the men you don't want to leave out."

"I can prepare guest suites upstairs."

"There isn't enough room for everyone; nobility can't be stuffed together like chickens going to market. Plus our upstairs has nothing of the finery they're used to."

Mamma doesn't speak. It's unlike her to yield quickly, though even I am impressed by the number of arguments I've managed to amass.

I move along the bench closer to her. "If we do it in the city, I bet even Giuliano would come." Still she doesn't answer. I add, with a boldness I didn't know I had, "He's my friend."

"Indeed?" Mamma touches my cheek. Her face is quizzical, as though she doesn't know who I am. "Your friend?"

"Don't be surprised, Mamma. I just happened to meet him. And he talks easily and gaily. It was pleasant. I imagine he's everybody's friend."

Mamma's eyes change. That stunned look is replaced by her usual confident rationality. "If he would come out to the country to visit you on just an ordinary day, then surely he'll return for something as important as your party."

"He was out here on business at Greve." That isn't entirely true. The flower show isn't business. But it sounds more impressive this way. "So it was easy for him to wander over here."

"At Greve? But you were at Greve."

"He left before I arrived."

Her hands clutch her skirt. Her brow furrows. "You really think he won't come all the way out here, but he would come to a party in the city?"

I take her hand and smooth the crumpled cloth of her skirt. "City people . . . well, Mamma, they feel superior to country people."

"I know that, Elisabetta. I wasn't born yesterday." She gazes away. "Giuliano de' Medici. I knew he liked you. I could tell from the way he talked." She shakes her head in wonder, then turns to me. "If he likes you that much, he might persuade all the other nobles to come, too. Oh, Elisabetta, this accidental friendship might turn out to be a wonderfully useful thing."

I hadn't thought of it that way. I don't want to use Giuliano. I just want to have a party in the city. I don't want to be discounted as a mere country girl.

Mamma looks at me hard. "Paying for an appropriate place in the city—that would add to the expense quite a bit, Elisabetta.

And your father is already pressed. He'll be against this. But . . . I may have an idea."

"What?"

"Family has to be useful some of the time," she says mysteriously. "Let me talk to your father tonight."

The next morning I find myself riding horseback to Florence with Papà and Mamma. We are on a mission.

Last night Mamma started in immediately after our meal. She announced the party had to be in Florence. Before Papà could bring arguments against that, she complained that the house Papà owns in Florence, near the Santa Trinità church, is so dilapidated it isn't serviceable; it isn't even inhabitable; he should have repaired it years ago, like he promised; and on and on. Even I wanted her to quit after a while.

It worked, though: Papà responded not to our announcement that the party must be in the city, but to the claim that we had nowhere to hold it. He came up with this plan. We are going to convince Papà's cousin Fabrizio to host my party in his city house in early June—before the women and children leave for their country homes.

Yes, indeed, family has to be useful some of the time. I have no doubt that cousin Fabrizio's house, while Papà proposed it, was Mamma's plan all along. But if Mamma had made the suggestion directly, Papà would have bristled. He isn't on the best terms with Fabrizio, and Mamma knows that very well.

And now I must do my part: I'm going to invite Giuliano de' Medici immediately. I'll send a messenger straight to his palace. Then, when he says he'll come, I'll tell Cousin Fabrizio, and of course he'll agree to host the party. Everyone wants Medici family members as guests.

I remember Giuliano rubbing his knuckles on my palms.

His laughter. His words about my smile. My cheeks heat. Well, those words seem exaggerated in retrospect, but all the rest is true and sure. Giuliano really is my friend. Though such an idea would have seemed outrageous a month ago, I'm convinced of it. Giuliano may be a Medici, but he isn't the least bit snobby. He wouldn't have come all the way out to Villa Vignamaggio if he were. He'll say yes.

So I'm full of hope. And how could I not be, in this very moment in this very place? Spring has gone from the delicate arias of April to the rowdy chorus of May, the most glorious month in these hills. And I am amused at a new realization: our home's name, Villa Vignamaggio, means "May vineyard." I was destined to love May. What a marvelous day! And after the pitiful way yesterday went. We trot past mulberry groves and grapevine terraces. We trot past giant fields sown with rye, barley, wheat, oats, and smaller fields of lentils, peas, chickpeas.

And now Papà cuts across a meadow. The horses speed to a gallop. This meadow is tilled by no one, natural as the day it was created. Wildflowers cover the hillsides to our right in colors that seem to arrange themselves in perfect harmony. Red, yellow, blue, purple. The eye of God is clear.

Maybe that's why Papà is so pious. He also has a clear eye. It's what makes him a master at his job. Mamma is pious because it's the only defense of women. She says that outright, no beating around the bush. Piety and purity, the sword and shield.

But men have more freedoms. Papà could have chosen to stand outside the church, like many intellectuals, but he's a papist.

I don't know what I am. Not really. God is evident, of course. The hillsides prove that. And the silkworms. And . . .

"Aiiii!" Mamma's horse stumbles and falls. She disappears

under him. Her scream ceases—cut off in an instant, as though the air has been sliced.

I'm down from my own horse in a second and tugging on the reins of her horse, tugging and tugging, pulling him to the opposite side from where Mamma lies.

The poor beast is half-crazed. His eyes bulge; his mouth slobbers. He lifts his neck and paws at the ground with his front hooves, trying to rock his weight, get himself up any way he can. I smell his silent screams.

Papà pushes on him from behind. He curses. Papà never curses. I'm pulling and calling to Mamma. I can't see anything beyond the bulk of the horse. I keep calling, tugging with all my might. The air stinks.

Papà finally pulls me away, and I kick at him. He spins me around and grabs me from behind, locking my back to his chest. "She's dead, my little one, my baby girl. She died instantly."

"No!" I kick and thrash and break free. And stop. For now I see the side of the horse, the side I've been avoiding.

Mamma's head is at a sharp angle. I know immediately Papà's right. No neck could bend that far; it's broken. Her face is already white, the blood all drained away somewhere else. A hidden pool.

The horse's right rear leg is shattered. Bones protrude in so many pieces. An explosion of shards. Why are horse's legs made so thin, as though designed to break? He'll have to be destroyed. It must be his fear that fouls the air. Or maybe that's just the way death smells.

We'll have to dig graves.

A double funeral.

I taste blood.

Papà puts his hand on my shoulder. But I sink away, to the ground. The dirt yields to me. This plot of earth is riddled with mole tunnels.

Blood drips from my mouth, red on black. I must have bitten my tongue. But I don't feel it.

Two graves to dig.

"Come, Betta." Papà has caught my horse. She neighs in terror. She stamps and throws her head back. "Mount. We have to go for help."

"I'll stay here."

"She doesn't need you now, daughter. Get on the horse."

"No."

He stands a moment. "Hold these reins." He hands me the reins, down on the ground where I sit.

He looks around and finds a heavy rock. "Look away, Betta."

But I won't look away.

He slams Mamma's horse in the head, at the very top between the ears.

My horse screams and rears, dragging me a little way before she stops and paws the ground.

That one blow crushed the skull. But the poor animal gushes blood from his nose. He's somehow still alive. Papà kills him with a second blow.

Then he takes the reins from me and pins them to the ground with the rock. "I'll be back as soon as I can." His face is grooved with pain, though his voice stays steady. "If you want to leave, ride home."

He's gone.

I sit here, hands loose, nothing to do.

Gradually my horse stops stamping. She grows quiet. She grazes, pulling the rock along with her.

I sit. I can't feel my legs anymore. Nor my arms. Nor any part of me really.

Birds catch the edges of my vision. Insects have already discovered the wells of blood.

I sit.

The day moves forward as though nothing has changed.

Sparrows.

I have walked in the meadows and the woods so many times, reveling in being the Lord's smallest sparrow.

But I don't want Mamma to be a sparrow.

Oh, everything has changed.

Mamma is dead. The woman who calls me her sweet delight is gone. Oh sweet delight she was to me. I should have told her that. I should have told her every day.

My heart breaks.

I bury my fingers in the soft soil and weep.

CHAPTER Eight

AND SO WE MEET AGAIN." Giuliano de' Medici comes up beside me. His voice is hardly more than a whisper, yet I recognize it before I even turn to face him. "I'm so sorry, Monna Lisa."

I've been brave. The hostess that Mamma would want me to be. Greeting everyone. Thanking them for coming. But now my bottom lip trembles. The last time he called me Monna Lisa I smiled. He said that calling me that was the key to my smile. Wouldn't it be lovely if there were such simple keys to happiness? I swallow. "Thank you. Thank you for coming." I try to be clever. "Maybe funerals will be our regular meeting place."

"Don't say that." Giuliano shakes his head. "Anyway, we don't meet only at funerals. We met once before, near the Duomo."

My mouth opens in disbelief. "You remember that?"

"And why not? You do."

"But you're famous. Anyone would remember meeting you."

Giuliano gives a small smile. "Are you fishing for a compliment?"

"I'm sorry I said that. I realized what it sounded like immediately after the words came out of my mouth. Please, let us start over." I curtsy in greeting. "Hello, Ser Giuliano. Thank you for coming."

"We were ten." Giuliano rubs above his lip, though I can't see anything there. And I remember how he did that last time we were together. Is it his habit? "You talked a lot in those days. Or at least you talked a lot that time."

I don't remember talking a lot. I might have said twenty words. But maybe to a ten-year-old boy that was a lot. He's thirteen now. Only a couple of months older than me. Thirteen, without a mother or a father. I, at least, still have my beloved Papà. But Giuliano does have siblings. Thank the Lord for that. If one of us had to lose both parents, I'm glad it's him rather than me.

What a dreadful thought. I'm ashamed of myself. But I can't help it; thoughts invade on their own.

"Did your brothers come, too?"

"Alas, no. Cardinal Giovanni lives in Rome now. He only came home briefly for my father's funeral. And Piero, well, he sends his regrets and condolences."

"Good." I put my hand to my mouth. I did it again. "I'm so sorry. I should bite my tongue."

"Why? All you did was voice your true feelings."

"Nothing excuses rudeness. That's the kind of behavior that made Mamma worry about me."

Speaking of her—saying *Mamma* aloud—cracks my skull, so the truth of it all seeps in again. Mamma is dead. She won't come back. My eyes brim with tears.

Giuliano looks away.

I cried through the funeral Mass, which was all right, because I was hidden behind the black veil. But that's enough. I should be finished with crying. Mamma would want me to be a dignified hostess. It shows strength of spirit and good breeding to hold in tears at times like this. Besides, crying means I can't talk. And I want to talk with Giuliano. I swallow again and gather myself. "Did you come alone, then?"

"Aunt Nanina brought me."

My eyes smart with embarrassment. "Of course. I wouldn't have expected you to come on your own." This sounds wrong. I feel confused now. "I mean, that's what aunts do, they make people . . ."

"No one makes me do anything. I came of my own accord. To see you, Monna Lisa. To offer comfort."

Before I can speak, Giuliano steps partway behind me and jerks his chin toward the other side of the room. A man and woman wend their way through the crowd from Papà to me. I immediately understand: Giuliano's yielding his place so I can greet these next visitors, who have come to pay their respects.

Francesco di Bartolomeo di Zanobi del Giocondo and his young wife, Camilla. My ears catch the long string of names but hardly process the words that follow. I want to be talking to Giuliano. There's something I want to tell him, I realize now. And the realization makes it feel urgent. But I must pay attention. These kind people have come to Mamma's funeral. I force myself to nod at appropriate moments, to murmur thanks.

Francesco kisses my hand. Camilla kisses my cheeks. She's older than me by only a few years. And she's married to a man probably ten years her senior. A friend of my father's, in fact.

I think of Silvia and her hopes to do just what Camilla has done. She wants to entice a husband today, in fact. She wears my old green dress and holds her mouth shut—for we had a frank talk and I told her my fears about her language. She's determined not to let her tongue expose her social class until after a man is already smitten with her.

And all this is going on at Mamma's funeral. But it doesn't bother me. Rather, it seems a natural part of the sadness. For it's a widower Silvia hopes to lure. Widowers often take young wives.

How else can a man provide loving care for his small children when his wife dies? And so many wives die. There's nothing wrong with such a match.

All the same, I pity those girls, tied to aging men. I never want to be one of them. I pity this Camilla. And if Silvia succeeds, I'll pity her. It's awful, but I can't help how I feel.

What is this way of thinking, excusing terrible thoughts on the grounds that I can't help it? I've done it twice in the last few moments. I must be a firmer master of myself. Mamma is no longer here to guide me.

I turn my attention back to this young Camilla in front of me now and look into her eyes and wonder if she's happy. She's plain and a little stooped to one side. Was she desperate? Her husband stated his father's name, Bartolomeo, and his father's father's name, Zanobi, but all he said of her was "Camilla." He didn't say her childhood family name—as though being married to him is the only thing about her that matters. Is she without a history, without ties beyond the broad girth of the man whose arm her hand rests on? I have no sense of her. In her eyes is only a steady silence. And below her eyes a bit of a shadow.

Ah, sleep-deprived. Yes, I remember now: this Francesco recently became a father. Mamma talked only last week about how lucky he was now. For his first wife died in childbirth along with the babe.

Why don't her eyes show the delight of having that baby? But how stupid I am. Her eyes wouldn't twinkle merrily at a funeral. Not while she's talking to the daughter of the deceased. I must be losing my mind. Even if this young mother is joyfully giddy at her life, she's too well-bred to show that here. Someone raised her right.

I should behave like I've been raised right. Mamma tried so hard.

Mamma.

Mamma was younger than Papà. But her situation was different from this Camilla's, I'm sure. She didn't marry him out of desperation. She loved him. She loved him with all her heart. I know she did.

All this time Francesco has been talking. And I've been lost inside my head. I hope I haven't been rude.

They move away and I can finally turn to Giuliano. But no. Behind them, waiting his turn, stands Ghirlandaio, the painter who has just finished his work on the choir chapel of Santa Maria Novella. Papà calls him a master of colors, and if there's anything a silk merchant understands, it's colors.

He looks ill. I have the urge to lead him into the kitchen and set him down with a bowl of hearty *ribollita*—a soup made of layers of bread and beans and red cabbage, topped with onions and olive oil and soaked with beef broth. Silvia made it and brought it over last night. She filled a bowl and put it in front of Papà. She's so good to him, even knowing he doesn't like her family. She's never said as much, but I can tell she knows. I love her for not holding grudges. For simply seeing need and giving.

Papà ate hardly any of that wonderful soup. There's plenty left. I should take this painter by the hand and urge him to eat it and grow strong again.

But my hands hang at my sides, and I don't speak my crazy urges. I act proper.

And, finally, I am left in peace. I look over my shoulder at Giuliano.

He steps neatly from behind me to my side. "As I was saying, I came with my aunt Nanina. And, obviously now, with her husband and his two nieces and the husband of one of them. The men sat outside on the coach bench, but I was stuck inside with three gossiping women who were annoyed with me." He gives a little apologetic laugh.

His words confuse me. What's obvious? And which women, I wonder. I should be able to picture immediately this Aunt Nanina. I should see in my mind who she's married to, who her husband's nieces are, who the husband of one of them is. But I can't think so well through the thick cream of grief that clogs my brain.

Besides, the Medici family is too large to keep track of. And everyone has the same name anyway. Too many men called Giovanni. Too many women called Camilla. Mamma thought it was important to memorize every single link between every single family. But the whole thing is a muddle to me.

A big family. What a comfort a big family must be.

Most noble families are large, like the Medici. Nobles have better food than peasants— and nobles have doctors—so it's natural that we thrive. It's Mamma's poor luck that I have no siblings, nothing else. Papà has always put good food on the table. And the best surgeon was called when I ran a horrible fever last year. But good food and care can't make someone become with child. And the sorceress Mamma went to failed. She seemed to suffer from the same infertility her own mother suffered from.

What I wouldn't give to have a sister beside me now. I hug myself.

"I should leave you to your mourning." Giuliano bows his head and steps away.

"Don't go. Please."

"I thought you stopped talking because . . . All right, I'll stay.

We don't have to talk." He stands beside me again and folds his hands over his abdomen solemnly. His eyes lower. He is clearly doing his best to act proper in the face of grief.

Just like me, trying to be a proper hostess.

What a sad world, that we should be cast in these roles so young.

"You were better at this than me," I say. "You managed to act brave when your father died. You even laughed when we were together."

"My father was sick for months. I had time to get used to the idea. You didn't."

He's too understanding. I feel tears coming again. I give a little tug to Giuliano's sleeve and walk quickly from the room through the hall out the rear door. I'm stumbling over the gravel walks in our garden, blind with tears, crying so hard, my ribs hurt.

I drop onto a bench, weak.

Giuliano sits beside me and offers a handkerchief.

Snot runs from my nose into my mouth. I must look disgusting. I wipe myself up thoroughly. When I can speak, I say, "I want to tell you something. I have to tell you something. There's no one else to tell."

He looks at me and waits.

I wave my arm around the garden. "See all those flowers in pots? They were supposed to be for my party. The one that was to follow my thirteenth birthday."

"So?" says Giuliano softly.

"So, it's my fault Mamma died."

He blinks. But he doesn't talk.

"We were going to Florence to prevail upon Papà's cousin to hold the party in his house. We'd have never been in that meadow if it weren't for me."

"Stop it, Lisa. Don't think like that. You were just living. Doing ordinary things. If we take responsibility for the accidents that happen out of doing ordinary things, we'll all go mad."

"But it wasn't ordinary. I insisted. Mamma wanted the party here. I was afraid that people would look down on a party in the country. I was afraid they might not even come." I close my eyes. I feel like I'm in the confessional, only this time there's no one to give the penance that will make it all go away. I look at Giuliano. I have to tell him. "I used you to convince her. I said that if we had the party in the city, you would come."

"What treachery," says Giuliano in feigned horror.

"Don't make fun of me. I acted like a spoiled brat."

"Then be sorry you acted badly. But don't take the guilt for your mother's death. It was bad luck, Lisa. Daughters—and sons—act spoiled all the time, and their mothers don't die because of it."

"But I was thinking as we were riding across that meadow—I was thinking about religion. And I was questioning my own beliefs."

"So God punished you for doubting? He looked at you and saw a spoiled, doubting brat. He tripped your mother's horse to teach you a lesson? Do you really believe God works in such a clumsy, brutish way?"

"How do we know how God works?"

"I can't answer that. But if He doesn't do better than what you've just said, He's a rather poor specimen of a god."

I look down at my hands in my lap. My head feels so heavy, I think it will drop into them.

Giuliano stands.

I look up at him in dismay. "Are you going?"

"No. I just thought this would be the easiest way to make you look up. I have something for you." He reaches inside his vest and takes out a thin sheaf of papers. He puts one on my lap.

It's a drawing of a horse. But not an ordinary drawing. The horse is skinless. "All those muscles," I say slowly. I know about the bones under them. I saw the bones under them. Shattered. A spasm goes across my shoulders.

Giuliano sits beside me again and points. "And those are sinews. And those, tendons."

A woman comes down the path. She's Franca someone. I can't remember. The wife of someone Papà has business with. She's already greeted me. I don't know why she's here, but I'm glad she's interrupting. I may scream if I keep looking at that horse.

"Oh, Monna Elisabetta, you're out here. And Ser Giuliano." She smiles kindly. "I didn't mean to disturb. I just needed a breath of fresh air. I get nauseated easily these days." She puts her hand to her abdomen and I realize she's telling us she's with child.

"Congratulations," I say.

"Well, it's a secret yet. What's that?" She looks at the horse drawing and gasps. "How revolting."

"It's not revolting at all," says Giuliano.

"It's grotesque." Franca covers her mouth.

"It is ugly," I say firmly. I touch Franca's elbow. "Perhaps in your condition, it's better not to look."

"Perhaps. Yes, I think I'll keep moving." Franca wanders away.

"Do you really think it's ugly?"

"I wouldn't put it on my walls."

"But look how perfectly this muscle wraps around the bone and . . ."

"When Mamma's horse fell, his rear leg broke, clear through the skin. I've seen enough of the inside of horses. Forever."

"How thoughtless of me. Forgive me, please." He slides it inside his vest. "But give me another chance. Look at this one." Giuliano puts a second drawing on my lap.

In the middle of the paper is a dog paw. One half is covered with fur and the other half is skinless. To the top right is a dog, with skin and fur everywhere this time, a normal dog digging a hole. I feel Giuliano's eyes on me. Hopeful. He's persistent.

"Do you find this ugly, too?"

"Not so much, no."

"Look closely. What do you think it's about?"

I study the drawing now. It's a dog, digging. And the insides of a paw. The digging. The paw. "I guess it's telling me what happens inside the dog when he digs."

"Exactly," says Giuliano. "Paws in motion. That's science. How can it be ugly?" He puts another drawing on top.

A dragonfly. Every marking on every wing shows. The precision catches me now. I can see the points of energy. "It's as though I'm holding it in my hand, not breathing lest it fly away."

"Yes. That's it exactly. Do you like these last two?"

"The dog is instructive. I understand that, even if I don't find it beautiful. In fact, I think it's ingenious; the artist perceives the world in a more profound way than normal." I shrug uneasily. "But if he intends these for people's walls, well, I'd have to suspect that he's showing off his cleverness. The dragonfly, though, that's something else. It's quite remarkable. Strikingly beautiful."

"Leonardo da Vinci made these."

"My goodness." I pull my hands away from the paper. "What a fool you must think me, to have spoken so brashly and said all that rubbish."

"To the contrary, every word you said makes sense. And the horse and dog paintings are studies Leonardo did for himself.

You clearly appreciate his art for what it is. I'm so glad I asked him for them—to give to you."

"To me? Papà says people will pay outrageous sums for anything by Leonardo, even doodles on a piece of paper. I can't accept these."

"You have to. They're an early birthday present."

"You knew my birthday was coming up?"

"If a Medici wants to find out something, he finds it out."

I look again at these two drawings. The dog one intrigues me now. And, of course, the memory of the horse one is vivid. "It's so curious, how Leonardo draws things inside and out."

"It's his philosophy. He says if you want to paint, you need to know how things work, how each limb moves. He cuts open cadavers and animal corpses." Giuliano raises an eyebrow at me. "I helped him cut up a horse once. But not the horse in that drawing." He laughs sheepishly. "And what I just said isn't even true. It was right after my mother died. Why on earth he trusted a seven-year-old boy to move a horse leg or hold back a muscle so he could peer under it, I don't know. I couldn't help anyone do anything really. I just said it to impress you. Like I took you to see the lions to impress you." He shakes his head ruefully.

The queerest sensation goes across my cheeks and into my ears. Both Giuliano and I will always associate the inside of horse legs with our mothers' deaths. It is the strangest thing to have in common with someone.

Silently, Giuliano puts another drawing on the pile.

I jerk back in surprise. "But that's not an insect I recognize."

"Look closer."

"It isn't an insect at all, is it? It isn't alive. Is it some kind of child's toy?"

He laughs in delight. "You're so smart. It's a model of a flying boat. Leonardo is trying to convince the Duke of Milan to build it."

"A flying boat? You mean, in the air? People up in the air?"

"Exactly."

"High up?"

"Over the treetops."

"I don't think I'd have the courage to go that high in the air. I would have made a very bad bird."

Giuliano laughs. "So you like this drawing?"

"Leonardo has a quick mind. It lives in another world. Inventive, indeed," I say. "But I like the drawings of animals better, with or without skin."

"Really? You're not squeamish like that foolish woman?"

I shake my head.

"I thought not."

"And, on second thought, I'll even accept the horse one. Is that all right?"

"Yes, of course. That's wonderful." He looks satisfied. "And now, ta-da, I saved the best for last." Giuliano puts the final drawing on my lap.

"What a funny goat." I have the urge to touch it. But I don't want to do anything that might harm such a valuable drawing. "Floppy ears down to his knees. And look, his tail touches the ground. Leonardo must have been having a fantasy when he drew it."

"Do you like him?"

"He's a darling."

Giuliano jumps up. "Well, then, that's only half your present. Come with me."

"First I must put these drawings someplace safe."

"I'll keep them safe for now." He carefully tucks them inside his vest again. Then he leads me around the outside of my home to the front.

I peek through the open doorway, to make sure Papà is all right. Guests stand in groups talking. A man walks across the floor looking at Silvia, and I can tell he's taken with her. She is stunning. In my green dress she seems almost regal with that long neck and almond-shaped eyes. I'd be jealous of her if she weren't my Silvia.

And there's Papà, listening to a plump young woman. She looks familiar. She's animated. It isn't right for her to be so animated at Mamma's funeral.

"Who are you looking for?" asks Giuliano.

"I was just checking on Papà."

He looks past me into the room. "I see Caterina has already snared him."

Snared? Giuliano is crazy. He can't possibly mean it in the way it sounded. Mamma is barely cold. "You know her?"

"Of course. That's Caterina di Mariotto Rucellai, the sister of Camilla—the one you were talking with before. I thought you knew. They're the nieces of my aunt's husband."

"Do you call them cousins?"

"I could, I suppose. They are, distantly. By marriage, at least." Giuliano offers the crook of his elbow. "Come. Please."

I take his arm and we go to his coach. He opens the door.

Naaaa. A little goat instantly butts his head against my chest.

"Why, he's the very goat of the picture."

"Drawn just for you."

"I can't believe he's real." I pet his head and he pushes harder against me. "His ears are like silk."

"Amazing praise from the daughter of a silk merchant." Giuliano eases me aside and the little goat jumps out of the coach.

"The Sultan of Egypt gave us lots of strange animals. But these goats are the only ones that thrived. He's yours, if you want him." He looks at me hesitantly. "You said you love animals."

A funny little billy goat. That's the oddest present ever. I watch him, and my heart goes tender. Someone new to love when I have just lost someone to love. My tears come again, but I smile through them. "Thank you."

"You're smiling. Another smile from my dear Monna Lisa. Indeed, that makes it worth having ridden in the coach with those women, even though they scolded me the whole time because of the goat smell."

I look at Giuliano's luminous eyes and sleek black hair that curls under. He's not handsome in the conventional sense. But his looks please me. Very much.

I should move, or do something else. But I stand here, too flustered to move.

CHAPTER *Nine*

PAPÀ LOOKS AT THE MEAL with surprise. "So, you took a night off from cooking, did you? Well, you certainly deserve that. You work too hard as it is." He puts the first bite of quail into his mouth. It's stuffed with juniper berries and glazed with Marsala. His eyes close briefly in appreciation. "Sandra still cooks well for such an old girl."

"I made it."

His eyes widen. Then he blinks. "You've learned a lot in the past few months."

That's the truth. I cook all the meals, though until now I've made only simple things. I oversee Valeria's mother in laundry and mending and cleaning up. I check Old Sandra's storing of the pantry. I run the household. And I do it well. I do everything Mamma said a good wife should do; I honor her memory. And when I'm not busy with household duties, I work in the silking building. That's not for Mamma's sake, though—that's for my own peace of mind. Silk is the thread of continuity for me.

Papà gobbles his meal. "This is delicious, Betta. You amaze me repeatedly."

I take a bite of the quail. Papà spoke true: it is just as good as Old Sandra's. I sit up proudly. Papà hums. A lightness enters me. I haven't felt light like this in so long. It helps to do things that make others happy. Maybe Mamma was right—maybe learning the culinary skills really will bring me joy.

We finish the meal without further talking. But it's not really silent. Uccio tramps back and forth in the hallway bleating—*naaaa, naaaa.* He used to be a quiet kid, but now he makes a ruckus whenever he can't come someplace with me; Papà doesn't allow him in the dining room. He says he should be in the pen with the other goats.

I wish Papà wouldn't shut him out like that. Not because of Uccio—he has an insistent happy energy that nothing can daunt. No, I worry the noise will bother Old Sandra and her husband, Vincenzo. They moved into the parlor behind the kitchen back in July, after the first time Papà stayed in Florence overnight.

I'm grateful. I hated that night I spent alone. I closed every shutter, even though it was horribly hot. And Uccio made it worse, because he sleeps with me, and his body pumps out heat like a stove. But even with Uccio right there beside me, I quivered at the night noises. Me. Me, who loves to wander in the woods alone. It was dark and I was scared. I didn't tell Papà such an absurd thing; I couldn't. He had asked me a dozen times if I was sure I'd be all right alone and, of course, I had said yes with disdain at the question. I'm lucky Old Sandra took one look at those closed shutters in the morning and put two and two together and told Papà. So he asked her to move in.

Papà dips his fingers in the water bowl and rests his arms on the table, one on each side of his plate. "We've had sunshine two days in a row." It sounds like a complaint.

"But that's good," I say. "It's been such a rainy November so far. This sun feels like a gift."

"If it's dry tomorrow, it's the right time to harvest the olives, because the rain could come back at any time."

I nod. Olives should be picked perfectly dry. That way they won't rot before pressing. And they won't be so full of moisture that the oil comes out tasteless.

He sighs and drops his head.

"What's the matter, Papà?"

"I was planning on riding to Florence tonight. I made appointments for the next several days. And I told our workers here they could take short jobs with others till I get back." He shakes his head. "I'm going to lose business if I'm not there—and I risk losing the harvest if I'm not here. Nothing works out."

Papà goes to Florence often. These days the city has parties nonstop. Piero de' Medici loves them, and the rest of the nobles follow suit, for he has, indeed, taken over the role of his father; that wretched man rules Florence. Papà says there are so many parties, the street cleaners can't keep up. Garbage litters Florence.

All those parties are good for us, though, because they mean a greater demand for silk. Still, there are many silk merchants, all vying for the same customers. Papà has to keep up personal contacts, or he'll lose out.

His face is so tired. It's wearing him out, racing back and forth between the city and Villa Vignamaggio. I think that's what he wants, though—to be worn out so he can't think, so he can't miss her so badly. But he'll get sick if he keeps this up.

"I'll do it."

He juts his chin forth and his eyes fasten on mine.

"It's children's work anyway," I say.

He opens his mouth, then shuts it, then opens it again. "A noble girl shouldn't work outdoors in . . ."

"Don't say it." He's just echoing what Mamma would have said anyway; he's always really liked having me around his work. "I've watched every harvest my whole life. I can oversee this one. Silvia will help me."

He blanches. Well, that's so stupid. Silvia and I do everything together these days. Without her I'd have fallen to pieces—just like he would have without his trips to Florence. Why won't he accept that and treat her nicely?

He opens his mouth and I prepare to interrupt at the first bad word about her. I won't abide a single one.

"You're right. You're so capable, Betta. You always have been." His voice cracks. "You know I treasure you, don't you?"

"Of course, Papà." His voice is so sad, I am about to stand and rush to him.

But he's already on his feet and leaning across the table looking at me. "You can do it without the men. Put Cristiano in charge of the boys. He'll enjoy playing big shot. And he'll follow your orders. Especially if he doesn't realize I'm gone." He goes to the corner and picks up a travel bag I didn't notice before.

"Why, you're already packed." The realization makes something inside me quiver.

"I packed yesterday. I didn't think the sunshine would last." He comes around the table and kisses my cheeks in parting and goes to the door. Then he stops and turns. "I won't let you work like this for long, Betta. You won't be one of those girls who nurses her father through old age. I promise you." He leaves, shutting the door behind him.

I stare at the tiny quail bones on my plate. Tears threaten. It's not the harvest that bothers me. I'm glad to run the harvest. It's that Papà has addressed a fear I hadn't let myself recognize yet. Nothing is the same since Mamma died. There's no talk about my future anymore. No talk about a party or betrothing me. It's all we can do just to get from one day to the next without dissolving in our grief.

I don't want to be a spinster, at Papà's side till he dies, then withering slowly. But I do love him. I love him so much.

I open the door and let Uccio bound in. The dear goat butts me affectionately. I kiss him on the bony ridge above his eyes. "I'm so lucky I have you," I murmur. He jumps up on the table and eats the remains right off Papà's plate. I stand back and watch with surprised gratitude. "We need a little naughtiness around here."

The next morning Silvia and I string nets under the olive trees.

The team of boys follows us: Valeria's four big brothers, under the charge of Cristiano. The oldest brother is only eleven, so they listen as attentively to Cristiano as they would to a full-grown man. And Cristiano seems full-grown. It's as though he's matured into a man since that day we had our sad encounter in the woods. His chest is broad. His shoulders and arms bulge. When he sees me looking at him, I flush and turn away.

The boys beat the branches of the first tree with sticks, standing on ladders for the highest ones. Little Valeria runs around rescuing the olives that fly beyond the nets.

After the boys finish their part, Silvia and I climb high into that tree and inspect. A few olives cling here and there. Faithful little things. We wrest them off by hand, calling encouragement to each other as we go, for neither of us is fond of heights.

Uccio runs around the bottom of the tree. *Naaaa, naaaa.* The perfect little fool.

I glance around quickly. The boys are finishing off the second tree; no one is watching us. Well, I didn't want anyone to be watching. No, I certainly didn't. I don't care where Cristiano's eyes go. I know who he is; he knows who I am; there's nothing more to be said. We were born different. It's just annoying, annoying and rotten, that the one man interested in me is a peasant, so he doesn't count, he can't count.

I declare the first tree done. We climb down and Uccio butts me. I hug him tight and lift one of his long, soft ears, and whisper to him, "Giulianuccio."

That's his full name: Giulianuccio—"sweet little Giuliano." But I never call him that in front of anyone except Silvia. To the others he's just Uccio—just the ending that means sweet and little. No one else must find out I named him after Giuliano. I don't want people suspecting something stupid about my feelings, especially since I haven't heard a word from Giuliano since the funeral.

Silvia gives a quick, loving pat to Uccio and we climb the next tree. Uccio goes back to bleating piteously.

Paco comes gallumphing through the grove, drawn by Uccio's bleating, no doubt. The two have become unlikely friends. They play tug with rags that Paco steals from Valeria's laundry line.

Uccio disappears with Paco while Silvia and I go from tree to tree, working together. It would be faster to separate, so we can work two trees at once. But it cuts the fear to share it.

We break for the midday meal. I shoo little Valeria home and pull Silvia toward the house with me, to eat separate from the boys.

Cristiano watches us go. He nods to me. Just one quick nod. Then he takes a hunk of cheese out of a sack, cuts it toward his thumb with a small knife, puts the slice in his mouth, and chews large. The whole time his eyes are on me. I know, because I keep glancing back, even as I lead Silvia inside.

Silvia enters the kitchen warily. "Your father won't want to eat with me."

I put cheese and bread on the table. "Papà's gone to Florence."

Silvia visibly relaxes. "He left you on your own to oversee the whole olive harvest, then?"

"And why not? It's fun."

She makes a face. "Ain't he the lucky one that you like to work so hard." Her tone is an accusation.

"Papà works hard, too. That's all he does."

Her face softens. "Sorry. I'd get mad at you, too, I would, if you said bad words about my pa." She pulls two buns out of a hidden pouch. "I made these last night and saved a couple."

I take a bite. It's stuffed with chopped rucola. A memory invades: Mamma's rucola-rich hands on my cheeks. Loss makes me instantly hot all over.

"Elisabetta?" Silvia furrows her brow. "What hurts?"

I shake my head and stare at the ceiling. "Sometimes, Silvia, sometimes I run upstairs and bury my face in the skirts of one of Mamma's dresses and stay there till my heart slows enough to allow me to stand without fainting."

She puts her hands behind my head and pulls me to her. We stand a moment, forehead to forehead.

Then we sit and eat quietly, till we hear Uccio at the back door, bleating to high heaven. Paco must have ditched him to chase a rabbit or a squirrel, the poor little goat. I grab what's left of the food on the table and carry it outside to share with him.

We hunt down little Valeria and send her to round up the boys again. All together we empty nets into the two-wheeled cart. When the cart is full, we wheel it away and dump it into the wagon waiting near the road. Net after net. Cartload after cartload. Valeria and Silvia and I climb into the loaded wagon bed and pick out as many leaves and stems as we can. Uccio keeps jumping in, which means Paco jumps in, too, and we keep chasing both of them back out. I refuse to imagine what goat droppings might do to the taste of our oil.

Dark comes quickly. We're forced to stop. We cover the wagon bed with canvas. Tomorrow Cristiano will drive this wagon to Greve to have the olives pressed. I might go with him. I haven't decided yet.

Cristiano hardly talks to me since Mamma died, and when he does, it's respectfully. Still, he harbors feelings for me; that much is clear no matter whether he says it or not. His eyes don't hide it. But I can handle that; I handle it every day. My hesitancy at going with him in the wagon is due to something else entirely.

The question is the money. Papà pays the olive miller a tip to put us first in line. Would entrusting that tip to Cristiano tempt him to steal away a part for himself? I don't want to be the instrument of his moral decay. But there's the other side: he might rise to the occasion and be glad for the opportunity to prove himself.

I have to think this whole thing through.

Silvia stops by her home first, then she comes back and we eat together. We eat the cold strips of tripe I boiled this dawn with onions and parsley, and the mix of vegetables I lightly steamed and then seasoned with the end of last's year's oil. I chopped those vegetables so small, they're close to a mash. That way the flavors blend on the tongue.

Silvia makes appreciative murmurs as she eats. When Papà is away, her mother lets her take her dusk meal with me. We don't make a fuss over it. We sit at the counter and eat and talk and shriek now and then. The shrieking is because of Uccio. One of his favorite games is to nibble at our toes.

"This food is good, Elisabetta."

"Your bun at lunch was good, too," I say.

She laughs.

"What's funny?"

"You." She pats the back of my hand. "To talk about a simple bun as though it's equal to such a fine meal. Tripe. It ain't the same as game, you know, something anyone can catch. The most tripe I ever tasted before now was when I rubbed a crust of bread in a dirty cooking pot your Sandra had set out to wash. You're very funny." She picks something from between her teeth and looks at me thoughtfully. "It takes time to mince vegetables this small. You must have got up early to make all this."

I did, and willingly. After last night's success with the quail, I can't wait to try more recipes. Maybe I'll even try some of Mamma's. In my head I see her beaming at that idea. "I love cooking."

"It shows. But then you worked till dusk. You know, your day ain't so different from mine anymore."

I almost say I love the work, too. It felt so good today—so good to be as capable as Papà believes I am. I ran the whole olive harvest, and it went without a hitch. Well, really, Silvia and Cristiano and I ran it. Still, I was in charge. But saying I love the work would erect a wall between us again. For Silvia doesn't love it. Why should she? Villa Vignamaggio isn't hers.

I clear things away, then we finish off with pomegranates and goat cheese.

"Mamma handed me a sack of chestnuts." Silvia shrugs in apology. "I better go. I have to finish them tonight for her morning baking."

"Where are they?"

"By the back door."

"Fetch them," I say. "I'll start the fire."

"Don't be daft. You don't want to work all evening after working all day."

"Neither do you."

"I ain't got a choice."

"You think I do?" I say. "You think I want you to get all the cakes?"

She laughs. "Glutton."

I build a fire in the living room hearth and we set the chestnuts to roast on a reed bed beside it. Silvia and I sit on chairs with our legs tucked under so Uccio can't get at our toes. When the chestnut shells split, we husk them and grind the nutmeat into flour. Her mother will make cakes from it tomorrow. I used to think of chestnut cakes as peasant food. But Silvia has shared so many with me the past few months that now I simply think of them as good.

Food doesn't need to be fancy in order to be worth eating. It needs to be tasty. I have to remember that as I go about my cooking from now on. Not all my recipes have to be complicated, like the quail.

I toss two burned chestnuts to Uccio, who eats them whole, shell and all.

"How long's he gone for this time?" asks Silvia.

"I don't know. I suspect at least a couple of days."

"Depending on how he's getting on with her, I guess."

"What?" I stop grinding and hold the mortar firm in my sloping lap. "Getting on with who?"

Silvia looks at me. "I was afraid of that. You don't know, do you? Your father's courting."

"That's not possible. Mamma just died."

"Half a year ago."

Half a year? Lord, I've really lived half a year without her. Everything's jumping around inside me. My mouth goes dry. "Tell me what you know."

"Valeria's father told my pa: it's a lady from one of them really fancy families. The Rucellai."

"Caterina di Mariotto Rucellai," I say slowly, as certainty blooms. I've known it deep inside all along, or I wouldn't remember her name.

"So you do know."

I shake my head and hold in tears. "She caught his eye at Mamma's funeral. Giuliano saw it. I thought he was crazy. But it's Papà who's crazy."

"A man has got needs."

"Don't say that!"

"It's natural, Elisabetta."

"For an animal. Men don't act like that. It's disrespectful of Mamma's memory. Widowers wait a year at least."

"To get married, sure. But they start courting the moment they eye the right girl. You know it's true. How do you think so many widowers find a wife exactly at the end of that year? Your father ain't no different from the rest of them."

"But he should be! Papà should be!"

"Why?"

"Because." Because Mamma loved him. Because he loved her. But I don't say that—not to Silvia. She doesn't believe in love. I'm grinding that pestle down into the chestnuts harder and faster. "It isn't right."

"Who are you to say what ain't right?"

I stare at her apoplectic. "Don't take his side."

"I'm taking yours, you fool. Don't make life so hard, Elisabetta. Let him do what he needs to do. He's still your pa. He still loves you. And that's the truth."

"I know that." I do, I do. I just don't want this. Not now. Not yet. Every part of me is flying around the room, bashing into things, all wild and helter-skelter.

"He could pay a prostitute easy. But he ain't doing that. He's taking up with a nice lady. And at least part of why he's doing it is you."

"Me?"

"He doesn't want you out here alone." Silvia empties her mortar of flour into the big bowl on the table. She refills it with chestnuts and sits to grind again. "You got to know that. Anyone can see it. And he's made a good choice."

A good choice? I remember Caterina's animated face at Mamma's funeral. Papà didn't make a choice—she did. "What have you heard about her?"

"Her pockets is ripping with gold."

"She's young, Silvia. Not much older than me."

"Good. Maybe she'll last a while."

"Don't say that. Really. I can't stand it."

"I'm sorry. It was a dumb thing to say anyways, what with how many women die in childbirth." Silvia sighs. "Valeria's father said this girl's mother died that way."

I blink as her words sink in. "Oh, Lord, what if she wants children with him?"

"He could use a son," says Silvia.

I drop my pestle in the pile of flour and stare at her.

"Don't act daft, Elisabetta. His life has to go on. Just like yours does. Maybe we'll both get lucky and marry and move away and get a chance to see something of the world beyond this piece of land."

"No. No, Silvia. I don't want him to forget Mamma so soon."

"He ain't never going to forget her. He's just got to keep going. That girl'll help him."

"I don't want to put up with a girl in my mother's bed. A girl telling me what to do. It's intolerable. I hate her."

"Ain't it early to hate her?" says Silvia. "And, anyways, in the meantime you ain't got her. You got me. We got each other. At least for another half year. Let's make the best of it."

And all the swirling parts of me fall together at last, weighted by the sense of her words. Silvia's unflinching honesty could save anyone. "You're right."

"Ain't I always?" She smiles.

I'd pinch her for being so self-satisfied if I weren't grateful right now. "I'm not in a rush to leave home, you know. Villa Vignamaggio has so many beauties. You shouldn't be in such a rush, either."

Silvia pauses in her grinding. "This beauty belongs to you, Elisabetta. Ain't nothing beautiful belong to me."

An idea comes. Oh, let it work. "Stay here."

I go upstairs and head for my room. But when I pass Papà's, I suddenly turn back around and go inside it. Mamma's closet is against the inner wall. I stand still and for a moment I feel numb, like on a January day when I've been out in the cold too long.

I open the closet. It's empty. In the dark, I feel around, touching the air to be sure. Mamma's things are gone. I think back to the last time I raced up there to clutch her skirts. It couldn't have been more than ten days ago. So in that period Papà had them whisked away. Well, of course, I tell myself. A man has to supply his bride a new wardrobe. Papà's making room for that.

But he didn't ask me what I might have wanted to keep. Maybe he was trying to protect me in some misguided way. Maybe. Like maybe he's courting Caterina so that I won't have to take care of him in his old age. Maybe that's what he was trying to tell me last night. Maybe he's a mess of good motives and mistaken actions. But that doesn't excuse him. He threw out things I treasured. Pieces of Mamma, gone. I am bereft, as though someone has scraped raw my insides, leaving me as empty as this closet.

I go to my room and open my wedding chest. There are surprises in here I've never looked at. Mamma put them in. And I won't look at them until I marry. But on the very top is something I put in: the sheaf of drawings by Leonardo da Vinci that Giuliano gave me. The horse one is on the bottom, I know. I ease it out.

I carry it downstairs and place it on the dining room table. "Come take a look, Silvia. Brush your hands off on your skirt first."

Silvia comes over, wiping her hands. She stares at the drawing.

I haven't been able to bear looking at it since the day Giuliano gave it to me. But I look now. In the flickering light cast by the fire, the lines of the drawing seem to move. It is a strange effect— a skinless horse moving.

"I ain't never seen nothing like it," says Silvia in a whisper. "I didn't know you was capable of such grand drawing."

"I didn't do it. Leonardo da Vinci did. He's famous. Florence's most famous artist."

"Do you know him?"

"Yes. But he lives in Milan now. I saw him at Lorenzo de' Medici's funeral."

"Did he give you this grand thing then?"

"No. Giuliano gave it to me."

Silvia doesn't speak. She's got the habit of not speaking when I mention Giuliano. I appreciate that. She doesn't press and she doesn't laugh.

"What do you think of it?"

"Well, I don't know. I just feel it. I feel how grand it is."

"Is it beautiful?"

"It ain't trying to be, is it? It's just saying this is what the horse is. Inside and out." She taps her right hand quickly up her left arm and across her chest and stops at her heart, letting her hand beat there for a moment. "We're like this horse. Just skin over all that stuff inside. Yeah, Elisabetta. It's beautiful."

"It's for you," I say.

"What? But Giuliano gave it to you!"

"So I'm free to do with it what I want. Now something beautiful belongs to you."

"I don't want you giving me something so grand." But her eyes stay on the drawing as she speaks.

"It hurts me to look at it, Silvia. It makes me think of Mamma's accident. But it's too wonderful to sell, though it would bring an enormous amount of money. It's a perfect gift for you. My best friend."

"It ain't my birthday," she says slowly and softly.

Birthdays. Mine was dreary this year. Papà and I ate quietly, then sat in the garden. We didn't talk about how it was supposed to have been, how it would have been if Mamma hadn't died. We just sat with our arms hooked, missing her, till it finally grew dark. Then we climbed the stairs. He went right to bed. But I changed into my nightdress and went back downstairs and outside to count the stars.

That's when Silvia came over, carrying a bowl of *cinestrata*. It's broth and beaten eggs with Marsala, cinnamon, nutmeg, and enough sugar to make your tongue sweet all night. She sat with me as I ate, then whispered, "*Sogni d'oro*—golden dreams."

I made *cinestrata* for her on a Sunday in her birth month, too.

August. In fact, I made a big meal and invited her father and mother and Cristiano, as well. We had pasta with spinach, and sautéed chicken giblets. It was too hot for such food, really, but I wanted to do something splendid. We waited till late at night to eat, after it had cooled down some. Papà didn't object to sharing a table with Silvia's family, because Papà didn't know. He was in Florence.

I guess he'll be in Florence more and more now.

But Silvia's always here. With me. "You and me," I say, "we don't need a birthday as an excuse for gifts."

"I don't have nothing to give in return."

"Is that the kind of thing a friend says?"

Silvia looks at the drawing. She wipes her hands till I think the skin will come off. Then she touches it just barely. "Thank you," she whispers. A tear balances at the corner of her eye.

CHAPTER *Ten*

IT WAS ALREADY THE NEW YEAR when Papà finally told me he was betrothed. The wedding would be in April. A full month short of the first anniversary of Mamma's death. "No!" I said. "It's a dishonor to Mamma to rush like that."

But Caterina set the date to coordinate with the annual dove festival in Greve. She has a passion for birds. So Papà wouldn't even discuss a change with her. He didn't want to upset her. He upset me, instead.

He said, "She's only nineteen."

I said, "I'm only thirteen."

"You're almost fourteen."

"She's almost twenty."

"Betta, my amazing treasure, be reasonable. Let Caterina have her way on the most important day of her life." He tilted his head slightly and his eyes were gentle.

I wanted to hit him.

I ran and found Silvia and ranted to her. I said, "Birds! She loves birds! She's planning her wedding around the dove festival. That's her excuse for dishonoring the memory of my mother. Can you imagine?"

Silvia shrugged. "Maybe it's homage to the saint she's named after."

Well, I know the Santa Caterina story, of course. Her father was about to force her into an unwanted marriage when he saw a dove over her head and decided to let her enter a convent to marry God, instead. "Then let her go become a nun."

Silvia laughed. "At least Caterina loves animals, just like you used to."

"Used to? I still love animals!"

"You don't go down to the pens anymore. When's the last time you pet any of them other than Uccio?"

"Who has the time? I work every moment of every day. Anyway," I said, "Caterina doesn't love animals. She loves birds."

"Birds is animals."

I wanted to hit her.

It's the twenty-sixth day of April. Papà and Caterina are to be married today, the day after the dove festival. Our entire villa is decorated with gilded cages of doves. The cooing is quite deafening. I'm glad; it will make it hard to hear the musicians.

Caterina has planned everything with the help of her little sister, Camilla. The two of them find the most frivolous things worthy of long discussion; they seem equally mindless. Camilla's the mother of a one-year-old—Bartolomeo, the infant she gave birth to just a little before Mamma died. He's grown into a curly-haired, fat thing who loves milky almond pudding.

I want to hate him like I hate them. But Bartolomeo giggles a lot. He rolls on the floor and crawls after Uccio and pulls tablecloths off, sending things crashing. I watch from afar. I was the one to witness his first steps. His mother and aunt were gabbing away stupidly, all wrapped up in each other, while he pulled himself to standing with the help of a table leg. Then he grinned and took a step toward me. And a second.

"Are you walking, love of my life?" said Camilla, looking over.

Bartolomeo promptly fell on his cushioned bottom and refused to try another step for days. The fine fellow. He's nothing like his spoiled mother and aunt. Silvia was right: they're rich. Extraordinarily, it seems. I suppose that makes it clear that Caterina is not marrying Papà for security. Why, then, is she taking my papà? He's a step down for her in society. And he's not even good-looking.

The Rucellai are known for extravagant weddings. The actual ring ceremony will have no pomp, of course. But Caterina's uncle, the famous Bernardo Rucellai, is sparing no expense on the feast afterward. He even paid for a new fountain in our garden. Most formal gardens have fountains, but ours didn't because a stream runs along the side of the vegetable terraces. Mamma liked it better than an artificial fountain. Natural things are always better. But the Rucellai are too stupid to appreciate natural things. The fountain will be unveiled at the feast. It's outrageous. That was Mamma's garden. Caterina had no right.

Who knows what else Bernardo Rucellai has paid for. The villa is being decorated in our absence—while the family members are away at the ceremony hall.

I ride in the coach with Papà to the hall, these thoughts rankling in me. Cypresses flank the road. The air is redolent of evergreen. It would be the perfect day for a wedding, if it were anyone else's wedding.

Papà and Caterina are having the ring ceremony in the public meeting hall in Greve instead of at her family's home in Florence. And, then, instead of her riding horseback through the streets of the city so everyone can admire her gown, she's taking a coach to Villa Vignamaggio for the feast, just like the guests. Papà told me that privately, in stentorious tones: "Caterina has chosen not to go horseback." I believe he wanted me to think she's making a sacrifice for my sake. Because of how Mamma died. I hope he's wrong. I don't want her doing things for my sake.

I'm wearing my old yellow dress. The one I wore last year to Lorenzo de' Medici's funeral. A month ago Caterina said I should have a lovely new gown of green, all flowing silk. Did Papà tell her green was my favorite color? What a traitor, to give away parts of me like that. But if she came to green on her own, that was worse. Then she put a drawing in front of me—she'd taken the liberty of designing it—and she stood there, hands clutched, her face all hopeful. One glance and I knew the dress would be marvelous on me. I was furious. That ninny, who was about to slip into my papà's bed, thought she could seduce me so easily? I refused vehemently.

I look like a neglected waif in this dress. It pinches me now, it's so tight. And Giuliano will be at the wedding feast. He's part of Caterina's family, after all; his aunt Nanina is married to Caterina's uncle Bernardo. Giuliano will think this yellow dress is the only party dress I have. And it is—all because of me. I hate to have him see me like this. I hate not having a flowing green dress. I hate myself for not saying yes to Caterina. Spite made me stupid. What a thoroughly awful day.

I've been to Florence three times since Mamma's funeral. Twice over the Christmas holiday and once at the Easter holiday. And even though we stayed long each time, through the *carnevale* in winter and the passion plays in spring, I passed Giuliano only once. We were both on our way somewhere. We exchanged a couple of words about Uccio and he was gone.

But at least Giuliano laughed. And at least I smiled.

I'm starting to feel strange about my smile. It's been so long since I've smiled at anyone but Giuliano, it's as though my smile belongs to him. I wanted to smile at baby Bartolomeo the other day, but I stopped because it felt somehow disloyal to Giuliano.

When we get to the hall, Papà turns his back on me. He will stand beside the notary while the bride stands with her father on the other side of the notary. I am to stand with the bride's family, people I don't even know. Papa asked me if I'd prefer to stand with him, even though that goes against custom. I hate it that he keeps acting so solicitous, as though that will make me forget he's marrying too soon. I told him of course not. Still, as Papà walks off now, I want to call him back. I feel lost. I wish ring ceremonies were not limited to just the family—I wish Silvia stood with me.

The notary asks, "Does anyone here have reason to object to the marriage of these two people, Antonio Maria di Noldo Gherardini and Caterina di Mariotto Rucellai?"

No one speaks.

I want to shout: it's only eleven months since Mamma died.

I look at Caterina for the first time today.

She stands in a white silk dress with gold brocade. Who ever heard of a bride in white? It's dramatic, I'll say that for her. Her hair is woven with pearls. She smiles steadily at her sister, Camilla, and holds on to her uncle's arm. That's when I understand her father must be dead. I didn't know that. She's an orphan. Like Mamma. My arms and cheeks tingle.

But I won't feel sorry for her. Not her.

Her pink face is round, like her big cheeks and breasts and bulging waistline. Overall Caterina's as different from the slight, stooped Camilla as any sister could be. She'd make a fine peasant's wife, hale and hearty. Her eyes glisten. She's happy to be marrying Papà. I'd have to be an idiot not to see that. She's bursting with joy. Papà is right: this is the most important day of that girl's life. I swallow the lump in my throat.

The moment for objections passes.

The notary asks Papà, "Do you enter into marriage to Caterina di Mariotto Rucellai consensually, by your own will?"

"Indeed, I do," says Papà. He looks at Caterina. "I give you my body in loyal matrimony."

"And I receive it," says Caterina in a breathy voice.

The notary asks Caterina, "Do you enter into marriage to Antonio Maria di Noldo Gherardini consensually, by your own will?"

"Oh, yes," says Caterina. She looks at Papà. "I give you my body in loyal matrimony."

"And I receive it," says Papà.

The notary takes Papà by the hand and brings him to face Caterina. Papà puts a gold ring on Caterina's right hand, on the finger beside her pinky.

The notary steps back. "You are man and wife."

I bow my head. A tear runs down my nose and dangles from the tip. It's done. I have never felt so alone.

We exit the hall to an unending line of waiting coaches. Why, the entire nobility of Florence has turned out. I should have expected it. A Rucellai wedding, after all.

I ride back to Villa Vignamaggio in the Strozzi family women's coach. It's the fanciest coach I've ever seen. Leather tooled with real gold lines the inside walls. Black velvet covers the seats. The lace of the curtains is intricate and delicate. I squeeze my arms in to my sides with my hands on my lap. I was harvesting the asparagus just yesterday. I wonder if I cleaned under my nails thoroughly enough.

The women chatter happily. They tell me how lucky I am to

have such a sweet stepmother. One of the younger girls says it will be so much fun to get to know me now.

I nod and try to look agreeable. Nothing is as I thought it would be. Caterina hasn't stepped down in stature; rather, Papà has stepped up. And apparently pulled me with him. I should be happy at that. But all I feel is confused.

We arrive at Villa Vignamaggio and I make a dash for the front door, leaving behind those women and girls, who were all so nice to me. Papà and Caterina stay in their coach while everyone else heads for the house.

I enter my home and stop immediately. White silk drapes across the walls of the living room. Lilies and carnations and jasmine vines, all tied together in great white ribbons, sit in vases on small tables that dot the wall at regular intervals. They exude the sweetest perfume. I'm transfixed. White everywhere, dazzling in its purity.

A girl holds out a basket filled with shiny white paper doves. I take one and it sits perfectly and lightly in my palm. The little thing is entirely the product of tiny, precise folds; nothing cut, nothing glued. Papà's new wife is possessed with doves. Through the small hole in this dove's back where the edges of the paper come together I see gold inside. I put my eye closer. Teeny gold paper stars. How dare they be so darling! But I will not be taken in—I will not be enchanted. This is Caterina's doing—and there is nothing at all about her, nothing nothing nothing, that should enchant anyone.

I move to the side and watch everyone file in. I scrabble to remember names. Mamma would know all of them. But my head holds nothing. Until Giuliano enters. He's swept inside in a group of already rowdy young men, bumping into one another and joking like overgrown calves. And he's immediately lost to my eyes, somewhere on the other side of the room. He didn't look around—he isn't looking for me.

A shiver comes from nowhere. I quickly hug myself.

But now Silvia arrives, thank heavens. I invited her, of course, and Papà even managed to suppress a sigh as he consented. Her hair is done up on top of her head and she's got on my old green dress that doesn't look old on her at all. She's breathtaking.

The music starts. It's a single flute, played exquisitely well.

"I feel like crying," I say to Silvia.

She pinches my side. Hard.

"Aiii!"

"Complain again and I'll pinch harder. You live with her now. So you got to kill that envy."

"Envy? I don't envy her."

"Ain't you the girl that was supposed to get betrothed a year ago? I'd wish all this celebrating was for me, too." She shakes her head. "But it ain't. It ain't for either of us. It's for her. So just shut your mouth."

Cheering breaks out as the bride and groom enter. Everyone rips open the charming little paper doves and sprinkles golden stars in the couple's hair as they walk through the crowd, greeting the guests.

The brilliance of adorning the room in white is now obvious to me. All the guests wear bright colors. But Caterina is in white, like the walls and flowers. Eyes are naturally drawn to her. This is her party, totally and absolutely hers.

People spill happily into the music room and the map room and the library.

"Let's go see," says Silvia. And she pushes me ahead of her.

These other rooms have been transformed with flowers, too. But flowers of all colors now. Especially red geraniums.

A bell summons us to the dining room. Long narrow tables and benches have been set up. I don't see how we can all fit, but, oh, it turns out the organization has been perfect; we take our places with decorum. Rosemary and sage have been strewn down the center of the tablecloths. Pink rose petals circle the plates and glasses. The china itself is pink. I'm surprised at the bad taste; it's as though a child chose it. Good. Let everyone laugh at Caterina.

The meal has too many dishes to count, all set out at once, of course. We feast on chicken, duck, pork, venison, trout, veal stuffed with kidney, all these things surrounded by cardoons, baby artichokes, new peas, asparagus, leeks, even spinach, though I have no idea where they found spinach so early in the season. Sauces and stuffings are pungent with porcini, *ovoli*, morels, and, oh, the little white truffles that Mamma loved. A whole roasted peacock sits in the center of each table, with the feathers all placed back where they belong so carefully that they look like they're sleeping. Beyond that there are the cold dishes scattered everywhere: we eat tiny almond cakes and marzipan candies and goat cheese and dried fruits and all kinds of nuts, dipping our fingers in bowls of rose water as we move from one dish to another. I am seduced against my will, memorizing fantastic recipes nonstop.

The very best thing of all is the pasta. It's cut in the shape of doves that float in a light chicken broth with one raw egg yolk in each person's bowl. I cannot believe all the hours that went into making just this one dish. But it's worth it, oh my, yes. I can almost forget the bitterness of the occasion.

After many toasts with many wines, we move back to the living room, some half-stumbling from drink. Laughter drowns out the cooing of the caged doves. And soon the music prevails—an ensemble now of flute, drum, and lute—and people dance.

I wander, feeling like a stranger in my own home. Caterina has taken over so thoroughly that not even Mamma would recognize the place. Mamma. A shaft of grief immobilizes me. I retreat against a wall.

Silvia finds me. "Introduce me to someone," she whispers in my ear.

"I can't," I whisper back. "I've forgotten their names."

"Pah! You're useless." She sighs and slumps against the wall beside me. "It wouldn't help noways. Look at all them men who came up to me at your mother's funeral, and ain't none of them stayed once I opened my mouth. You were right; they hate how I talk. Maybe I should cut out my tongue."

I shudder. "What a hideous thought."

"Ain't it, now?" She gives a sharp little laugh. "Don't take it too serious. It was a joke." She stands up straight. "All right, I'll stay right here and help you."

"Help me what?"

"Look for him. That's what you're doing."

"I am not. You're not always right, you know. Besides, you've never even met him. You couldn't pick him out. All you know about him is what I say."

"And how you say it."

"You're crazy."

"You can tell me more lies later," whispers Silvia. "You got a guest now."

"Little Elisabetta." A woman comes toward me. She grabs my wrist and smiles. There's gold jewelry up that arm, at her throat, in her hair. She was at the hall this morning for the ring ceremony, so she's clearly in Caterina's family. I curtsy.

She laughs and kisses me on both cheeks, then stands on my other side, hooking arms so that we look out on the wedding guests together. "You don't know who I am, do you? I'm Caterina's aunt Nanina. Your aunt Nanina now, too. Please call me that."

The wife of Bernardo Rucellai. I am to call her Aunt Nanina. Is this a dream?

"Aunt Nanina," says the voice I know so well. Giuliano comes up on my other side, from which Silvia has discreetly disappeared. He kisses his aunt. "May I steal this lovely young woman from you?"

"Enjoy yourselves. Be dancing fools."

And so Giuliano takes my hand and the circle makes room for one more couple.

The dancing of the people around us is stiff. Men have recently taken to lacing their vests tightly and women to wearing corsets, so their torsos can hardly flex. And some of the men have ruffs around their necks, preventing them from turning their heads.

But Giuliano and I have no such entrapments. Giuliano's lack of participation in the latest styles surprises and delights me. Perhaps he enjoys freedom of movement as much as I do. We sway, cut, slide, stamp. The footwork is easy and all dancers do the same steps so, even though this dance is unfamiliar, I quickly catch on. His hands hold mine firmly when we swing each other. His arm guides my back securely when we move forward and backward. And his eyes meet mine every time we face each other. The patterns change from a giant circle to columns to smaller circles. The music and movement have gravity, but all I feel is a lightness, as though we're the thinnest filaments of silk practically floating in the air. This is so good. Let this last forever.

"May I steal my daughter?" It's Papà. And using the same term: "stealing" me.

I don't even try to hide my disappointment. We dance off together.

"Are you enjoying yourself, Betta?"

"I was, Papà."

"Caterina knew you would," he says gaily, missing the fact that I used the past tense. "She said you'd be happiest if we did everything out here, in the country. I guess she was right."

"Perhaps."

"She's wonderful with her sister, Betta. I'm sure she'll be wonderful with you. We're going to be a happy family. Just you wait and see."

My mouth fills with a sour taste. But I manage to hold in angry words. I look away from his eyes.

Someone announces that the fountain is to be unveiled. Papà hurries to Caterina's side. Everyone troops through the rear doors to the garden, which is as unrecognizable as the house, with so many added flowering bushes. Evening has fallen, and women servants dressed in yellow hold torches to light our way. Men servants, also in yellow, come from all sides carrying the dove cages. They set them on the ground behind the fountain and, at a signal, they open them, and prod the mindless creatures out. The air goes white with doves.

Someone pulls the sheet from the fountain to reveal the statue of a man and woman, naked, embracing in a passionate kiss, under a shower poured from an amphora by a baby angel. The wide, round basin they stand in catches the water. Silk ribbons in all colors dangle from the basin lip.

It's stupidly romantic. I look around, expecting guffaws under the hands that quickly rose to cover those mouths. Finally, Caterina will get the scorn she deserves.

But everyone's exclaiming how beautiful it is. No one else finds it absurd.

Caterina stands close to the lip of the basin and reaches her hand out to touch the falling water. I see Silvia in the crowd on the other side of the fountain, watching Caterina with awe on her face. The traitor! I hate Caterina. She's cast her spell over my only friend. It's unbelievable. I hate her!

That's when Uccio comes racing from the terraces and bounds with a single leap right into the fountain basin. Water splashes up the front of Caterina's pearl-studded dress. Ha! Immediate satisfaction warms me. A red ribbon catches on one of Uccio's horns and flops there ridiculously. And now the horror hits. My cheeks flame. No! Oh, I wanted things to go badly, I longed for everything to be ruined—but not this way! Not via Uccio. Oh no, oh no, what will Caterina do to him now?

I rush to grab my dear little goat and tuck him behind me for safety.

But Caterina grabs him first. She's laughing and hugging him. She's hugging my goat! And everyone is laughing now.

A hand snakes around my waist.

I practically jump to face the owner.

"Close call. After such a stunt, I thought perhaps our little friend would wind up on a dinner table as the main course." Giuliano grins.

I smile wide. He's here. And he's understood my worst fear. He understands me.

Giuliano moves in even closer with a conspiratorial lift of the eyebrows. "Which might not be so bad. Roast kid is among my favorites."

I gulp and pull away. And I realize that roast kid was absent from the wedding feast. That must have been Caterina's choice, since everything else was. "What a disgusting thing to say about my pet."

"It was a joke." He lowers his head so that he manages to look up at me, though I'm shorter than him. "Don't be angry. Can't you let it pass as a stupidity?"

A joke. A revolting one. Like Silvia talking about cutting out her tongue. "Of course. It's already gone. I was just thinking about something my friend Silvia said."

"Silvia? Who's Silvia?"

"She was standing beside me when you came to take me dancing."

"Ah! The girl in green."

My cheeks tighten. "You noticed her."

"Who wouldn't? She mustn't be a very good friend of yours, though."

My insides shake. "Why would you say that?"

"You didn't introduce her to Aunt Nanina. I watched."

My hands fly to my cheeks. "Oh, Lord, I didn't. I was so surprised at Aunt Nanina that I got all flustered. What must Silvia think?"

Giuliano shrugs. "You can apologize. She'll understand."

I look down. Everything keeps changing. I was so happy when I found Giuliano's arm circling me. Then everything went wrong. Giuliano noticed Silvia—and I didn't introduce her to Aunt Nanina— and both things make me ill.

"Come on, Monna Lisa. It isn't that bad. Tell me, do you truly forgive me for joking about roasting goats?"

That he can ask so dearly is enough. "Yes."

"Then you believe in forgiveness. Silvia will forgive you. That's what friends do."

I take a deep breath and look up at him.

He gives a tentative smile. "Let's do something happy, Lisa. Show me some secret. Something special in this home of yours."

I'm instantly shy. There is nothing at Villa Vignamaggio that could amaze someone as urbane as Giuliano. And then I realize the perfect thing.

"Are you willing to work a little for it?"

"Is that a challenge? Lead the way."

We go out to the silking building. Uccio breaks away from the crowd and follows us. I close him outside, of course. He doesn't kick the door or even bleat, for he knows I won't relent when it comes to this building.

Luckily there's a tray with complete cocoons, waiting as though by order. I light the fire under the silking pot and fill it with water and rub oil over the pulley hoop.

It's dark in here and the fire is the only source of light. Oh, I hope Giuliano can see well enough to make this work.

Giuliano has been walking up and down the aisles all this time, touching here and there gingerly. Now he comes to my side. "When do I help?"

"Soon." I drop three cocoons into the hot water. "Watch."

The cocoons fuzz up as the silk loosens. I use the hand broom to whisk around them till the filaments can be separated. In seconds I've caught the end of a filament from each of the three cocoons. I twist them together and thread them through the hoop and over the pulley.

"Here. You take them now and wrap them around the reel."

Giuliano follows instructions.

"The rest is up to you. Pump."

And the reel squeaks as it spins.

"Watch. This is the secret part."

The white cocoons dance wildly on the dark surface of the water, leaping like joyful spirits.

"Isn't it amazing? I mean, you know they're held by the

filaments, but you can't see that in all this steam. So it feels like they're alive."

"Yes, yes." Giuliano's face is flushed from the steam, but I can see in his glistening eyes that he knows what I'm talking about. He feels it, too.

"This is my favorite part."

He laughs, and the reel spins slower.

"Keep pumping. You have to do it fast till the entire cocoons are gone."

The reel spins fast again.

He's lucky. The threads on these three aren't as long as some can be. They soon grow transparent.

"Stop."

He stops and I scoop out the cocoon shells with the wooden spoon and crack them open and save the chrysalises inside them in a jar, like always.

"Okay, pump again."

Giuliano pumps until all the thread has been reeled in.

"That's it," I say.

"That's it," he says, throwing his hands in the air.

I put out the fire.

The room is instantly black. Without the squeak of the spinning reel, the air feels empty. The magic of the moment is gone.

Did he really feel it?

Dancing cocoons. Why, they're the most mundane things ever, really. What a stupid thing I am to think he might have been entranced.

"I guess it's time to go back," I say limply.

"This was a wonderful secret."

"Do you mean that?"

"It was like a fantasy. Thank you, Lisa." Giuliano takes my hand in both of his and presses it to his lips.

And the strangest thing happens: I tremble. We danced together with my arm hanging from his and I didn't feel anything like this. But here, alone in the black of the night, this lightest of touches is wondrous. I cannot stop myself from leaning toward him. I am almost falling.

CHAPTER *Eleven*

THE MESSENGER WAITS beside his horse while Caterina reads the letter he's just delivered. Papà is at her side. He's so love-smitten, he follows her around like some clumsy, overgrown pup. I half expect to see his tongue drop from his open mouth. "Elisabetta," she calls, knowing without looking that I'm watching from the kitchen window.

I come outside, drawn more from curiosity than obedience.

"A party at the Martelli summer villa. Look." She happily thrusts the invitation into my hands. "Shall we say yes?"

"You do whatever you wish. I have no interest."

"Oh, please come. It's a pity you missed the last party. Camilla and I had so much fun. We . . ."

"There's a lot to do to keep Villa Vignamaggio running properly." I hurry inside.

Old Sandra waits at the chopping counter where I left her. She takes one look at my face and her own squinches up. "What a scowl. Bad news?"

"Another party invitation," I say in disgust.

"A girl your age should like parties. A year ago you was going to have one yourself, if I remember right."

"Well, nobody's thinking about a party for me anymore."

Old Sandra slaps the bird carcass down in front of me. "You're as silly as this goose."

"What's that mean?"

"How can they guess your mind when you act so contrary? Tell them, dear girl."

How dare she make assumptions about my wishes? "Please just finish teaching me this recipe, Sandra," I say with as much dignity as I can muster.

I chop garlic into smaller and smaller bits, my knife flashing so fast, the movements blur before my eyes.

A party at the Martellis' summer home. This is exactly what Mamma wanted for me—a step up into the highest echelons of society. But not like this, for it happened only because she died. And what's the point of going, anyway? Every time I hear hoof-beats, I run to the window. But it's never anyone for me. Giuliano hasn't come back since the wedding, over two months ago. I thought maybe on my fourteenth birthday, he'd send a message, at the least. He doesn't want to see me—that much is clear.

I split quinces and press the minced garlic into them and take a handful of salt and rub it into the goose's prickled skin. I rub and rub and rub and rub.

Old Sandra puts a staying hand on my shoulder. "That goose is already dead—you don't need to kill it."

And so tonight I place a fine meal on the supper table. Again. And Papà gobbles it with noisy hums of appreciation that I should be allowed to enjoy. Again. But Caterina has to ruin everything by repeatedly saying how utterly wonderfully I cook and what a failure she is in the kitchen—always with her phony sweetness. Again.

As Papà finishes, he clears his throat. "Dear Betta, and dearest Caterina, I owe you both an apology. Betta, you've become engrossed in work, and I've relied on you too heavily. It's hardly a surprise that you've forgotten what it means to be nobility.

Caterina, I beseech you, take my precious girl under your wing and make a proper lady of her."

"What!" I jump to my feet. "Have you lost your mind? What on earth are you talking about?"

"Society, of course. What else would I be talking about? The invitation to the Martelli party has made it obvious. Your reaction shamed me. Sit down, little Betta. Sit and listen."

I lower myself into my seat and glare at him.

"That's better. You don't do what noble ladies do. You spend all your time in the silking building or the olive groves or the kitchen or . . ."

"Mamma spent hours in the kitchen every day and she was a noble lady!"

"Yes, you're right. Of course you're right. But the other work— you shouldn't be doing it. Not to the extent that you do, at least. Not to the exclusion of pleasurable activities."

"I take pleasure in the silking building. You have no idea what matters to me."

"Please, Betta. You know what I mean. You constantly find new jobs to do. You even help me keep the ledgers now. And I let it happen because I took comfort in your partnership—just as you seemed to do. But it's not right, and I should have stopped it long ago. I am determined to remedy it now. And Caterina is the perfect means, for Caterina is the perfect noble lady. She'll be the friend you so clearly need."

I have to bite my tongue hard to keep from screaming.

"I'm sure that Elisabetta has not forgotten ladylike ways," Caterina says slowly in a gentle tone. "Let her do what she enjoys, Antonio. I understand that you want us to grow closer. But we will find our own ways to know each other. Things cannot be rushed."

I blink, but I will not be taken in by her. My stepmother is at best presumptuous and at worst duplicitous.

Starting the very next morning, I practically live outdoors. And without hat or sleeves. The sun darkens my skin in no time. Silvia and I look like two berries off the same bush. That's how it should be. I'm a country girl—this is what I love. If I were to go to a party now, I'd cause a scandal. So there, Papà! When I visit Mamma's grave each day, I beg her forgiveness. And I know she does forgive me. She was right: she understood me.

One day in midsummer, Caterina says, "Will you help me with a project, please, Elisabetta?"

This is a common question of hers; she has so many projects. I shake my head, expecting her to entreat like a child, as is her habit. She's clearly unused to being denied.

"Ah, and Camilla was so sure you'd want to be part of this."

Camilla comes for short visits often. And she never stays more than a night. Despite the way she and Caterina giggle together, her visits would be bearable if she'd only bring her little son, Bartolomeo. But she comes alone. She says newlyweds shouldn't be imposed upon. I wonder if she considers me an imposition? I'm quite sure Camilla has no notion whatsoever of what I'd like to be a part of. I don't bother to respond.

"Well, then, I'll just have to rely on Uccio."

"Uccio?" I yelp.

"Uccio and Cristiano, yes." Caterina's eyes twinkle. "You'll see."

She's got me and she knows it. I squirm against my curiosity.

That night, when the little goat romps up the stairs ahead of me to bed, Caterina comes out of her room. I expect her to give him a quick pet, like usual. Instead, she gives him a lingering hug, while her eyes look at me over his head, inviting me to ask.

I go into my room. Uccio pulls away from her and scampers in after me—good little goat.

The next morning a bleak drizzle turns the world gray. Brief cold spells in summer are always welcome in these hills, but I'm particularly grateful now, as I watch Caterina leave early in a wagon with Cristiano, for I know she's chilled. It feels more like March than July. She should have put off her little excursion a few days till the sun returned. Such determination would impress me if it were anyone but her.

I walk in the garden with Uccio, who promptly jumps into the fountain. He settles on his knees, immersed so only his head shows. He bathes here often, regardless of rain. And Caterina never complains; she seems to take delight in it. When Camilla visits, the two of them exchange stories—Camilla's are mostly about little Bartolomeo and Caterina's are mostly about Uccio. That, too, is annoying of her.

Paco comes racing through the vegetable terraces and plops into the fountain beside Uccio. That dog loves water. But he's a thief—he snatches Uccio away from me. Of course. The dog is lonely without Cristiano. Spinone dogs are loyal to their masters. So even when Paco plays, he wants to know where Cristiano is every moment.

I walk past the fountain and, oh, at the far corner of the garden Mamma's cherished muse statues have been gathered into a circle surrounding black roses, the very type I saw at the Greve flower show two springs ago, the type that grow in the Medici garden in Villa Careggi. Nestled among the muses are sprays of wild orchids. And I know these orchids, as well. They're the type Cristiano was going to enter into the flower fair at Foiano della Chiana that same spring.

Cristiano's been helping Caterina on this project. Somehow

she discovered his passion for flowers. She's an observant one, insidiously so.

I feel left out, which is absurd; it's been my choice not to know about Caterina's doings. And it isn't right that she should take such liberties with Mamma's garden. Papà pampers her—like he used to pamper me. But more.

I turn around now and my eyes take in the whole garden. The various places where those statues used to stand are bare and the area around them seems bland now. That can't last; Caterina hates bland, so much so that our home has become a shock to the eye. Tablecloths and bed linens scream in the high-pitched voices of reds and oranges and yellows. She's hung violet tapestry in the dining room, too. She indulges herself terribly. Clearly, she is now about to indulge herself in redesigning the garden. With Cristiano's help. But what part does Uccio have in all of it?

The wagon returns at dusk, loaded with flowering plants. Just as I expected.

The next morning, however, there's a surprise: wagons come slowly up the road, burdened with heavy loads. Three men, arms bulging, appear at the rear door. I go off to my chores in the silking building with Silvia, but we sneak peeks, peering through the light but persistent rain.

By the end of the day, flowers circle so many statues, all of animals grouped according to some plan that only Caterina sees the logic of: dolphins and mermaids together here, a harmonious pair—but fawns and lion cubs there, a doomed pair. The only lone statue squats beside the fountain: the goat god Pan playing on his reed flute. I rest my hand on his head and wonder if Caterina thinks of that as Uccio's choice. In any case, even I can't deny that the total effect of all this profusion is quite disarming.

Before supper Caterina finds me in the kitchen. "I saw you in the garden. Don't you love it?"

It's Friday, a day of fasting from meat, so I'm making *cacciucco*, a fish stew. The traveling fish vendor from Livorno gave me the recipe just this morning. He took advantage of the cool weather to come inland to sell. He promised everything was as fresh as in winter. Conger eel, gobies, stargazer, dogfish, scorpion fish, sea toad, prawns, squid, and octopus—all lie cleaned and ready on the counter. I slice them into bite-size pieces without a word.

Caterina tucks a lock of my hair behind my ear. Then she leans close and whispers almost sadly, "It looks like it's going to be a very fine stew."

In the following week, Caterina's behavior toward me changes. Her invitations and questions cease, until she barely talks to me. Fine; I have no time for her nonsense. Papà still goes often to Florence for business deals, though he rarely spends more than one night there unless Caterina accompanies him. But I'm the one who makes sure that we meet the obligations he binds us to; I oversee the silk production. And I run this house, as well. Papà makes no further objections. And Caterina, well, she merely lives here. I really truly do not have time for her.

Besides, my work has, ironically, increased since Papà's ridiculous outburst. The three young men that Caterina hired to place the statues in the garden now live in the workers' cottages, for she convinced Papà to hire them even though money is still scarce and Papà had already let go other workers. Rocco and Tomà are peasants; they know the earth and livestock. But Alberto comes from a servant family in Florence. He found no work there; times are as hard in the city as in the country. He, of course, is a stranger to farmwork. And not a one of them knows about silk production. So it falls on Silvia and me to teach them. Every step must be done carefully and on time, or an entire batch of worms will be ruined. And these men are not used to the demand for precision. We must check on them regularly and give encouragement and correct errors before they become gross. I have no idea how Papà thought he could have managed all this without me.

Yes, I am far too busy to bother with Caterina.

Late in August Camilla arrives, for five days. This will be her first extended visit since the wedding, and she's bringing her son. Caterina is so excited, she waits out front for her, and I stand alongside—not to greet Camilla, of course, but to see little Bartolomeo. Caterina gets to see him every time she goes to Florence, but I never leave Villa Vignamaggio. I've missed the child, against my will.

Camilla literally leaps from her coach and promptly vomits.

Caterina throws her arms around her sister. "Elisabetta, go quickly. Ask Sandra to prepare a sick bed."

"No, no." Camilla laughs even as she wipes her mouth with a handkerchief. "Don't go anywhere, Elisabetta. No one's sick. That was simply my announcement."

"Announcement?" Caterina opens her mouth wide in happy realization. "Oh! What better way to say another child grows within you! What a delight, Camilla."

Camilla squeezes Caterina to her. "You're next, good sister. Do hurry, so our babies can grow up together."

"Oh, let it be true!" Caterina turns to me with an excited laugh. "Elisabetta, could you make that sweet-crusted pie with hare meat and candied orange peel for tonight's meal, the one you do so fantastically well? Antonio loves hare."

"Don't forget the parsley." Camilla giggles.

"And rucola," adds Caterina, giggling herself.

I remember Piero de' Medici talking about amorous prowess.

Women discuss sex freely among themselves, for everyone needs to know the best times and positions for getting pregnant. But it's my papà they're talking about here. I have to get away before they say more. Fortunately, little Bartolomeo, abandoned and forgotten in the coach, calls me to lift him down. I hug him close and dance in a circle, then I take him to find Silvia, and the two of us entertain him until it's time for me to begin cooking.

A few weeks later, Caterina says to me, "Camilla's coming tomorrow. Could you take the day off from chores and help us again with Bartolomeo? You know, so it will be a special welcome."

"I didn't take the day off last time. Bartolomeo simply accompanied Silvia and me in our work."

"I've got a treat in mind," says Caterina. "You can't work and do it at the same time."

A treat for Bartolomeo? I'm tempted.

She comes closer. "Silvia's invited."

So the next day when Bartolomeo arrives we lead him into the kitchen and all four of us girls spend the day making the boy jellies shaped as little men and animals. We let him add colors to each jelly—from saffron, sweet almond milk, and herb juices. We even make reddish-gold ones from the juice of tomato, a new fruit Camilla has brought. But those are just for show; you can't eat this kind of fruit.

And thus begins a ritual: every few weeks, Camilla returns with Bartolomeo. The toddler cannot get enough of Vi-Vi, as he calls Villa Vignamaggio, and of his doting aunts—Caterina and Silvia and me. Silvia, of course, is an honorary aunt. But I'm a real aunt; the wedding made me an aunt overnight. Dear Bartolomeo calls me Zi-Bi, for Zia Elisabetta. He rushes into my arms on arrival without fail. The warmth of it makes me happy.

Bartolomeo makes Old Sandra and her husband, Vincenzo, happy, too, both because he loves them (he loves everyone), and because when he visits, Caterina sings. She fancies herself quite a singer, in fact. She stands by an open window and belts out songs for whatever audience she can gather. Silvia has little patience for it, but I enjoy it actually, and Old Sandra and Vincenzo clap with enthusiasm, as does Camilla, the ever-insipid sister. The songs are well-known poems that Caterina sets to music. She reads Latin and Greek fluently, as well as our own Florentine tongue. She has the education only the wealthiest noble girls are offered, and even fewer decide to accept. Her books lie open on the library tables now.

And so the summer ends. The air turns cold. Christmas comes and goes. I make the slight concession of attending the festivities in Florence with Papà and Caterina. We stay in Camilla's house, with Bartolomeo and her husband. It's a very fine home, with an inventive cook who is surprised at my initial inquiries—noble ladies don't generally come into his kitchen seeking help—but then flattered enough to share secrets with me. But in the end, I wish I hadn't come, for, though I search tirelessly, I don't see Giuliano anywhere, and no amount of wonderful recipes can fill that hole.

On a dark afternoon in January, Silvia and I sit in the silking building after the workers have finished for the day. Her hands lie folded in her lap, a quiet pose unusual for her. "Cristiano's leaving."

I jerk to attention. I've been making a list of winter projects— the outbuildings need repair—and I was planning on starting him on them soon. "For how long?"

"For good." The shadows hide Silvia's face; still, I hear the tears in her voice.

I shake my head. "But he's so young."

"He turned seventeen last month. He's almost as old as Alberto."

Seventeen. Why should that surprise me? I'm but a half year from my fifteenth birthday. I put my hand over hers. "Where will he go?"

"He said he'll wander till he finds a place to work as beautiful as here."

"If he thinks Villa Vignamaggio is so beautiful, why leave?"

"What else could he do?"

I won't ask what that means.

That night I lie in bed and wonder how we will manage without Cristiano. I've worked with him so closely for so long now. I rely on his intelligence and doggedness. He's a good model to the other men and he's a kind but firm leader to the younger boys. When he hugs me good-bye, should I try to dissuade him?

The next morning, I sit by the back door, pulling ice from the soft spot in the center of the underside of Uccio's hooves. The dumb little goat made the mistake of following Paco into the fountain basin on the coldest day so far this winter. Spinone dogs love frigid water, but a goat isn't made for it; the ice has cut into these fleshy spots and made him bleed. So Silvia took Paco away while I dragged Uccio home. Poor little limper. I'll have to lock him inside for the rest of the day.

Cristiano appears with a satchel over his shoulder. He stops in front of me. "Good-bye, Monna Elisabetta," he says. So formal.

I push Uccio off my lap and stand to hug him, but Cristiano has already turned away. "Good-bye, Cristiano," I call. He walks down the path to the road. I watch till he's out of sight. My arms hang empty.

Bark! Bark, bark, bark! It's Paco, somewhere back behind the workers' cottages. He must be tied up, not to come running. I've never heard that dog bark before. It's as though he knows something is very wrong. Poor Paco. He'll be heartbroken once he realizes his master is gone. How can Cristiano leave him like that? But a dog would be a hindrance for certain kinds of work, and Cristiano needs to keep his options open. Cristiano has learned to harden his heart against impossibilities. I hate knowing that. I hate it, because it's what I'm struggling so hard to learn, as well. Paco barks all day.

That night snow falls deeper than I've ever seen. I watch from my window, hoping Cristiano has found shelter. Whatever he thinks of me now, if he does still think of me, is buried as deep as this snow. I'm both sad and relieved to see him go.

Silvia keeps Paco tied up for the next two days, till he stops barking. On the third morning, she lets him free. He disappears instantly. We stand together and call. We walk the fields and the woods, calling till we're hoarse. We hold each other and cry.

Then I go inside and chop dried vegetables for soup. I chop smaller and smaller; I let the movement of the blade absorb me. Caterina and Papà exclaim it is the best they've ever tasted. That night I say a prayer—that Paco might find Cristiano, that Cristiano might find a beautiful place to work. I repeat it, night after night.

February comes with a wet cold that chills to the bone. I make Rocco keep a fire blazing in every fireplace night and day. I worry about Old Sandra's husband getting congestion. But I don't have to worry about little Bartolomeo, at least, because Camilla is so heavy with child now, she announced at her visit yesterday that it was her last. From now on, Caterina must go to Florence if she wants to see her sister.

That news saddens Silvia and me. We've had fun when Camilla

has come with Bartolomeo. Somehow the very act of entertaining that sweet child leveled us. We were no longer a contrast of peasant on one side and city nobility on the other, with me uncomfortable in the middle; we became just four girls together, enjoying the moment. And, as time went on, Caterina cozied up to Silvia and me as much as she cozied up to Camilla. Now that's over.

It's late morning and Papà is in Florence. I pass Caterina's open bedroom door. She sits naked on the edge of the bed, weeping quietly. Blood stains the sheet. Each moon's bleeding must bring her such sadness. I have the urge to circle her inside my arms and stroke her hair. I take a step into the room and a floorboard squeaks.

Caterina pulls the bedclothes up to her chin and gives me a blank, dead look. Of course. She can't imagine why I'm here. Comfort is the last thing she'd expect from me.

I turn and leave, closing the door. But I can no longer pretend I know nothing about my stepmother. She is vulnerable. And sincere. The sweetness I took at first as forced is, instead, completely natural to her; it never flags.

The next week Caterina comes to me with a travel bag. "Pack, please. Come with me to Florence to see Camilla and Bartolomeo."

"I don't go horseback."

"I know that. Of course I know that. We can go in the coach."

That many hours alone in a coach with Caterina? "I don't feel that well."

Caterina's face falls. She had dared to be hopeful.

"But we can make jellies for you to bring to him," I say. "If you have the time."

Caterina postpones her travel for a day, while Silvia and

Caterina and I make the jellies. And Caterina sugars almonds herself—the boy loves almond flavor. She does it expertly, not burning a single nut and making the sugar coating exactly the right thickness. Could it be that she isn't the failure in the kitchen she has always claimed to be? I press my fingers to my lips as I watch her work.

Silvia and I stand together the next morning and wave at her departing coach. "I wonder why she doesn't go to Florence more often," I say. "You'd think the country would bore her."

"Maybe she feels about the country like I do about the city," says Silvia.

"How do you feel about the city?"

"Anything can happen there. You know, the grass is always greener and all that."

Anything can happen. I feel a cold spot of fear for Caterina. She wants something to happen out here at Villa Vignamaggio. I think of the bloody sheet.

Caterina comes home four days later and walks into the kitchen without a word. She sets a card on the counter beside where I'm working. It's an invitation to a wedding in April. My hands are too dirty to open it and see who's getting married. It could be anyone. All the girls my age have been betrothed for a while now. I look at Caterina.

"I can help you design a dress if you want." Her eyes study mine. "You'd look lovely in blue." Her voice is tentative, ready to retreat. Her mouth is worried.

The *no* that normally surfaces so quickly sticks in my throat. I am without response.

"Elisabetta," she half whispers, "no one can replace your mother. I would never try to do that. But I can be something to you . . . something more than what I've been so far . . . if only you'll let me. There's a whole wonderful life ahead of you. Please." Her voice quavers. "Let me help you find it. Stop hiding here. Let's begin with this party."

Hiding? My initial reaction is to rise up in denial, but I can't. Caterina has spoken too frankly. She knows my need. And I can hear hers in her voice. My strange behavior hurts her. How very odd, and yet how natural, given that it's her. And I might as well face this particular pain. Everyone's getting married now; I'll look mean-spirited if I don't join the celebrations. "Blue's all right," I murmur.

She smiles so wide, I'm embarrassed. "It will be truly magnificent. A Medici wedding always is."

"Medici?" I say with a croak. Could Giuliano be lost to another?

"Contessina di Lorenzo de' Medici is marrying Piero Ridolfi," Caterina announces as though she takes pride herself in this event. "The most noble young woman of Florence marrying the richest banker—everyone will be there."

And I am breathing once more. Of course it's Contessina's wedding. A younger brother doesn't marry before his sister.

Three weeks later, I stand at the mirror in my bedroom, inspecting how the bodice of this dress fits. Silvia lies prone on the floor, inspecting how the skirts fall.

"Valeria's mother did a fine job," I say. "Don't you think so?"

"The bottom's even enough." Silvia gets to her feet and smiles slyly. "I ain't never seen such a low cut on the top, though."

"It wasn't my idea."

"Sure."

"It wasn't. Caterina insisted. That's how they do it in Florence these days. She wants me to fit in."

Silvia nods and looks away. But her lips twitch.

"What?"

"I didn't say nothing."

"But you want to. So do it. Just spit it out."

"You're going to fit in—like Caterina says. You'll be part of Florence now." She nods. "I knew it was going to happen sooner or later. I'll miss you. But it's good. Good for you."

"Don't act daft. I'm just going to a wedding. I'm not moving to the city."

"We'll see. Nobility is nobility. Anyways, you look like the sky. Soft and gentle."

"You mean that?"

"He'll think the same thing."

My breath catches. After all this long time, I haven't learned Cristiano's lesson; my heart is still tender with hope.

CHAPTER *Twelve*

THE NEXT WEEK I stand in the entrance hall to the Ridolfi house, holding my breath and not feeling at all like the sky. In contrast, I feel tiny and insignificant. For the first time I'm actually grateful that Papà and Caterina's wedding was so extravagant. It prepared me for this; otherwise I might be standing here agog at the flowers and lanterns and sugar sculptures, like a country mouse in a city pantry.

We've already eaten; tables were set up in the streets, so the whole city could feast. But, though I have become insane for new recipes, I hardly tasted what I put in my mouth. My attention was fixed on finding Giuliano, while not letting anyone else realize I was looking for him. We're now inside the Ridolfi home. Only the top nobility are invited inside for the dance. So, while the room is crowded, it's filled with tens, not the thousands outside. My eyes search the room.

A girl rushes up. "Elisabetta! You really came! Finally. Well, of course, who could miss this?"

I look over my shoulder in panic at Caterina, who obligingly steps forward to my rescue. "Your dress is wonderful, Barbara." Ah, so that's the girl's name. "May I join you young girls just for a little while?" Caterina smiles warmly.

Barbara links arms with me and draws me to the circle of girls my age. But it's Caterina who says hello to each girl, calling them by name, slowly and clearly: Ginevra, Bianca Maria, Lucrezia, Laudomia, Piccarda, Maddalena, Donata, Alessandra. It is only Alessandra that I remember immediately, for I sat with her in the coach little more than a year ago, on Caterina and Papà's wedding day. But the others, it's as though I never met them before. Without Mamma's constant litany about these families, I have lost touch entirely. Still, no one seems to notice my hesitancy, nor my ignorance about almost everything they say. They fold me in, as though I've been one of them forever.

Well, I guess I have been, sort of. Nobility is nobility, like Silvia said. But now that I've become part of the extended Medici family, via Caterina's uncle's marriage to Aunt Nanina, everyone wants to tell me their secrets. And everyone wants to know mine.

I have so many secrets. The way I pass my days is a secret. But secrets are exactly that. The only one who knows all mine is Silvia, and that's the way I'm going to keep it. Since the winter has faded my skin to a respectable paleness, it doesn't give me away. And this dress is certainly appropriately fashionable.

Soon Caterina is whisked off to the dance floor on the arm of a young man.

"So who do your eyes search for?" Maddalena comes closer. "I saw how you looked around the room when you came in. You're older than me, aren't you, but you're not yet betrothed. Do you want a rich banker, like Contessina got?"

"She had to marry him," says Ginevra. "Her big sister married a banker. Her brother Piero wasn't about to let her marry anyone less. I'm happy with my betrothed—he's handsome and young and he will be rich if he follows in his father's footsteps."

"I'd take an already-rich banker in a flash, even if he was old," says Bianca Maria. "Comfort is worth a lot."

"You're still a child," says Maddalena. "What do you know?"

"I know what Mamma tells me," says Bianca Maria. "Other things fade, but money lasts."

"Other things?" says Ginevra with a knowing look. "Does your mamma describe these 'other things' to you?"

They giggle. But I know this talk is far from silly. They're discussing their future. Their chance for happiness. Nothing could be more serious. They chatter on.

Piccarda sidles up and whispers in my ear, "No old man for me. I want those 'other things.' I want to scream in joy in the bedroom. Don't you?"

I blink. No one's ever talked this way to me. I can't believe it's coming from Piccarda. She can't be more than thirteen. Do people really scream in the bedroom?

"And I'm going to get it." Piccarda practically puts her mouth to my ear. "I'm going to get Giuliano."

My hand flies to my mouth to hold in the gasp.

"So you think me silly? You think with all the mess going on, he'll wait a decade or more to marry, and then choose someone half his age, don't you? That's what everyone thinks."

My heart's beating so fast, I can hardly understand her words. What mess is she talking about?

"Well, I'm not silly. My father wants to find me a suitable match now. But I'm begging him to wait. I've caught Giuliano's eye, I'm sure of it. I just need more time. And with how rich he is, he's as good a catch as any older man."

Piccarda's so young; she might not understand things yet. Whatever Giuliano's eye has done, she might have misunderstood. But she is pretty. Alas, very. And her jewelry shows her wealth. Her father will pay a handsome dowry, I'm sure.

"May I have this dance?" A young man bows to me. I accept his invitation eagerly, for it is nothing less than escape.

When the dance ends, another young man sweeps me away. And when that dance ends, a third man, much older, makes me his partner.

No sooner does that dance end than I hear: "Quite the popular one, aren't you?"

I swirl around to face him so quickly that I knock into him. Why am I always so graceless?

Giuliano makes a show of staggering backward, but he's grinning. "At least you haven't knocked anyone down on the dance floor. Or not yet, that is."

"So you've been watching me?"

"It's impossible to take my eyes off you."

I have nothing to say to that. But I'm smiling. Lord, how I'm smiling. At last I manage, "Congratulations on your sister's good fortune."

"Thank you. We'd better dance or someone else will snatch you from me." Giuliano offers his arm and we join the dancers.

"I haven't been watching you," I say as we twirl away from each other. His eyebrows rise and his mouth falls. We twirl again and come together again, and I swallow, then add, "Because I haven't managed to catch even a glimpse of you till now."

He grins again.

"We saw each other at two funerals in a row, your family's then mine. We saw each other at two weddings in a row, my family's then yours. What do you think is next?" I try to keep my voice light. "And how long between?"

His face goes solemn. "I haven't been to parties this year. I'm sorry I haven't taken the pleasure to dance with you in so long." We part and twirl and come together again.

"I haven't been to parties, either. Not since Papà's wedding."

He blinks in surprise. "Any special reason?"

"Special, no. I wouldn't say that. And what's your reason for not going to parties?"

"All these squabbles. Every time I show my face at a social event, people want to interrogate me about what I know. It takes away the fun."

"What squabbles?"

"About the troubles everyone predicts. Or, well, not everyone. Just that Savonarola. And now Giovanni's involved."

"Cardinal Giovanni? Your brother?" I shake my head in confusion.

"You don't know anything about it, do you?" He turns me once neatly under his arm. "I like that. It's a relief. And, come to think of it, it's an opportunity, too. I want to hear your reaction. Let's talk after this dance."

The music ends and we walk to a spot near the wall. "I wish we could speak in private," says Giuliano, looking around at the guests. "But the streets are as crowded as this hall. We risk being overheard no matter where we go."

"Speak under your breath. I'll listen hard."

"Come." Giuliano takes two chairs and pushes them close. We sit side by side and look out at the dancers with feigned interest.

Somehow being together but not on the dance floor feels more intimate. I become intensely aware of our physical selves. I look down and my eyes take in his hands. "Your fingers are studded with rubies," I say in surprise.

"Contessina dressed me. Don't breathe too deeply or you'll swoon from the perfume in my shirt."

I laugh, though I feel I could swoon regardless of the perfume.

"It's so good to hear laughter. And so rare." Giuliano shakes his head. Then he whispers, "The banks falter briefly and everyone makes a commotion."

"Falter?" The very idea shocks me. I am instantly alert. "Papà calls Florence's banks the foundation of modern society."

"And so they are. These problems will pass, Monna Lisa. But in the meantime Savonarola exploits everyone's fears."

"What can a monk, of all people, say about the banks?"

"Nonsense, that's what. He says the Italian states are going to ruin because the rich throw away money on extravagances."

I view the dancers in front of me with new eyes. "This wedding is extravagant. Will the feast really go on for three days?"

"A Medici wedding must be like this." Giuliano sits taller and from the corner of my eye I see his jaw clench. "The cooks prepared thousands of chickens, herds of calves. We are as grand as ever, and this wedding shows that."

I can't stop myself from reproving: "At huge cost."

"It's nothing compared to the past. My grandfather spent six thousand florins on his daughter's wedding."

My head spins with how much that sum could do. I squeeze my folded hands tighter in my lap. "And you think Savonarola is wrong to decry extravagances?"

"A sumptuous wedding feast portends a fecund marriage. Even Savonarola can't be against that. What he rails about is Italian states spending money on foreign treats. He says other countries use Italian money to grow more powerful than us. Especially Florentine money. And, of course, he points his finger at my brother Piero."

"Are other countries more powerful than us?"

"How could they be? Florence is the center of the civilized world. The nobility here are the richest anywhere. Piero easily found the money for this wedding in the banks. But Savonarola can't be reasoned with. He's even stirred up the Pope. So the Pope sent my brother Giovanni home from Rome to tell Piero how to fix things. As though the Pope understands the material world."

"The Pope must understand money. Papà says no place is richer than the Vatican."

He shakes his head at me, but his eyes are wide. "Monna Lisa, regardless of what the Pope knows, Florence isn't a papal state. He can't tell a republic how to behave. It's wrong." His voice cracks. "And it's wrong to pitch brothers against each other."

I turn my left hand, the hand closest to Giuliano, upward and extend it toward him instinctively. "You're caught between them, aren't you? Between your brothers. That must be awful."

From the side, I see an older man approach. "Am I interrupting?" He looks pointedly at my extended hand, which I quickly drop, and—oh!—it's Leonardo da Vinci!

"Ser Leonardo!" Giuliano stands and embraces him. "You came from Milan. I'm so glad."

I hurry to rise.

"No, no," says Leonardo. "Please stay seated, Madonna Elisabetta. Put your hands like they were a moment ago." He takes my hands and arranges them. "The right hand facing down, the left facing up—and your eyes looking toward that left hand."

Did this artist's discerning eye catch the emotion in my gesture toward Giuliano? I shake my head and pull my hands away, hoping my cheeks are not as red as they are hot.

"Don't be shy with me. I need you as a model. Please. Just for a moment." Leonardo takes my hands again and gently arranges them as before. "That's perfect." He snaps his fingers. "That's what I've been looking for."

"May I be so bold as to ask what you're talking about, Ser Leonardo?"

"Il Moro has asked me to do a special painting, and you have given me the idea for how to pose the central figure."

"Who is Il Moro?"

"That's what they call the Duke of Milan," says Giuliano.

"Maybe it's because of his dark Moorish skin or . . ." Leonardo lifts one corner of his mouth. ". . . his dark soul." He bends toward me and talks softly. "I've done portraits of a handful of his mistresses." He straightens up again. "Now I'm doing the last supper."

The last supper? With Jesus and the apostles? How on earth could I have given Leonardo something to use in such a painting?

"But hasn't that already been done so many times?" asks Giuliano.

"The subject will never be exhausted." Leonardo smiles. "And Milan needs it."

"But the Milanesi come to Florence to see Fra Angelico's paintings. He's done three versions of it."

"Mine will be better than traditional frescos," says Leonardo. "I'm using tempera and oil on dry plaster. Jesus' wrath will shine forth more. After all, it's a moment of impending betrayal."

"Betrayal, yes! That's what it's really about. I'm sure you'll make it extraordinary, as you do everything." Giuliano looks around briefly. Then he steps closer to Leonardo. "Circulate, Ser Leonardo. Let everyone see you are here. Let them know that you don't play the artists' games of betrayal. Remind them that the best artist in the world is a friend of the Medici family."

"I understand," Leonardo says solemnly.

I don't.

But before I can ask, Leonardo turns from Giuliano to me. "May I have this dance, dear model?"

I let him lead me onto the dance floor, knowing Giuliano will find me again soon. We take our positions among the couples.

"You've saved me days of wandering, you know," says Leonardo.

"I don't know that at all. What do you mean?"

"I search the streets of Milan looking for men whose visages and poses would be right in my painting. I spend hours at it every day. And there you were, perfectly posed. Thank you, Madonna Elisabetta. Returning to Florence feeds my soul."

"If you miss Florence so much, why don't you stay?"

Leonardo narrows his eyes at me. "Little Madonna, what you don't know. The arts are slipping away here."

"What an absurd thing to say. The school of art in the Medici gardens near San Marco is world famous."

"And who works there now? Michelangelo has left. And Botticelli. And the della Robbia brothers." His voice has a bitter edge. "They don't take secular commissions from the nobility of Florence anymore. From the likes of your friends— and mine. They've gone over to Savonarola's side. That's the betrayal Giuliano was talking about."

"So they believe the nobles of Florence are decadent?"

"Sweet Madonna, I love your innocence. But beware ignorance—none of us can afford it these days. I remember you describing the silk business. You understand how things work. Art is a business, too. Those artists' defection is not about morality but money. Right now the church has it, and the nobility don't. And artists love to eat."

I cannot tell if Leonardo is sad or angry, but I am distinctly uncomfortable. I don't know what to think about any of this.

We dance without further conversation. As the music ends, I look around for Giuliano, but another man comes up and asks me to dance. And at the end of that dance, another. There is no short-age of dancers tonight. But, though I scan the crowds constantly, both during a dance and afterward, the evening passes and Giuliano doesn't reappear. It's as though he's vanished.

In the morning, we vanish, too, for Papà announces we are skipping the rest of the wedding festivities. He won't relent, no matter how much I implore.

I can hardly sit still in the coach home. My mind races over the things Giuliano said. The fight between Savonarola and Piero worries me, yes—and I can just bet that some new rumor about the banks is behind Papà's whisking us away. He and I have shared enough hours poring over the financial ledgers of Villa Vignamaggio for me to understand how he views money matters. I can't say I don't agree with Papà; if the banks are faltering, the rich of Florence should tighten their belts. That's how we've kept Villa Vignamaggio from going into ruin, after all. And I hate it that the artists are somehow defecting. Florence's reputation as the center of culture relies on them.

But that's not what fills my head here in the coach. Giuliano said he'd been watching me. He said it was impossible not to. And he wanted my reaction to the present state of things. Mine.

I'm so distracted over the next few days that I can barely do my work properly. Caterina suggests I help her embroider things for Camilla's coming baby. I accept, to keep from losing my mind. She's so surprised, she squeals, actually squeals.

I sit now in my room embroidering the edges of a baby sheet. I'm working by daylight, which is a gift. The short days of win-ter have already passed. The extra hours of sun give my spirit a much needed lift, for the sight of this sheet is a bit discouraging. My skills with an embroidery needle are indeed limited. But the baby will know no better. And the little animal I have sewn for Bartolomeo, as a prize upon becoming a big brother, is decently done. It perches on the top of my wedding chest. I made him a goat stuffed with crushed chestnut husks. It's pliable and sturdy, and though it is certainly no paragon of sartorial mastery, I know he will love it, for he loves my Uccio.

But, oh, the day has gotten away from me. I rush downstairs and heat up the sauce I made this morning. It's oxtail ground up with so much rosemary you can't tell meat from herb. Vinegar and honey tease the tongue together. Camilla's cook, Jacobo, gave me the recipe when we were in Florence for the wedding. He's quite content in my appreciation of his skills, and that gets realized in his generous sharing. The smell is exquisite. I boil long, thick strands of pasta to serve it over. There will be only two dishes. The other is *biancomangiare*: pancreas and thymus in a chicken broth enriched with egg yolk, Vinsanto wine, almond paste, milk, cinnamon, coriander, nutmeg, and clove. I twirl around the kitchen, from one task to the next, quite content myself.

We all sit down to eat. I help myself to the pasta first, eager to see if the taste holds up to the smell. Caterina and Papà follow suit.

But Papà holds his fork above the plate and hesitates. Then he sets it down sharply and smells the air with loud sniffs. "Spanish rubbish." He drums his fingers on the table. "I won't allow Spanish rubbish in this house. The odor taints the food."

"What are you talking about?" asks Caterina, eyes wide.

"Tomatoes."

Tomatoes sit in the center of the table as a decoration. Camilla put them there, and I think they're quite lovely. If they're giving off any odor, I can't smell it, and I'm the one with the best nose.

"Tomatoes are Spanish? You're quite wrong. They're the rage in Florence. You find them only in the very top stores. I brought these back after our visit to Camilla last week and they cost extremely dear."

"Despite your education, Caterina, you are the one in the wrong."

Caterina's naturally pink face goes red. "Explain yourself, please, Antonio."

"Ever since Cristofero Colombo discovered the New World, Spain has been selling us things like this. Ridiculous things that we pay enormous sums for, and look what happens: Florence grows poor while Spain grows rich." His speech gathers momentum as his anger mounts. "This, on top of the fact that Ferdinand of Aragon captured Granada, uniting Spain. One giant Spain now!" Papà shakes his finger at Caterina. "Mark my words: Spain is more powerful than the Republic of Florence."

This is what Giuliano was talking about; Papà must be on Savonarola's side.

"I wasn't aware we were at war with Spain," says Caterina archly.

"Wars aren't fought only with artillery, my dear. This is an economic war."

"I seriously doubt that our enjoyment of a few tomatoes as a centerpiece will make the banks of Florence crash. And I certainly can't smell them over the wonderful aroma of this sauce." Caterina puts a forkful of pasta into her mouth.

The act is so defiant, I'm at a loss for what to do.

Papà looks at her. She chews without looking back at him. And I see his anger deflate just like that. In its place is something worse: defeat. He puts his elbows on the table and props his forehead in his hands.

*

I cannot see his eyes. I tap Caterina's foot with mine under the table.

Caterina looks at me, then at Papà. She drops her fork and goes to Papà. "Speak to me, Antonio." She strokes his ear lightly.

Papà wraps his arms around her waist. He buries his face in her abdomen. She caresses his head. The scene is so tender and private, I quick look down at my food.

Papà clears his throat. "It's everything, Caterina. Everything taken together. France united even before Spain, and it's richer and more powerful every year. The French king threatens to invade the Kingdom of Naples. Everyone sees the Italian states as markets or potential conquests." He sighs and a sob catches in his throat. "We are in trouble, my lovely bride."

"We? Our family?"

"All of Florence." Papà squeezes Caterina so hard, I see her wince.

"We will make it through this, Antonio. You are a sensible man. I will never bring home tomatoes again. I'll throw them to the goats. We can toss this pasta to the goats, as well." She frees herself from his arms and makes a dramatic throwing motion toward the window.

Papà gives a sad laugh. "Jewel of my life." He laughs again. "Yes, dispense with the tomatoes. But there's no need to waste the pasta. Besides, we don't want to kill the goats with surprise at such remarkable luck."

Caterina smiles at him. She carries the tomatoes into the kitchen and returns to her seat, and, amazingly, the meal goes on. Somehow men and women do that—they comfort each other and move on, no matter what's happening around them. I want to do that, too. I want to help Giuliano. "May I accompany you the next time you go to Florence, Caterina?"

She looks at me with delight on her face. "You must. For the very next visit will be to meet our new nephew, of course."

"I want to go to Florence often."

"Contessina's wedding feast had an effect on you, I see." Caterina looks at Papà and he looks at her. A message passes between their eyes.

"Ordinary visits to Florence will not please you much, I'm sorry to say, little Betta," says Papà. "The streets are overrun with gangs of wild boys. Still, Florence is good for special occasions. I've been thinking," he says. "You'll turn fifteen in June. This seems the right year to hold a party for you. In the city."

"A big one," declares Caterina—and her look says it all: they have been thinking of me. I will have a party, my party, that thing that has become a phantasm. It's hard to believe.

We eat the rest of our meal quietly. As we finish up, we hear hoofbeats. A man bursts through the door without knocking. The pained look on his face is alarming.

"Cousin Ruggiero," says Caterina.

He comes to stand near the corner of the table between Papà and Caterina.

"What is it?" asks Papà.

"Your sister, Camilla." Ruggiero hangs his head. "I'm so sorry."

With dizzying speed, we are once more thrown into a grief that dissolves us from the inside out. Camilla died in childbirth. The infant died, as well. She was a girl. Lost mother, daughter. Lost sisters. We are hollow.

PART Two

CHAPTER *Thirteen*

SEPTEMBER IS NEARLY UPON US," says Caterina. "Just another couple of weeks. I'm thinking October is a good party month—toward the end, when the nights are cool. Aunt Nanina, don't you think a party is due for our Elisabetta?"

"Overdue," says Aunt Nanina, and the way she says it feels rehearsed. They've been talking about this without me, I'm sure. "We'll throw it in my city palace." Aunt Nanina sits in her favorite chair like a queen on a throne, ready to give orders, which makes sense, since this is her domain—we're in her country house today. We've been helping her pack up to return to her city palace for autumn. "Let's make the guest list."

The two women look at me expectantly.

A terrible stone of worry tumbles in my middle. If we really plan a party for me, something major is bound to happen and stop it. For this is the party we would have had when I turned thirteen, if Mamma hadn't died. And the one we would have had when I turned fourteen, if Papà hadn't married Caterina and I hadn't recoiled from both of them in spite. And the one we would have had at the beginning of this summer, on my fifteenth birthday, if Camilla hadn't died in April.

Poor Caterina. Is she ready for a party? She marches brightly from day to day, acting cheery, especially around little Bartolomeo. But there are moments when such a savage loss fills her eyes

145

that I have to turn away to keep from crying for her. I've gotten good at making pasta in the shape of her beloved doves, which I serve her often.

"Let's wait for spring," I say. "In October everyone's thinking ahead to the winter festivities. No one will want to take the time to come to a simple party for me."

"A simple party?" Aunt Nanina points to her footstool. "Sit down here, Elisabetta." I sit obediently. "In my family we don't do simple parties. Everyone will happily make the journey for this party."

"Everyone will be ready for a celebration by then, anyway," says Caterina. "The summer started so badly. But people are feeling more optimistic now. It should be a good olive harvest, after all."

She's right. In June it rained so hard, the Arno overflowed and flooded the cornfields. Since the corn was near ripe, the harvest was lost. It was disaster; though corn is a grain that came to us only recently, it's already become crucial. And not just for animals—everyone but the very rich eats it nearly daily. But the new crops are doing well. And the fruit trees bend under their loads. Yes, October will be a good time for a party. And, truth be told, now that I face the real possibility of a party, I don't think I can wait much longer; I haven't seen Giuliano since his sister Contessina's wedding. I hug myself at the rush of feelings that come unbidden. Nothing bad can happen this time. "All right, let's make the guest list. First of all, Silvia."

"I don't recall a Silvia."

"She's my best friend."

Aunt Nanina looks at Caterina. "What family is she from?"

Caterina comes to stand beside me. She rests her hand lightly on my shoulder. "She's the daughter of Giacomo, a worker at Villa Vignamaggio."

"Well, now, let's not be ridiculous," says Aunt Nanina. "It's time for more suitable friends."

"They're very close." Caterina's eyes flash warning at Aunt Nanina.

Aunt Nanina's eyes flash right back. She looks at me. "This girl cannot come."

"We grew up together, Aunt Nanina. We tell each other everything. We . . ."

"Country ways are regrettable. And you are old enough now to realize that, Elisabetta. In the presence of the Florentine nobility, you will do nothing regrettable. And certainly not at a party in the Rucellai palace."

"But . . ."

"Caterina and I will make the guest list together, without your help, Elisabetta. In fact, we'll do all the party planning. This is the best thing for you. Trust me. Now go take care of little Bartolomeo."

I open my mouth to object, but Caterina's hand clutches my shoulder so hard, I have to hold in a yelp.

"He's in the kitchen," says Caterina. "Go be with the sweet joy of your life."

I blink back tears and seek out my nephew. He comes quickly to me, holding the toy goat I made him by the neck. It's quite limp and worn now, for he takes it everywhere. I lead him out the rear door and into the grasses, where we roll in the sunlight.

Bartolomeo's time is split between Aunt Nanina's summer home and Villa Vignamaggio, where he comes for weeks at a time. After his mother's death, the child was forlorn, going from room to room saying, "Mamma?" There are still moments when he seems confused. We make him jellies then, all in different shapes and colors. Caterina sings to him and I roll with him in the grasses.

But now I'm rolling not to comfort him, but to gain comfort, for Caterina is right: Bartolomeo is the sweet joy of my life. Holding him feels as though I'm being held—all safe and simple. Oh, I wish things were simple now. I have no sense of how to tell Silvia she can't come to my party. Her exclusion is wrong, very very wrong. But I want this party. I want it so much. My head feels like it will explode.

The next day, we ride in the coach back to Villa Vignamaggio. Caterina talks to me over Bartolomeo's head. "You're so good with that child. You belong with him. And he with you."

"I love him." I run my fingers through Bartolomeo's curls. "I'll love him all my life."

A small cry flies from Caterina's throat. "Just as my sweet sister Camilla would have."

"Caterina . . ." I look at her beseechingly. "Silvia is as close to a sister as I've ever had. Is there nothing I can do to change Aunt Nanina's mind about her?"

Caterina shakes her head and her eyes grow shiny. "Silvia wouldn't feel at ease at the party anyway. You must know that, Elisabetta. She practically merged with the walls at my wedding feast. And that was in a home she knows well. She would suffer at the grand Rucellai palace."

I turn away and look out the window. Caterina is wrong—Silvia will suffer much more from not coming. But I won't press. Not with those tears in her eyes.

I'm surprised that Caterina noticed Silvia's behavior at her wedding feast. That must mean she noticed mine, as well. I search my memory for details of that day. I felt beastly then, but I hope I didn't do anything too beastly. I don't want Caterina to remember how I acted when I hated her, especially since she was so nice to me through it all. She actually laughed when Uccio jumped in her new fountain and splattered water all up her wedding gown.

We arrive home cranky and tired. So it's only right to wait till the morrow to talk with Silvia. That's what I tell myself, as Uccio and Bartolomeo and I all curl up together to sleep.

In the morning, I take Silvia by the hand for a walk in the woods. "I'm going to have a party at the end of October," I say softly.

"The blessèd event at last." Silvia squares her shoulders and smiles with satisfaction. "I hope it's in time. My pa's breathing down my neck. He wants to marry me off to Rocco or Tomà or Alberto. He doesn't care which. All he wants is to get rid of me. Next week is my fifteenth birthday—I won't be able to hold him off much longer. But I think I can make it to the end of October."

I look at the ground and pretend to pick my way carefully. "Oh, yes, your birthday. I'll make you a special dinner again. Tripe—you love tripe. I remember. With carrots and celery and new onions and . . ."

"Hush about my birthday. It's the party that matters." She squeezes my hand and hurries along through the undergrowth. "Every bachelor within a day's travel will come, I bet. We'll both find husbands."

"Silvia, you're rushing . . ."

She slows down. "Sorry, I'm just so excited."

"That isn't what I meant. Silvia . . . Silvia . . . you're not coming."

"What?" She stops and moves to stand in front of me.

"You're not invited."

She looks stricken. "You don't want me?"

"Don't be daft." I take her hands. "I fought, but Aunt Nanina won't allow it."

"Aunt Nanina?" She pulls her hands away. "Who cares about her? It's your party."

"In her palace."

"Then don't have it in her palace. Villa Vignamaggio is perfect for a party. You saw how beautiful your pa's wedding was. We can . . ."

"It has to be at Aunt Nanina's. And Caterina says you wouldn't be at ease in such a rich palace."

"Oh, so it's for my own good that they shut the door on me. Ain't that just the cunningest reasoning ever."

"You're right. Caterina said that just to comfort me, I'm sure."

"Comfort you? I'm the one needs comforting. I'm the one hurt."

"It cuts me, too, Silvia. You're my very dearest friend. I want you there."

"Then fight harder."

"Aunt Nanina has decided."

"And she's in charge, eh? She ain't even blood related to you. She ain't even blood related to Caterina. So why's it got to be at her palace? Oh! Her noble palace. In the middle of Florence. I understand. I see it all now." She holds her nose and marches past me. "It stinks like dung here." She breaks into a run back toward the house.

I run after her. "You don't understand."

She twirls around. "Of course I do. I know you, Elisabetta. You want to seal things."

"Seal things? What are you talking about?"

"You have your party in some rich palace and everyone sees— everyone knows you're top nobility now. So Giuliano chooses you. This is all you hope for in the whole world. Don't lie to me. Lie to yourself if you want. But don't never lie to me."

I feel like all my blood has flushed away. I throw my arms around Silvia and cling to her. "I'm sorry. I'm so so sorry." And I'm sobbing.

She stands in my arms like stone.

"I'll have the party at home," I say.

"No, you won't." Her words are ice.

I step back and swipe at my tears and look at her. "I will. It's better that way anyway because . . ."

"Hush." She puts a warning finger up in front of my face. "Not one more false word. Not one, or I might just rip your hair out." She digs her fingers into her scalp and looks as if she's about to rip her own hair out. "It's unfair." She breathes slowly and deeply and loudly. "But life's unfair. Nobility and peasants—they don't have real friendships."

"That's not true! You're my best friend!"

"Hush! I mean it. Aunt Nanina and Caterina and whoever else has been part of this decision—they're right. An October party should be in the city—then everyone's sure to come. It's your best chance." Her hands fall limp to her sides.

"Silvia . . ."

"I don't want to hear it. Save your excuses for yourself. We both got hardly no choices of our own anyways. That's how it is. That's how it's always been. Ain't never going to change. But, hell, I'd sure trade my world for yours right now." She turns and walks away.

And I'm left crying.

CHAPTER Fourteen

OVER THE NEXT TWO MONTHS Silvia avoids me. It is impossible to do that entirely, of course, for we have the same habits now. We've come to recognize what chore needs to be done next, and so we wind up side by side without a word passing between us. But when that happens, she quickly turns to another task, abandoning me to work alone. Our eyes never meet. She's here but not here. I miss her far worse than if she had gone somewhere distant.

I turn again to little Bartolomeo for consolation. When he's here, which is often, he's my companion on any task that isn't delicate and doesn't present him dangers. And I grow used to Caterina's friendly words. I even come to count on her greeting whenever I come in from chores. She clearly enjoys the preparations for this party and her persistent cheeriness prevails; despite the gaping maw in my center left by Silvia's absence, I find myself more and more excited.

And so on the twenty-fourth day of October, I sleep at Aunt Nanina's city palace. It's the night before my party—the blessèd event, as Silvia called it. I remember her words and wince.

This is my first night in the city since Camilla's funeral. I expected us to stay with Bartolomeo at his father's home, like we used to do when we came to the city. But Caterina announced it was more proper for us to stay with Aunt Nanina, and it is a great pleasure to be in such an astonishing palace. I'm grateful Papà has still not found the funds to repair our own city house, otherwise we wouldn't have the excuse to stay here.

I open my eyes the next morning and Uccio jumps onto my bed immediately.

Naaaa. He falls on his front knees and nuzzles my face insistently. I lift one of his long, soft ears and whisper to him, "Giulianuccio."

If Aunt Nanina saw, she'd throw a fit. Uccio isn't even supposed to be in my room. He's supposed to be tied to the metal loop in the kitchen wall. Aunt Nanina had her slave girl install that loop just for this visit—like she installed a loop in the kitchen at her country home. But I sneaked the goat up last night.

A noise comes from the street. Noises start in this city before dawn and continue through half the night. It's so different from the dead quiet that can blanket Villa Vignamaggio.

Naaaa. Uccio knocks his nose against my chin now. "You're in a rush to get outside and do your business," I say, jumping up. "I understand. I'll hurry." I take care of my needs and slip on my simple shift and give a quick glance at the green gown hanging ready for the party. Caterina and I designed it together, and I finally gave her the satisfaction of choosing green, which I suspect she has known all along is my favorite color. The waistline is high, with a wide belt and folds and folds of soft, flowing, fine silk. I can't wait to put it on. But I mustn't risk getting it dirty ahead of time. Guests won't start coming till late afternoon.

I grab my shoes and sneak Uccio down the stairs.

Caterina's by the bottom step. She sees Uccio and our eyes meet. She chews her bottom lip. Then she calls loudly, "Just stay where you are, Aunt Nanina. I'm coming." She flags me out the door behind her as she rushes into the other room.

I let Uccio outside. "Wait there for me. One minute, okay?" And I run back inside to the kitchen and snatch a dried fig from the basket.

Aunt Nanina's cook takes hot bread out of the oven. Six round loaves. The smell itself tastes delicious. She cuts me a generous hunk. Then she looks over her shoulder furtively, and, secure in the knowledge that we're alone, she cuts a second one, wraps it in paper, and hands it to me. "For that little rascal," she says. She likes Uccio. I kiss her cheek.

I pour olive oil and sprinkle salt on my piece of bread. And a pinch of rosemary, too. Then I grab another fig for Uccio and walk out the door eating.

Uccio's not there.

Uccio is a smart goat. At home he waits outside whenever I tell him to. But the city is full of surprises. I can't blame him for exploring. Besides, the weather is perfect. It's warm for so late in October. I don't even need a shawl.

I lace on my shoes and look around. It isn't right for me to go far; a girl shouldn't be in public alone—city life has such particular rules. But it's so early that shops aren't even open. No one is likely to see me. I walk along the street eating and calling to him. The crisp air invigorates me. This is going to be a wonderful day.

"Hey, beauty," says a boy, coming around the corner. He's younger than me. With a filthy face and worn trousers.

A group of boys appears behind him. Five in all. Ruffians.

"What's a pretty gal like you doing wandering the streets so early?"

"Looking for someone?"

"A lovers' tryst, perhaps?"

"Ain't you the sassy trollop."

I lift my chin and walk quickly past them. Boys that age can be such fools. "Uccio," I call. There's trash down every street, so he could have gone anywhere. Everyplace must smell delectable to him. Papà's old continual grumble about too many parties for the street cleaners to keep up with is truer than ever.

I pass a man sleeping. Drool and who knows what else is crusted in his facial hair. His shirt lies in tatters on his back. I look down an alley that reeks of urine. Two men hunch there, one behind the other, both in blue silk doublets. Rich men, locked together. I turn my head away quickly, my heart thumping hard. I remember being at Lorenzo de' Medici's funeral and seeing that man defecating in the street. He was one lone man in the middle of a clean city. Now there are so many dirty homeless people in the middle of rubbish everywhere. And they are joined by rich people practicing ways people only speak about in whispers, all out in the open.

I hug myself. My eyes burn with unease; how vulnerable they are. Oh, I know too well that walls give but the illusion of safety, for Camilla died in her own bed. Still, how people can give up that illusion—that's beyond me, that makes me want to cry for them.

A rat scurries along the wall. I jump. Rats, in broad daylight?

"What's that in your hand, beauty?"

The boys have been following me! I move faster. They rush past to stand in front of me now. The one in the cap snatches the paper from me and I see that he's missing the last two fingers on that hand. He unwraps Uccio's hunk of bread slowly, so slowly I get the feeling he takes pleasure in making people try not to stare at his three-fingered hand. He looks at me, takes a big bite, then passes the bread around.

Another boy points at the fig in my other hand. It's just a fig— who cares? But before I can toss it to him, a third lunges at me and rips it away, leaving a line of grime that runs from my wrist down my palm. A spasm of disgust jerks my neck stiff. I turn to go the other way, but they immediately surround me. They give off a stink like old onions.

"Tasty, don't you agree, boys? This gal here, she's a tasty one."

They laugh and close in on me. I can smell their breath now—rot. One of them has a leaky eye. All of them are skinny, but they look strong. I don't see a single weak link in the chain around me. My breath shortens. Panic threatens.

"She's going to be fun, all right."

The one with the fig touches my neck. I slap his hand away.

"Let's start with a serenade, boys, what do you say? A serenade first? Remember them jolly words?"

And they're singing the most ribald lyrics. I'd be embarrassed if I were truly a city girl. But I heard cruder things than this from Cristiano and his friends when I was only ten. These boys are mistaken to think such words can make me cower.

But it's their closeness that feels menacing. And that finger on my neck made my skin crawl. Boys like this only feed on fear, though. I stand taller and will my face not to give me away.

Gangs, that's what Papà calls them. Boys gone wild. There's nothing to do but wait them out. It's daylight and we're on a public street, after all. People have got to pass this way soon. They've got to.

When they finish the song in their rough and ugly voices, the one with the cap and the claw hand, the leader, I suppose, puts his fists on his hips. "It's your turn now, beauty. A song deserves a prize. What have you got for us?"

My eyes flit to his hand, to the site of the missing finger, and away again.

"I don't have a purse on me. You can see that."

Another boy whistles. "Yes, we can see what you've got. A body wrapped in cloth. Is that what you're peddling?" He steps forward with a puffed chest, knowing I cannot retreat without pressing against the boy behind me. He smirks. "Just as we guessed now, huh? You should put on something more revealing than that shift if you want to fetch a good price." And he leers.

"I haven't insulted you," I say in a steady voice. "You have no cause to insult me."

One of them whistles. "Get that, boys? No more insulting the lady." His tone is sarcastic.

And all at once I understand. Because I'm dressed so simple, they've taken me for a servant girl. I look straight at the leader and curtsy. "I'm Elisabetta di Antonio Maria di Noldo Gherardini."

He grins, as though I've made some big joke. "All right, then, now that you've set us straight, Monna Elisabetta blah blah blah, what are you doing out here?"

"I'm looking for Uccio."

"Uccio, Uccio," calls one of them, mimicking me.

"Does Uccio by any chance have a long long tail?"

"And dangly ears?" The leader puts his hands by his ears and swings them, the claw hand looking particularly grotesque.

My stomach lurches. "What have you done with him?"

"You already owe us something for the song. Ain't that so, boys? Monna Whatever owes us. Now for this new information in addition, well, I suppose we'll need some florins."

"Give me Uccio, and I'll give you florins."

"Florins first."

"Uccio first!"

Naaaa! Uccio comes out the same street the boys did.

They race at him.

I'm racing, too. "Uccio!"

And Uccio charges. He butts the first boy in the groin.

The boy gets up, limping, and one of them says something about Uccio's long horns and all of them take off down the street.

I would laugh from relief if there weren't tears streaming down my face. "I didn't know you had it in you," I say as Uccio nuzzles my fingers, looking for food. "Greedy. I bet your stomach's fit to burst, you've eaten so much garbage. Let's get home. Fast!"

"Monna Lisa, Monna Lisa, Monna Lisa," comes a singing voice. But this one is anything but rough and ugly.

There is only one person anywhere who calls me Monna Lisa, and when he does, I feel different, as though the name itself transforms me. The whole incident with the boys is swept away in an instant, and I turn with a smile so big it hurts my cheeks. "Good morning, Ser Giuliano."

Giuliano bows deep, then smiles back. He has grown noticeably taller since I danced with him at his sister's wedding, a half year ago. His hair curls around his ears in a playful way. His white shirt and breeches, trimmed in blue along the tops of the shoulders and down both sides, leave his hosed calves and bare forearms showing his strength. He's robust and glows with energy that seems to flow from him to me, because I find myself bouncing on the pads of my feet. My skin is all atingle.

"In the street with a goat," he says. "Exactly what I was hoping."

"And what on earth could you mean by such strange words, pray tell?"

"I stopped by Aunt Nanina's to find you, and your agreeable stepmother said you'd be in the rear garden. She added in whose company. When you weren't there, I hurried to find you. And here you are." He grins. "Only you would take a goat as a chaperone in the streets of Florence." He grabs hold of one of Uccio's horns and shakes it. "Want to come watch me play kick ball?"

That's why he's dressed like that. It's a sports outfit, of course. My heart falls. "I have a party to go to today. Haven't you heard?"

"I would never miss it. Nor will the rest of high society. You've become quite the talk of the town."

A warm blush rises in my cheeks. "I repeat, what on earth could you mean by such strange words?"

He laughs. "I speak but the truth. You're the mysterious girl from the country. Everyone wants to know what you're like. Still, I wish it were not so—no no, everyone should not be talking of you. I don't want this particular treasure sought after by everyone."

I blush hotter and deeper. Inside my chest tiny birds flap their wings.

"Anyway, gentle lady, the party isn't till much later. But the tournaments are now. Come with me."

"Tournaments? What's the occasion?"

"Every day is an occasion. At least according to my brother. Florence is a continual festival. Piero says it's important, for the morale of the city. But this won't be in Piazza Santa Croce, like the annual kick-ball tournament. We're playing south of the river." He touches my cheek and his face goes serious and gentle. "Lisa, are those streaks from dried tears?"

"Only of relief. I thought some stupid boys had done something to Uccio."

"Boys?" Giuliano's face immediately tightens. "Boys here in the street? A gang?"

"I suppose."

"What did they do to you?"

"Do to me? Nothing more than insults I won't repeat. I was

only worried about Uccio. I wasn't scared for myself. Not really, anyway. Not much."

"You should have been. Three days ago there was a gang war outside the Duomo. They threw stones at each other. A boy was killed. Don't walk the streets alone again—especially not at dawn or after dusk—not when there aren't plenty of people around."

"A boy was killed?" I stand still, stunned.

"Stay away from empty streets."

"Giuliano, a boy was killed? Here? I know people are afraid of the streets in Naples and Rome and Genoa and Milan and so many other places. But no one's afraid of the streets in Florence. Not our Florence."

"Things have changed. And there's worse than that."

"What could be worse?"

"It's not to talk about in polite conversation."

What a formal thing to say. "Is this polite conversation?"

"You'll know when it's not." His eyes linger on my mouth.

I look down, flustered.

"Listen to me, Monna Lisa, there are reasons why girls should have proper chaperones, not goats. Stay away from empty streets." He stresses each word.

I look down at the line of grime the boy left on me when he stole the fig. I rub it away and fold that hand inside the other and press them to my chest.

"Please," he insists.

"I will. Rest assured, I will."

He takes a deep breath and I see his Adam's apple rise and fall in a swallow.

"Let's get you back to Aunt Nanina's, so you can dress up."

"Dress up?" I say, in a daze.

A slow smile crosses his face. "Of all the girls I've met, only you wouldn't care about public image. I bet you don't ever show off. And you're right, for your gentility glows through your face, no matter what you wear. Well, then, Monna Lisa, to the games." He offers the crook of his elbow.

I look at it stupidly, realizing I'm a fool. I should dress up. It was my simple clothing that led to those boys treating me so crudely. It's prudent to make one's social status known. But now that Giuliano's expressed admiration for my choice, I can hardly change my mind.

"If you're worried about the others, you can calm yourself. Caterina already agreed."

"Caterina is allowing me to go somewhere with you unchaperoned?"

He nods with a smile. "Once she found out Aunt Nanina and I had discussed this before you even arrived in town, she had little choice. I just have to have you back by midday. Caterina said to tell you Francesco is coming." His voice rises at the end in a question.

I shrug. "I can't think why she would have said that. Maybe she just meant that Bartolomeo will be here. My little nephew. That must be it. Francesco is his father."

"Ah, that Francesco. Well, shall we go, Monna Lisa, my lady?"

I take Giuliano's arm and walk unsteadily, Uccio at my heels. The incident with those boys, followed so closely by the news Giuliano brought, has left me reeling. In all Papà's fretting about Florence, nothing he's said prepared me for such things: a boy was killed by a gang. In the streets of Florence. Who ever heard of anything so vile?

And Giuliano said there's been worse.

Has the world gone mad?

I hold Giuliano's arm tight.

CHAPTER Fifteen

FLORENCE is not the center of heaven," calls a voice.

People have gathered around an unnaturally small man with a huge nose standing on an outdoor pulpit in the Piazza Santo Spirito. His right hand is raised high with two fingers extended as though pointing to heaven and blessing the crowd in one action, like in paintings of Jesus Christ. The sleeve of his monk's habit falls to reveal a very white and skinny arm. That arm and the fact that the habit hangs loose from his shoulders give the impression that this man is nothing but skin and bones draped over a firm spirit.

I linger, slowing Giuliano. "Is that him? Savonarola?"

Giuliano works us around the edge of the crowd. "He keeps building himself outdoor pulpits and inciting everyone."

"No, not the center of heaven," belts out Savonarola. "Nor is Florence the center of the world. No, fellow citizens, children of the Lord. Florence is not these things."

"I want to listen, Giuliano."

"It's best to ignore him." He pulls me along.

"But if we allow tyrannical governments," shrieks Savonarola, "if we allow evil, as in the likes of Piero de' Medici, then Florence will be the center of hell. Floods, plague, war, swarms of locusts—all manner of pestilence will rain down upon us."

"Outrageous," Giuliano mutters to me.

"You're right," calls a voice loudly.

"You're right," calls another.

And the air is full of voices agreeing with Savonarola.

"That's it." Giuliano stops. "Stay here and wait for me." He pushes his way through the throng to the pulpit. "Go back to your monastery at San Marco! Go, or I'll report this to my brother and he'll have you swept away like so much trash."

"Ah, it's Giuliano de' Medici! Little Giuliano. The most trivial of the Medici boys. The one who never dares to make a ripple in the pool of decadence he swims. Did you hear his tinny squawk, children of the Lord? Did you listen? And you, Giuliano, did you even listen to yourself? Are you hare-brained? You're saying your big brother would sweep me away simply for criticizing him. That's the behavior of a tyrant if ever there was one."

The crowd responds to Savonarola's point. Shouts come: "Let him talk!"

I'm bristling at the way the monk's remarks are so personal. It hardly matters if he has a point—he's mean and I instinctively hate him.

Savonarola puts up both hands to quiet everyone. "Ah, my cowardly young friend, Ser Giuliano, hear how the children of the Lord respond. You would do well to heed their concerns."

"Cowardly?" Giuliano's voice cracks; his wound is apparent. "I'm here confronting you as a warrior for free thought!"

"Bah. You're squawking. Squawk squawk. Go back to your hiding place behind your gluttonous, degenerate brother. His absurd red velvet cape can cover the both of you."

"So you can go back to your lies? Nothing you say has truth to it. Anyone can see that, you decrepit fearmonger!"

Savonarola turns his palms toward heaven in a questioning gesture. "In that case, what harm can there be in letting an impoverished, decrepit monk talk, little rich boy?"

"Indeed!" shouts a man. "Let the pious monk talk."

A chorus rises: "Let him talk, let him talk."

Giuliano's face goes white with rage. "Speak then! Spew your garbage. Anyone who stays to listen is a fool." He stomps back through the crowd and takes my hand and yanks me away. We practically run for the next block.

"Can you slow down, please?" I say at last.

Giuliano looks at me in sudden embarrassment. "I'm sorry." He slows to a walk. "I wish you hadn't heard that."

"He's clever in turning your own words against you."

"That's not what I meant. Yes, he is a clever orator, whereas I have no experience in public debate. I was impulsive to take him on like that."

"It doesn't matter. Anyone can see he's mean-spirited and vindictive."

"You think so? I wish that were true. He sets up his pulpit and says the Lord is on his side, and frightens the people into submission." Giuliano walks faster again as his words come harder. "He's a bully. Shouting of fire and brimstone. As though Florence isn't the best city in the world."

"But how can you say that, after what you just told me about the gangs?" I'm hurrying to keep up, speaking between pants. "Florence is dangerous."

"Death in the street is awful. Horrifying. But whose fault is it? My brother has nothing to do with urchins on the street."

"Not directly, no."

"What does that mean?" His eyes flash anger.

"Surely the leadership of Florence affects everyone," I say, mouthing the very words I've heard Papà say so often these past months, though he was talking about finances, not street violence. "If the leaders flag, well, there's danger for everyone."

"That self-righteous monk is more of a danger than my brother could ever be. So what if he predicted my father's death? Everyone knew my father had been ill a long time. So what if he predicted the death of Pope Innocent VIII a few months later? The Pope was ancient. Savonarola has no direct line of communication with the Lord. He just wants people to think he does, so they will fear him, so he can control them." Giuliano races as he talks. Uccio's hoofs clip-clop behind us on the cobblestones.

"Please slow down. Do you realize you have a penchant for running as you speak?"

"And do you realize you throw at me the very arguments Savonarola wants you to? You give in to the apparent. If you're not careful, you'll be his puppet, too." Giuliano pulls me over against the wall of a building, so we're out of the way of passing carts and people. His glowering brow is a dark scar that cuts across his forehead. "Savonarola is a charlatan."

I press my lips together. "I've never seen you angry before."

"I've never heard you speak nonsense before!"

I want to turn around and run back to Aunt Nanina's. But what a crazy thought. If I really want to know this boy, this man, I have to stand up and talk frankly to him. Mamma did it; Caterina does it. I say the most terrible thing I've heard: "Did your father really steal money from a fund meant to pay the dowry of orphaned women? Did your brother do the same? Is that how Piero paid for Contessina's wedding?"

Giuliano's fingers play above his upper lip for a moment. "Listen, Lisa. All the festivals for the masses, all the entertaining in the streets, the feasts, everything—that costs money. And the people of Florence expect such largesse. My father gave it to them. So Piero has to."

Giuliano walks to the other side of me, then back again. He seems like a wild animal caught in a small cage. I think of the lioness in the Medici palace pacing in front of us more than two years ago. I don't want to put Giuliano in a cage like this. But I also think of Mamma. "My mother was an orphan, Giuliano," I say steadily. "Piero must repay the funds he stole."

"How?" His face contorts and his hands rise to the heavens. "How can Piero possibly pay it back?"

I imagine gold flowing down the Arno, lost in the sea. "And so the banks really do stand on the edge of ruin?"

Giuliano makes just the slightest heart-weary *tsk*. He looks around at the passersby. "Please, may I take your hand?" His voice is hardly more than a whisper.

It's so strange for him to ask this gingerly when but half an hour ago he ordered me to wait while he argued with Savonarola. I offer my hand boldly. "Please take it."

He leads me down a side street. Uccio clatters happily past us, nosing the gutter that runs along one side. I'm instantly jittery. We mustn't be seen. A noble girl cannot be alone with a man outside of the public thoroughfares.

Giuliano stops and stands me with my back to the wall of a home and paces in front of me again. "All right," he says at last but still quietly, still gently, though I sense a tremendous force held at bay beneath the words. "Let's have it. Please. Do me the service of telling all your misgivings about me. Down to the most vile ones." He takes a deep breath and looks into my eyes. The sadness in his is bottomless. "Please. Let us clear the air and see if we both still breathe."

"My misgivings aren't about you." I know that's true the

moment I say it. "I have never known you to be anything but honest and worthy."

Giuliano hesitates. "My brother lacks self-restraint." He grits his teeth at this admission. "But he is my brother. I love him." He takes my hands and turns them upward, cradling them in his own. He looks at them as if for answers. "Please, do not be fooled. There is a difference between stupid self-indulgence and real evil. Savonarola wants to control people's minds. If there ever was a true tyrant to fear it is Savonarola, not my brother." His thumbs move lightly on my palms, then stop and dig in forcefully.

Quick and unexpected delight. My cheeks flash hot. I flinch.

"Forgive me." He lets loose my hands. "I didn't mean to be impudent." He blinks and turns toward the street we came from, clasping his hands behind his back. "Shall we continue our walk?"

I want to say no. I want us to stay here. I want back that delight that began so frighteningly sharp. "By all means."

We go slowly now.

Uccio seems to catch the new air of decorum between us. He prances just a couple of meters ahead, as though leading a formal procession.

We cross a street and turn a corner at the same steady pace.

"I have been raised to put loyalty first," says Giuliano at last. His tone is reflective, almost as though he's speaking to himself. "I'm in the fifth generation of Medici to govern this city." His voice trembles just the slightest.

"Loyalty is a virtue," I say.

"It is essential that I defend my immediate family to anyone outside it."

"I understand," I say.

"You are not in my immediate family." He pauses. "Not yet."

Pinpricks fly up my arms, my neck, my temples. They make my ears ring.

"I cannot speak as openly with you now as I will later. But I have listened to you today. Your words make me admit things to myself that I hate admitting." He pauses and sucks his top lip in under his bottom lip. "Monna Lisa, I promise you, I will never steal from anyone. I have ideas for a business venture. With this venture, I can live independently from Piero. I'll take care of you. There are villas to choose from in the Arno River valley. We can have the one in Fiesole, if you like. It's my favorite."

He looks sideways at me.

I am staring at him. At this beautiful man who smells faintly of apricot preserves and has a voice with modulations that play my every bone. This miracle of a man. Only moments ago he seemed lost to me, and now he has turned the tables. No, not turned, he has spun them. Like a top. I, too, am reeling.

"When we were little, we went to our villa in Fiesole all summer. It may not give you all the joys of Villa Vignamaggio—joys I see you value so highly. One of which you shared with me that evening we spun silk—a moment I return to often in my thoughts. Always with gratitude." Giuliano swallows, and that Adam's apple jumps again. "But this villa has other joys to offer. I remember it fondly. Poliziano tutored us there. Everyone says Giovanni is the brains of our family. But Piero wrote verse in Latin that was good. I remember a poem he wrote in praise of a pony—a nonexistent pony that he wanted Father to buy him." He lifts both shoulders in a shrug that seems so defenseless, I'm charmed. "He wasn't always a lout, Lisa."

"How did you avoid becoming one?" I ask sincerely.

He laughs heartily. "Lord, do I love your directness, Monna Lisa. You allow me to be a better person."

No one has ever said something so wonderful to me. "I can cook," I say in a burst.

"We'll have enough money to pay servants, Lisa."

"No, no. Listen to me. I cannot wait to cook for you. I've been practicing for years. I thought I was paying homage to my mother's spirit. And I was. But now I know I was practicing for you, too. I'll make you meals so fine, you'll hum your heart out."

Giuliano blinks. Then he smiles and shakes his head. "If you cook them, I'll stand on the table and sing." His hand takes mine and squeezes as he pulls me inside a private garden through the servants' gate.

We're alone again. I'm not jittery this time, though. I'm flushed.

His hand moves to my cheek, touching ever so lightly. His eyes flicker a question. His lips come close. And he stops. I can practically taste apricot now. It becomes my favorite fruit. I will eat apricot preserves every morning for the rest of my life.

He moves just the slightest bit closer. His arms circle me and press me upward till I am standing on tiptoe. The heat from his cheeks caresses mine. His face comes closer. His eyelashes are thick and black as night. Closer. Until I am aching inside. The infinitesimal span between us holds all the dangers and all the promises of life. And I am ready for them. Yes, Giuliano. I tilt my chin upward and my lips meet his midway.

CHAPTER *Sixteen*

GIULIANO PLAYS KICK BALL WELL, but nothing like Piero. Piero is a brute on the field. He attacks with vicious blows to belly and chest and has twice this morning rolled in a tangle of arms and legs with members of the opposing team, shouting obscenities to continue the scuffle. But he's also a natural athlete. He swiftly skirts around players coming right at him and aims the ball with alarming precision. He's made three of his team's five goals so far. I watch the game half-stupefied at the agility of this regrettable man.

The woman beside me leans closer. "Watching Piero, eh? Don't be too impressed. That scumbag does nothing but play ball all day. When he ain't killing someone, that is. All that Medici family, all their friends, all of them is scum really—the richer, the scummier."

I close my arms into my sides and try to shrink away. What a thoroughly awful woman.

And to say that about Piero. The man may be a lout, but he surely hasn't killed anyone. I put that woman out of my head.

Still, I can believe Piero fritters his day away on kick ball. He's astoundingly good, totally decisive. Giuliano, on the other hand, is tentative; he plays at the sides of the action, always checking, always questioning. These strengths of his in talking and reasoning are weaknesses in athletics. A warm sense of satisfaction fills me. A rational, trustworthy man will make a much better husband than a gifted athlete would.

We have talked, Giuliano and I, laying out as many details as we could in the brief walk here. Tonight, during my party, he will talk with Papà. They will negotiate the dowry informally, because Giuliano will accept whatever Papà offers. Papà won't have to pay anything like the fifteen hundred large gold florins that most fathers of our particular standing give. And Giuliano doesn't need more property, so Papà can keep his holdings. Papà should be delighted—the announcement can be made before the guests go home.

With each word from Giuliano's mouth, my heart is more his. He even came up with the idea of asking Leonardo da Vinci to paint my wedding chest, since it was Leonardo who brought us together in the first place. What could be more perfect?

I never imagined that it was possible to be this happy. Giuliano's proposal was like a gift straight from God. The rightness of it is solid as marble.

I scratch Uccio behind the ears and watch the game and gloat at myself—at how timid I was about facing my own hopes. But now I can let all my feelings run free. Like streams in spring, they flood the land of my soul. The only breath of sadness I feel is that Mamma won't dance at our wedding. But she'll be there in my heart.

It is a pity that Giuliano is the baby of the Medici family instead of the oldest brother. Giuliano would be a leader who could maintain Florence's history. Just as he said, we're the center of the civilized world. Look at literature—at the great poets Dante Alighieri and Francesco Petrarca, and the bawdy storywriter

Giovanni Boccaccio. All three penned in our language, proving it is just as good as Latin or Greek. That's what Caterina says. Indeed, there are more presses producing books in Florentine Italian than in any other modern language in the entire world.

And fine arts, ha! All people have to do to recognize Florence's superiority is keep their eyes open as they walk through the streets. No cathedral dome anywhere can be more beautiful than the one Brunelleschi built. No sculptures more fabulous than Donatello's. No doors more awe-inspiring than the bronze ones Ghiberti cast for the baptistery, the ones I pause before in admiration every time I pass. The grandeur of the spirit of Florence peeks out even from the corner eaves of buildings in the graceful ceramics of the magnificent della Robbia brothers.

We citizens of the Republic of Florence are heirs to the most remarkable heritage ever. Florence will not go down in ruin, no matter how dissipated a life Piero leads.

But Giuliano is not the oldest brother; he is in charge only of himself. He'll start a business. He hasn't told me what, but I trust him. Like Leonardo trusted him, when Giuliano was but a boy of seven. He merits trust. He isn't anything like his father. He won't have a mistress, like Lorenzo did, a mistress girls whisper about, saying she was the true cause of his premature death. Giuliano will love me and only me, always. And I will feel the same about him. We will make a good life together.

No, I have never dreamed of a city life. But I remember now the excitement I used to feel as a child when I came to town for festivals. The city has different charms from the country. And I will have a chance to understand so many of those charms better. I will learn to really appreciate art, not just gawk at it. Maybe I'll even read books for pleasure. Caterina can help me acquire some.

But, how silly I am: the Medici library holds every text worth having. We can take what we want to our new home.

Our home. Together. The sun warms the air gently as a dream, and I grow complacent on fat plans.

A man behind me shouts, and quickly people are shouting everywhere. A player lies on the field with another standing over him kicking savagely. Neither is Giuliano, thank heavens. The aggressor is a particularly talented player, better even than Piero. The crowd eggs him on. Blood splatters. Still the crowd calls for more. These matches started as military exercises, and their history lives on in their brutality. I know this—it's why Mamma and I never went before—yet I can hardly believe this thirst for violence. My innards churn. I close my eyes. Something gets resolved, for the game goes on.

The men near me set to whispering. I'm so close, I can't help but overhear. They complain because Piero de' Medici has aligned himself with King Alfonso of Naples, and Naples is in a giant dispute with King Charles VIII of France. Immediately, my eyes fly open, every nerve ajangle. Papà fears France terribly. He spoke recently of how the French army was on the move, already tramping through the north of Italy. I bow my head, so it's not obvious that I'm eavesdropping.

"We're risking war."

"And with the slime of the earth. The French army cuts off heads and burns homes to the ground."

"And rapes any woman in sight—even girls."

Papà never spoke about these things.

"The Neapolitans are worse. They treat their own people in the shabbiest way."

"They're a disgrace. Everyone hates the Neapolitans."

"Besides, business with France is important."

"If Piero doesn't shape up and see that the real power lies with France, we'll all be paupers."

"I've already lost my home to the bank. I'll never get back on my feet if Florence doesn't make amends with France."

I chew on my knuckles. Giuliano's business will be ruined before it's begun. No. They have to be wrong. Florence cannot be ruined. I back away.

The kick ball game dragged on too long, but finally now it ends and the jousting is about to begin. Giuliano said he'd walk me back to Aunt Nanina's afterward, but I don't want to wait. It's already close to midday. And I can't stay near these stupid naysayers any longer. I skirt around the edge of the crowd till I catch Giuliano's eye. Then I wave and leave before he can even think about coming over to protest. The streets are brimming with traffic now—there's no chance that I'll face anything like what happened this morning with that gang of boys.

I run back to Aunt Nanina's, Uccio trotting beside me. Mindful of Giuliano's warnings, I avoid the Ponte Vecchio, the bridge that's always filled with beggars and prostitutes. Besides, the reek there from the butchers' shops turns my stomach. I go out of my way to take the Ponte alle Grazie. I run over the bridge, all the way, all the way.

"Oh, Elisabetta! There you are." Caterina hurries to the entrance hall the second I arrive. She stands behind me as I close the door. "I'm sorry to say I have disappointing news."

"Tell me." And my heart already races. I knew something awful would happen—my party is doomed.

"Francesco got called away on a business matter, so he won't be with us this afternoon. But don't worry. He's sure to be back for the party. He wanted me to reassure you of that."

"Is that all?" I actually feel wobbly from relief. "How funny of him. Little Bartolomeo wouldn't enjoy a party anyway."

"Oh, your little boy is here. He's out back with a servant, chasing the peacocks. He already ate, with Antonio and Aunt Nanina. Because of the party preparations, we're just being casual for the midday meal, staying out of the way of the cooks. I haven't eaten yet, though. I thought I'd wait for you and we could share a quick cold dish."

"That sounds perfect."

She hugs me, then leads the way.

Her goodwill wraps around me, like swaddling around a baby. It was so sweet of her to wait to eat till I got home. I am overcome with gratitude at this small act of kindness. Caterina would clearly be a wonderful mother. Oh, I hope hope hope she becomes with child. I hope she gives Papà a son.

We eat, then Caterina ushers me up the stairs. "Aunt Nanina's servant girls have been decorating the dance hall since yesterday. You'll be amazed. And you wouldn't believe the amount of fish and cheese and sweetmeats that arrived this morning."

She chattered like that while we ate, and she keeps it up now as she helps me dress in this most delectable soft, green gown. She styles my hair without asking. I can do it myself, of course. But Caterina is a magician at it. She parts the center, then sweeps both sides into large loopy buns above and behind each ear. At the tail end of each loop she leaves a good hand's length of hair free, and rubs it quickly between her palms until each strand stands apart from the others. It looks like a spray, like filaments of silk when a breeze catches them. I watch in the mirror in wonder. Will my head float away? "It's amazing."

"Wait. I'm not finished yet," she says.

Now she teases free several strands of hair at both temples, so they wind down the sides of my face, all the way to the top of my bodice, like curling ribbons.

"See?" She steps back proudly. "You're a beautifully wrapped present. Your father's gift to the world."

Just the way she says it hurts my heart. This woman must have a child. I blink back tears. "Thank you." I kiss her cheeks.

Her eyes are happy. "You're like a sister to me now, you know."

Of course! She wants me to fill the hole Camilla left. It must be horrible to lose a sister. Maybe more horrible than losing a mother. "And you to me," I say sincerely.

"Your betrothal won't really change anything—for we are already bound. Wait here." Caterina goes out the door with a mysterious parting look.

My betrothal. Caterina is completely sure there will be one forthcoming. She takes it on faith—in me—in my worthiness. She doesn't even know yet that it's really true. I can't wait to see the delight on her face when Giuliano makes his intentions known.

A moment later, Bartolomeo runs in. "Zi-Bi," he calls. He sees me and stops. His mouth is a giant circle. "Aaaaa," he says appreciatively. "Pretty. Pretty Zi-Bi."

I kiss my sweet nephew and he places his shabby toy goat in my lap and reaches up his hands toward my hair, then stops. "Go ahead," I say. "You can touch." He bounces his palms under the tips of my two long curls.

Caterina beams from the doorway. You'd think he was her son, she's so happy. "But Zi-Bi can't play with you now, Bartolomeo," she says gently. "Remember, I told you. She's having a big party. That's why she's so pretty. You'll get to see all the guests before you go to bed."

"I'll spend tomorrow morning with you, though. I promise."

Bartolomeo takes the toy goat and rests his cheek on my knee just a moment. He's such a strange little dear. With one finger I trace the edge of his ear. Then Caterina whisks him back to the servant girl.

The rest of the day goes as Aunt Nanina and Caterina have planned. The dance hall is a heavenly vision of flowers in baskets hanging from the walls. Caterina whispers in my ear that the orchids were brought all the way from the Gargano peninsula. I think of the wonderful orchids that Cristiano found in the hills near Villa Vignamaggio, the kind that now grow in our garden in the midst of the Muse statues, and I feel a pang of sadness. He's never sent word home—Silvia has no idea where her brother is.

But I mustn't think about Silvia now. I don't want to be sad.

I walk around the dance hall marveling. Everyone has gone to so much trouble and expense just for me. I'm swimming through a wonderland. It's almost as though they know tonight will result in the best announcement. Could Papà and Caterina possibly have guessed at Giuliano's and my attachment? But I'm sure not. Even I didn't know the strength of it until this morning.

As evening breaks, servant girls scatter flower petals on the floor, forming a hush-hush carpet of white and yellow and pink and purple. Guests arrive in droves. Music swirls through everything. The food is so varied and abundant I don't recognize half the dishes. Some surprise me: crunchy pig ears, stewed calf trotters, venison sausage with a green herb inside I've never tasted before, and a salad with chicken livers, bacon, and poached egg. Some give off odd odors that make my nostrils prickle inside. I hear a woman murmur with approval that this is French food— and I blanch; Papà must not find out or he'll be furious with Aunt Nanina. It's best to keep him tipsy. Regularly I send over a servant girl to top off his wineglass. It's easy; we are awash in Trebbiano and Greek wines.

Piero is here. He drapes himself over the prettiest young women in the most offensive way. He laughs loud and shows no wear and tear from the tournaments this morning. His wife Alfonsina watches him hawklike, already giving a hint of what she'll look like in old age. Can anyone still believe they might be happy? Though they already have been blessed with two children, I am sorry for them.

Cardinal Giovanni is here, too. I knew he had returned from Rome, of course—Giuliano told me. And I've listened to noble girls making fun of him. His nickname is Tardi, for late to bed and late to rise. Tonight he eats until there's a pile of sucked-empty snail shells that rises practically to his nose. When he finally finishes, he stands in the middle of a fawning group like a round cupola in the middle of clouds.

But I can't really think much on him or anyone else, anyone other than Giuliano. He came to my side immediately as the dancing began.

People are noticing. Girls try to catch my eye, with inquiring glances, and Piccarda, naturally, with a painfully disappointed face. I would be sorry for her—after all, she recognized the inherent virtues of Giuliano. But I'm too happy to dwell on her right now. I look away, refusing to reveal the news yet. Papà and Caterina should be the first to know. But they're engrossed in conversation. And from the look on Papà's face, I'm guessing it's politics they're discussing. So he and Caterina haven't noticed that Giuliano and I are a couple. Maybe even if they watched us dancing together, though, they wouldn't guess; they'd think it too implausible. Even I can hardly believe it. Giuliano and I—a couple.

And what a couple. Our bodies move in perfect synchrony. Our eyes reach for each other. We separate only when someone snatches one or the other of us away.

That happens often, unfortunately. All the men seem to feel the obligation to talk with me, and most to dance, as well. Young and old alike. They recognize the intention of this party is to find me a husband, though none of the men seems astute enough to realize a husband has already been found.

Francesco arrives and comes directly to me, asking forgiveness for being late. He talks about Bartolomeo and tells me how much it means to him that I act so affectionate with the boy. I remember the first time I met him, at Mamma's funeral. He was the proud new father. Now he's doubly sad, widowed twice. And both times by childbirth. He must feel doomed. The poor man. Bartolomeo is the one light of his life. I have the urge to console him.

"I don't act affectionate with Bartolomeo," I say, interrupting his long stream of words.

He looks momentarily taken aback.

"I love him. Sincerely. He is the dearest child in the world."

Francesco's eyes melt with gratitude. And he seems to take this as a signal, for he talks again, talks and talks, ever faster, to the point where I begin to regret my little outburst.

Finally, another widower asks for a dance. He holds me too tight and won't let go of my hand between dances. Then a very old man with hardly a hair left on his pate leads me around the dance floor. At last Giuliano comes to me again.

"Happy, Monna Lisa?"

"I can't believe it. It's like a wedding feast."

"Not a Medici wedding," says Giuliano. "Ours will be extravagant." He smiles and gives me a knowing look. "Sumptuous."

I remember his words at Contessina's wedding: a sumptuous wedding feast portends a fecund marriage. Giuliano is one of seven children. He must want many of his own. My mother had one child, as did her mother. Lord, please let me be different.

"I bow to your wisdom," I say.

"The day your spirit bows to anyone—now that will be a day I'll have to see." Giuliano laughs. "I have asked your father if we may talk in private. We will do that at the end of this dance." He briefly touches above his lip.

Is that from nervousness? It is absurd that a Medici man should be intimidated by anyone. And it is enormously attractive, as well. This man enchants me.

Giuliano bows to me. We take our places on the floor, in a giant circle of couples for a pavan. We are dancing when the soldier comes. He barges in, sweating and dirty and out of breath. He goes straight to Piero.

The musicians stop playing. People turn, instantly alerted, almost as though they've been waiting for news. This is a messenger, clearly. Giuliano leaves my side and goes to Piero, as do Cardinal Giovanni and several other men. Faces pinch with fear. Men rush together and talk. Girls cluster and cling to one another.

Soon enough the news passes from mouth to mouth: King Charles VIII of France's march against Naples has come our way. His army is about to pass into the western part of the Republic of Florence.

Everyone knows what that means. Piero has maintained his stance as Naples's ally. He has denied the French army free passage through the Republic of Florence. So the King of France will have to march against Florence on his inexorable path to Naples.

And the French army is known for monstrous savagery.

CHAPTER Seventeen

DON'T. Please, Giuliano. Don't go."

"I have to."

We are pressed against the outside of the garden wall of the palace, hidden under an overhanging wisteria. A peacock struts along the top of the wall, pecking at the long-dried blossoms. Another calls to it from inside the garden, a raucous cry that vibrates through my chest and at once frightens and enthralls. Men rush by along the road, gesticulating as they talk. Arms fly wildly. Fear energizes the very air.

I look at the spot on Giuliano's neck that pulses so visibly. "Where?"

"Wherever Piero goes."

"What if you don't come back?"

"I'll come back."

I put my finger on that spot. I feel the pulse. I need that pulse. "War, Giuliano."

"Look at me, Lisa." He lifts my chin. "It won't come to war. We'll work it out. My father kept the peace. Piero will keep the peace."

"Your father was a master statesman. Piero is not."

"Even if there is war, and there won't be, war amounts to soldiers shooting in the air. Hardly anyone gets hurt."

"The French army is bestial."

"Don't believe everything you hear."

"They cut off heads."

"Stop it, Lisa."

"But some people do get hurt in a war. I heard people talking about it at the games this morning. Oh, Giuliano, some people must get hurt."

"Why should it be me?"

"Why shouldn't it?"

"It won't." His arms pull me close. Chest to chest. We kiss. His hair smells sweet as Malvasia wine. His taste intoxicates me. Our tears mingle in urgency. This has to last.

I pull myself away and tighten my hands into fists in front of my throat. "This morning you said you'd take care of me. But, Giuliano, we'll take care of each other. You want to start a business. Whatever business it is, I'll be by your side. The two years since Mamma died have been perfect preparation for this. You have no idea."

His hands close around my fists. "I believe you. I have never met anyone who speaks with me as you do, who stirs me as you do. I need you. I love you."

"As I love you." I bend my head and press his knuckles to my cheek. "You're only fifteen. There's nothing you can do to help now. Stay. Let others go."

"I'm my brother's right hand. He needs my counsel."

"You said he doesn't listen to Cardinal Giovanni. Why should he listen to you?"

"I'll talk sense."

"What is sense?"

"Peace."

"Peace." It sounds so right, so simple. "So you'll tell Piero to let the French pass through our republic unimpeded."

"I don't know. Naples is our ally."

"Everyone's against Naples. Everyone's for France. That's what people said this morning."

"That sounds like treachery."

"You and your loyalty. Oh, Giuliano, is loyalty worth going to war with France over?"

"There won't be a war, Lisa."

"You can't know that."

"I believe that. I have to."

The peacock cries again, repeatedly, loud and harsh and shocking.

"Why, Giuliano? Oh, why does it have to happen now? Why do you have to be pulled from me now, just when we've come to love each other?"

"We've loved each other all along, Lisa." And he's right. Of course he's right.

"I'll be back."

He kisses me again, and I'm falling into this kiss, falling and falling. He stops for breath and I kiss his cheeks, his nose, his eyelids, his eyebrows, his forehead. I cannot kiss enough of him.

He pulls away. "I'll be back."

CHAPTER *Eighteen*

PIERO RODE OFF with others. I don't know who. Their names mean nothing to me anyway. All I care about is that he took Giuliano with him. My Giuliano.

Papà stays up late talking with a circle of men in the library. I want them to stop and go away so I can have Papà to myself. I want to tell him about Giuliano and me. I want him to reassure me that Giuliano will come back, that everything will be all right.

But the men talk on and on. I ask if I can listen. I'm told women shouldn't know about politics, and I'm sent to my room.

Women shouldn't know about whether or not we're going to war? What on earth could Papà mean? He's always talked about politics freely—to Mamma, to Caterina—and always in front of me. I hide in the hall and listen and want to scream. They talk deep into the night, but their arguments go in circles. No one knows anything. Everyone makes stupid, panicked suggestions. What do their suggestions matter, anyway, with Piero and the heads of government not here to listen?

I go to bed at last. What would war with the French mean? I open and close my fists. I stare into the black. I poke and prod Uccio, who responds with a *naaaa* and a lick. I open the window, even though it's chilly, just in case I might overhear something in the streets.

Why does Piero have to be so stubborn? Everyone in Florence detests the King of Naples. That's what the man said at the tournaments this morning. And everyone here loves the French—or, rather, they love the money they make through business with the French—though they fear that army in the most ferocious way. Public opinion has to be worth something. This is a republic, after all. No one wants war with France.

War.

Giuliano.

I touch my lips. This is where he kissed me. And here and here and here. I hug myself till sleep finally comes.

The next day, the twenty-sixth of October, is Sunday. Uncle Bernardo and Papà run off early. I watch them leave from my window—separately. Uncle Bernardo slips off first, all alone. He must have come in very late last night, for he wasn't home yet when I went to bed. A few minutes later Papà meets with a man who's clearly waiting for him, and they head the other way. We women—Aunt Nanina and Caterina and I—go off to the holy Mass. The church is full of women, all of us praying for peace. That night Uncle Bernardo doesn't return, but Papà shows up at dusk in time for the evening meal.

"Papà," I say after supper. "I need to talk with you."

"I'm sick of talk."

"It's not politics. It's personal."

"The personal is the political, Betta. That's the lesson of these times. I know your hopes have been dashed—all our hopes have been dashed. Allow me whatever semblance of peace I can gather right now. We'll talk later, my treasure."

I think I'll burst. I am ready to press him—to tell him my hopes are not about betrothal with just anyone, but betrothal to Giuliano—and to find out whatever he knows about my dear love. But his eyes stop me. They stare vacantly at a point beyond the table. Deep blue pockets underscore them, as though sadness has pooled there. I pour him a glass of wine and hold my tongue.

Caterina clears her throat. "Can you at least tell us what Piero is doing?"

"He left today. To talk with the King of France."

"Alone?" bursts from my lips.

"Of course not." Papà looks at Aunt Nanina, then down at his wine. "But I have not been told precisely who accompanies him." He gets up and goes into the library.

The same thing happens on Monday. Papà talks about the mess all day; he doesn't want to talk about it all night, too. I imagine every household of Florence filled with women waiting for the men to finally talk to them. Silence wears on us. Caterina's eyes dart. The smallest noise makes her flinch. And Aunt Nanina, she's a shadow of herself, creeping around her own home. A messenger brought her the news that Uncle Bernardo is sequestered away somewhere with other friends of the Medici, trying to figure out what to do. That's all she knows.

A semblance of peace, that's what Papà tries to have through sitting alone at night. Whatever semblance of peace I have comes from being with Bartolomeo. I played with him all day today, as the hours dragged by. And I cooked with him, for the little boy loves throwing ingredients into a bowl. When stirring got too hard, he tossed the spoon on the floor and dug in with both arms, gleeful. I love him so much; just watching him makes me crumble inside. This child must not see war.

Caterina joined us in the kitchen at one point, with a wonderful recipe. I knew she was lying about being a bad cook. She's creative and bold.

But not bold enough to venture out of the palace.

I can't bear staying inside, in this forced silence, any longer, though. I need to know what's happening. On Wednesday afternoon, while Bartolomeo naps, I beg Aunt Nanina to let me accompany the servant Carlo on his errands. Papà is not home, of course, and Uncle Bernardo is still absent, so she is the one in charge.

Aunt Nanina looks at me with desperate eyes. "All right."

Caterina puts her hand on Aunt Nanina's forearm. "Is that wise? A noble girl in the streets right now?"

"Wear your shift," says Aunt Nanina. "Stay right behind Carlo, as if you were helping him. And bring that goat."

And so Uccio and I follow Carlo to the nearby candle maker's. Uccio frolics, happy to be rid of the kitchen rope. His joyous energy enters me and makes me hopeful. Giuliano will return safe and sound. He has to.

Now we head to the cobbler's, halfway across town. And the real purpose of my outing is realized, for the very air screams at a high pitch from every corner. People speak ill of Piero openly, not in harsh whispers like those men at the tournament on the morning of my party. They lean out windows and make proclamations to friends in the street. They don't care who hears. They say the city is decaying under Piero's leadership. He should be ousted. But how? He has no official post to oust him from. I think of Piero explaining to me the genius of the Medici.

On the way home we pass a piazza where a crowd has gathered. Carlo looks at me, then stops.

Savonarola's diminutive figure stands on a high, makeshift pulpit and he stares down that huge, hooked nose, and shouts that he is the mouthpiece of God. His voice extends to everyone's ears as they go about their daily tasks whether they want to hear him or not.

He talks of the same thing I heard him talk of last Saturday with Giuliano: moral decay and the damnation of Florence. He says the French army will rape our young women, and he puts the blame on Piero. He says he has always known this—alas, if Piero had only followed the pious ways that Savonarola has followed, none of this would have come to pass. The air reeks of his self-righteousness. Giuliano smelled it from the start. I am repulsed, for I get the feeling that Savonarola is gladdened by this imbroglio with the French. Gladdened that war may come. He cares more about being proven right than about what happens to Florence.

The crowd listens as though the monk is God's messenger, as though the Lord on high actually wants to preserve the business affairs of Florence. They pat their money purses, and quote Savonarola. They talk of closing their daughters and wives away in convents if the French should come. The chant of the day becomes "get rid of Piero." They seem convinced that without Piero, Florence will get around this mess between France and Naples and the world will go on beautifully and the rich can stay rich.

"Can we go now, Carlo?" I whisper.

We walk on. I don't care what happens to Piero. Let him get ousted somehow. So long as there is no war. So long as Giuliano comes back to me. When we get home, Caterina and Aunt Nanina and I stand in a huddle in a corner, and I tell all I've heard—in whispers, though there is no one around to overhear.

On Thursday afternoon, Uccio and I follow Carlo, who pushes a cart today. He's getting oil for the lamps and wood for the stove.

We pass another piazza where Savonarola stands preaching. Why, he must change piazzas every day. The whole city must be bombarded by that monk. Carlo looks at me, but I shake my head and we don't stop. I don't want to hear—the monk never says anything new, anyway.

But the people hanging out of windows and shouting to friends on the street, or standing together outside shops, they say new things. Today names besides Piero's are on people's lips. At first I don't know why. Then I overhear someone talk about them as Piero's staunch supporters in the government. People say they should be kicked out of office. That should slash Piero's influence overnight. I recognize one of the men I overhear. He's the one I saw meet Papà on Sunday morning.

When we get home, I go to my room and pace. Now I know why Papà won't talk to us. It is not that foolish thing he said in front of the men that night—about how women shouldn't know about politics. He's silent because he cannot speak his mind in front of Aunt Nanina, for Uncle Bernardo is one of Piero's staunchest supporters.

I dig my fingers in my hair and grip my scalp. It's all so absurd. How can people argue over money when war is at stake?

The next morning the news comes early: Piero has forged a peace with the King of France, after all. But in his efforts to appease the king, he has turned over to France the fortresses of Pisa, Sarzana, Pietrasanta, and Livorno. Papà is livid with fury. He storms out of the house.

I beg Aunt Nanina to let me accompany a servant on morning errands; I cannot bear to wait till afternoon. Caterina says she'll play with Bartolomeo in my stead, for the boy has been staying here with us. And so Uccio and I head off behind Enrico this time. Public reaction is heard on every corner, in every piazza— immediate and fierce: Piero's acts are madness. These four cities are the sum total of the strongholds of the Republic of Florence. Piero had no right to give them away without permission from the government. Who does he think he is, negotiating as though he's king? Florence has no king! Florence is a republic. He needs countersignatures.

And, on top of giving away those cities, Piero has promised the French king a vast sum of money. The merchants of Florence say they cannot possibly raise such a sum. "Get rid of Piero!" come the furious shouts.

I listen to hear where Piero is now. But I learn nothing. Nothing that might tell me where Giuliano is.

"Pack your bags," says Papà that night. "We're leaving in the morning."

"No!" I yelp.

He looks at me with apologetic eyes. "Now is not the time for happy announcements."

I'm taken by surprise. What happy announcements? But I shake my head. "Can't I stay with Aunt Nanina? Please, Papà."

"I need you at home."

"Silvia can do anything I can do."

Papà shakes his head. "Leave you in Florence alone?"

Caterina reaches out and puts her hand over mine. "She'll be safe here, Antonio. Please don't force her to leave Bartolomeo."

"We can take the child to Villa Vignamaggio with us."

"I already asked Francesco," says Caterina. "He won't allow it. He won't be separated from his son right now. Let Elisabetta stay, so she can pass the day with him. They're so attached. Besides, Aunt Nanina will welcome her company."

Aunt Nanina has been gazing down into her soup. But now she looks up. "I need the girl."

"But . . ."

"I need the girl." Aunt Nanina is resolute.

I don't know what's happening. It seems the women have formed a unit against Papà. But we haven't planned it. It's a tacit pact. What's more, Caterina's words may be entirely wrong. Staying in the home of a supporter of Piero's—one of the grandest palaces of Florence—may lead to finding myself in the middle of more trouble. Indeed, Bartolomeo probably shouldn't spend his days here. He's better off at his father's palace. Francesco is not so closely aligned with the Medici family to be in much danger. Yes, I will visit the child at his home from now on, rather than having him come here.

I say nothing of these doubts, though. Whether I understand what Caterina and Aunt Nanina are doing or not, I'm grateful. I must be here when Giuliano returns.

Papà hesitates, but what can a man do in the face of female unity, especially when one of those females is his young wife? I am left in this palace with Aunt Nanina, who promises she will retire with me to a convent if it becomes advisable.

Papà and Caterina leave early in the morning on November first. It's Saturday, only a week since my party, but so much has changed. I watch their coach disappear. Uncle Bernardo reappears moments later, as though he was waiting for Papà to leave before returning. He greets me as he rushes in. Not long after, he rushes out again.

"Can I borrow a servant to accompany me over to Bartolomeo's house?" I ask Aunt Nanina.

She jerks her head at me like a startled bird. "You want to visit with him there, instead of him coming here?"

"I think it's better."

She purses her lips. "Gossip can pass so quickly."

"Gossip? About what?"

"You in Francesco's home. A servant isn't a proper chaperone, you know."

I almost laugh. "Francesco's bound to be out on business. Besides, I don't think anyone cares about things like that right now."

"Everyone cares more now. More! Savonarola has turned neighbors into prudish spies." Her face puckers nervously. "All right, go visit the boy, but wear your shift so you look like a servant. And come back immediately after the midday meal."

I spend the morning in Francesco's palace, playing with Bartolomeo, who's delighted by the change in routine. His only disappointment is that I didn't bring Uccio, which I promise to do the next day.

When I return, I go directly to Aunt Nanina to beg to be allowed to accompany a manservant on his errands. She holds up her hand in the halt signal before I can get out a word. "Take Carlo; he's loyal and discreet. Tell him where you want to go, and he'll find an excuse if anyone should ask. And take Uccio; he makes you appear harmless." She grabs my wrist and squeezes hard. "Bring back news, no matter how wretched."

But, though I keep eyes and ears open, the outing proves fruitless. I hear only the same outrage as the day before.

That night, Uncle Bernardo says, "Francesco found out you went to his house."

"Found out? You say it as though I tried to keep it secret. I merely visited my nephew."

"Don't. Francesco doesn't want you on the streets. With the present situation, women should stay inside. That's what your father would want, too."

"What is the present situation?" I ask, for I want to know how he sees it.

"Beyond your understanding. Good night, Elisabetta."

I lie awake thinking of Bartolomeo and Giuliano and Caterina and Papà—and, yes, yes, Silvia, too—all the people I love. When will I next see any of them?

Sunday morning Aunt Nanina says she's not feeling well

enough to go to the Mass. She wants me to stay by her side. She doesn't look me in the eye when she speaks. Uncle Bernardo must have forbidden even the short walk to church.

He has friends over throughout the day, and I try to eavesdrop. But they shut the doors behind them every time.

That night, after Aunt Nanina has gone to bed, I catch Uncle Bernardo in the library, alone at last. "Uncle, can you tell me where Giuliano is?"

"Giuliano?" He looks at me vaguely. Then he frowns. "Which Giuliano?"

"Giuliano de' Medici, of course."

He blinks. "I wouldn't know." His eyes grow suspicious. "Why?"

"He's my friend."

Uncle Bernardo shakes his head and waves me away.

My uncle doesn't trust me. That means he fears for Giuliano's safety. I wince.

Monday morning, as soon as Uncle Bernardo leaves, Aunt Nanina says, "Carlo is ready. Make sure to get home before supper, before Bernardo returns."

Dressed in my shift, I wander with Uccio and Carlo. Through street gossip I learn that the central tribunal in the building adjacent to the Palazzo Vecchio, the seat of justice, has become a forum for public opinion. I head directly there, of course, but I'm not permitted to enter. Men go in but not women. So Carlo and I sit under an open window beside a huddle of women, all straining to hear.

People talk in angry rants. They say Savonarola is right about moral decay, right about the future of Florence, right about everything. Piero must be stopped.

No one sees Savonarola for the bully that he is. That's what Giuliano called him, and I know now that it's true.

But at the same time, Savonarola may be right about Piero. My understanding of politics is limited. But my understanding of business is not. A person who makes decisions when he has no right to, and whose decisions are costly to everyone around him—such a person will bring a business down.

But Piero isn't Giuliano. No one says a word against Giuliano. That night I sleep restlessly.

The next two days are repeats, the only difference being that the litany of wrongs people claim Piero has committed doubles.

Wednesday night a bell bongs. I jump from bed. A second bong comes. This is not an ordinary church bell, tolling the hour. I go into the hall and meet Aunt Nanina rushing along. "The bell of the Signoria," she says. "Get dressed. Hurry."

The government bell in Palazzo Vecchio. I've never heard it before, but everyone knows about it: it rings only for a crisis. A call to arms? I throw on a dress. That's when I realize the bell is now silent. It should have kept ringing to wake the whole city.

We meet at the main door: Aunt Nanina and her slave girl and the two men servants, Carlo and Enrico, and me. We race to the piazza, along with half the population of Florence, many carrying swords and knives, some even carrying firearms. Anxiety to hear everything hushes the crowd. But the Palazzo Vecchio is dark.

Whoever rang that bell had something to announce. Something urgent that couldn't wait till morning. And he was stopped after only two rings. This feels more ominous than any news could be. Aunt Nanina hooks her bird-thin arm through mine and draws me close as we rush home.

The next morning we expect the worst. The mystery of the bell leaves us skittish, jumping at noises, glancing over shoulders.

Aunt Nanina tells me to stay in today. She takes over the kitchen, saying it's been years since she made a meal. She throws chunks of old bread and pieces of aged pecorino into chicken broth, talking the whole time in coddling tones, the way she talks to Bartolomeo. The guileless attempt to take care of me, the need to protect someone in this crazy moment, makes her seem like egg-shells—easy to break. Her eyes have sunk into her skull. When was the last time she slept?

Finally, on Friday, the seventh of November, Uncle Bernardo tells us Piero is returning to Florence. All this time he has been with the King of France. He says nothing more—and we know not to question him further.

If Piero returns, Giuliano must show himself, too.

I can't stay still; I mend a pillowcase and help knead bread and walk in circles while Aunt Nanina plays the pianoforte. That night I can't sleep.

On the eighth, I make Carlo accompany me to the Palazzo Vecchio. I'm sure Piero will go there first. But he doesn't show up. No one knows where he is.

When I return to Aunt Nanina's, a man awaits me. It's Alberto from Villa Vignamaggio. Papà sent him to accompany me home in the morning. When I object, Aunt Nanina says I must go, for Uncle Bernardo insists I obey Papà.

Women's unity has collapsed.

I grit my teeth as I pack. Giuliano could well be preparing to enter the city just as I am preparing to leave. Another sleepless night.

But in the morning, it turns out the gates of the city have all been closed. No one can leave. I have a reprieve. And, though it's Sunday, ordinary church services are suspended. So I'm back in the piazza outside the Palazzo Vecchio, this time with Alberto, still dressed in my shift, but without Uccio. News comes that Piero is approaching the city gates with five hundred men on horseback.

One of them must be Giuliano.

But why five hundred men? The town won't open the gates. How could he expect they would, coming with a private army? Then the government, or what there is left of it, decrees that Piero can come inside the gates only if he comes alone.

The crowd in the piazza buzzes with energy at the news. Will Piero's army storm the gates? There's an edge to everyone's words. We're just people standing together, unarmed civilians, but I feel surrounded by swords; blood is about to flow.

A moment later Piero appears on horseback. He smiles. I'm shocked; his face shows no effect of suffering, while the rest of us are wrecked. Is the man entirely impervious? He scans the crowd, and I duck behind Alberto.

Piero's not wholly alone, despite the decree—a band of footmen precedes him and a few men on horseback flank him. I search their faces. No Giuliano. The crowds part as the procession rides up to the Palazzo Vecchio.

Piero is refused entrance. If he wants to go into the seat of government, he must enter alone, and not through the front, but through the small side door. Such humiliation is beyond comprehension. The crowd comes alive at the realization that Piero has truly fallen from power. The unoustable has been ousted. They jeer and throw stones.

Piero turns in a circle on his horse, looking every which way. The bravura of before is gone; his face is drawn and hard. He gallops with his men up the road in the direction of the Duomo, toward the Medici palace. Of course: he's going home.

We run after him. A surging mob, flowing like a torrent through the road. I'm carried along from behind. I couldn't get out of this current if I tried. Alberto has disappeared. There is nothing to do but hold myself high and run.

A cry rises, *"Popolo e libertà*—'Long live the people. Long live liberty.'" It's taken up by the mob. "Long live the people. Long live liberty."

Shopkeepers frantically run to protect their stores against an unpredictable mob. The bell of the Palazzo Vecchio rings. It's a call to arms now if ever there was one. It rings and rings. More people rush into the street with random and antique weapons.

By the time I get to the Medici palace, Piero has already remounted his horse and left. The mob goes wild. Some enter the palace. Some flow out over Florence, like a flood. People hurry to barricade their homes against it.

I press my back to the wall across the road from the Medici palace. Through the rest of the day people sack the palace, the cellars, the gardens. They steal furniture, glassware, chandeliers, statues, vases, anything that can be carted away. The palace bleeds a stream of gold, silver, and bronze. A man carries away the Botticelli that so entranced Leonardo da Vinci the first time I set foot in the Medici palace. I'm grateful Leonardo is in Milan, so he cannot see the undoing in a single day of a treasury of art that took five generations to amass.

Despite the sweat and grime, I recognize many looters, though I couldn't say names. Some of them talked with Papà the night Giuliano disappeared. Some are friends of Uncle Bernardo, or they pretended to be. Important men—respectable men. Even elite members of the government. Looting.

A man yanks a painting from another man's arms. They struggle. The first stabs the second. A scream escapes me. The stabbed man lies thrashing in the road. People race past. I wring my hands. Tears gush. I take a step forward.

But a young man stops, thank heavens. He kneels beside the wounded man. He cuts free the man's money pouch and runs. I clap both hands over my mouth to stop the scream this time, and press back against the wall again. I sink to a squat. The wounded man no longer moves.

Two men stop an arm's length from me and talk over their booty. One says the city has offered two thousand ducats for whoever should slay Piero, and one thousand for whoever should slay Cardinal Giovanni. There's no mention of Giuliano.

Evening comes. Groups disperse. The streets are nearly empty. I stand, my back still to the wall. I smell destruction before I see it: flames rise from a roof down the road. Whose home is burning? Someone loyal to Piero, no doubt.

Poor Aunt Nanina. Poor Uncle Bernardo. Poor little Bartolomeo. Oh, Lord in heaven. This is the end of reason. The end of everything. Savonarola said that Florence would become the center of hell. This is the stench of hell. I'm crying and I can't stop.

"He's safe."

I jump at the voice. A fat monk stands beside me. He pulls back his hood just enough for me to recognize him. Is this a specter? "Cardinal Giovanni?"

"Hush. Giuliano is gone. With Piero. To Bologna."

"Thank the Lord."

"He'll send you word."

"I won't be at Aunt Nanina's. I'm going home as soon as the gates open again."

"Is there anyone at home you trust?"

The question stabs like a dagger through the center of my being, for I can no longer be sure of Papà. He is against Piero;

who knows how he might treat Giuliano? But there is someone—and she can't stay mad forever. "I have a friend. Silvia. She
lives in a cottage to the northeast of our villa. I can walk there in
minutes."

"All right. Get off the streets now. Go."

Cardinal Giovanni walks down the road, away from the center
of town, bent forward at the waist like any monk in prayer. That
he can hide in sight so coolly, that he could deliver a message, that
he could even find me in the first place, all of it leaves me gaping.
One more surprise on this stupefying night. I watch till black
swallows him.

CHAPTER *Nineteen*

IT IS THE ELEVENTH of December. Caterina and I chop vegetables in the kitchen at Villa Vignamaggio. This is our new routine; it consumes our attention. Smaller and smaller pieces. This is our rope of salvation. Papà has grown haggard, sinking under the weight of the problems of this world—but Caterina and I are suspended. We swing together, in silence.

Silvia appears at the door and looks at me. When I first came home from Florence and told her all that had happened, she listened without a word. Giuliano's and my pledge to each other, the party, the messenger, the days of confusion and stealth wandering the streets, the plunder and burning of Florence, the message delivered by Cardinal Giovanni. She moved closer to me as I cried. She has still not spoken of forgiveness. But she no longer punishes me with coldness. We work as partners again. And we talk about everything, everything except our hopes for husbands.

I kiss Caterina on the cheek now, pull on the wool cape Old Sandra made for me, and rush out the door to Silvia and the rest of my daily routine.

Silvia links arms with me as we hurry to the silking building. The act is more friendly than anything she's done since our row. I squeeze her arm in gratitude. She clears her throat. "He did it. My pa is a stubborn blockhead. I'm betrothed."

"Oh no." I look at her, but her eyes stare straight ahead into the frigid air. "He can't really force you," I say. "You have to agree. By law. You're not chattel."

"Law," she says scornfully. "Law protects them who don't need protecting."

"That's not true. The law covers you."

"And if I disobey my pa and he throws me out, what then? Ain't no law going to give me a roof over my head and food in my belly." She forms a fist with her free hand and punches it into her middle.

"Don't do that!"

"I'm getting married, Elisabetta. I'm getting married, and ain't nothing I can do to stop it." Big tears roll down her cheeks.

I try to pull her close, but she rips free. When her sobs finally slow, I ask, "Who to?"

"Alberto."

I don't know what to say. "Alberto used to live in the city, at least. Maybe he'll return. Maybe that's why your papà chose him, because he knows you want city life."

"My pa chose him because of your pa."

"What are you talking about?"

"Alberto's the one your pa sent to Florence to bring you back home. He's won your pa's trust."

He's won mine, as well. The olive harvest was brought to Greve for pressing last week so I sent Alberto to pick up the oil today. He'll be in charge of unloading it and storing it away tomorrow. He's more reliable than the others, and I lean on him like I used to lean on Cristiano. But I won't say that now, of course. "I don't see what my papà's trust has to do with anything."

"Lord, Elisabetta, do you have to stay dumb your whole life? Workers are being sent away right and left, times are so bad. Pa figures that if he weds me to your pa's most trusted worker, there's less of a chance of his own ruin. And he's old now. If Alberto becomes the next head worker, then my parents get to stay living here."

We reach the silking building and hurry to light a fire for warmth. Rocco has left us a pile of tools on the floor, just as I asked him to. We pull on work gloves and sit down to oil tools.

"Maybe it's not that selfish, what your papà's done. I told you what I saw in the streets of Florence. Maybe he's right to put security first."

"And how will you feel if your pa puts security first?"

I jerk my head back in horror. "You're right. I'm so sorry I said that."

"It infuriates me. Pa says I live in dreams, while there he is, living in a nightmare. He's so stupid. This mess with France ain't going to last."

"How could you possibly know that?"

"If it was, your pa would be packing everyone up and heading for a different Italian state. But he ain't. He's staying put. That means Florence will be strong and rich again. And I'll be stuck in the country with a poor man for the rest of my days."

"Lord, you have a lot of confidence in Papà."

"He's the only rich man I ever known. Why shouldn't I have confidence in him? This is all turning out so bad for me. I have half a mind to pack a bag and walk down the road like Cristiano did."

"You're a girl."

"Ain't that the truth. And that says it all for the both of us, don't it? Here." Silvia takes the hoof trimmer from my hand and tosses it back into the tool pile. She passes me the clamp we use for castrating sheep and goats. "Make this one shine."

I take it and rub in small circles. The caked-on blood gradually gives way. I dip the rag in oil and rub harder. I rub till my hands ache. "Another day," I say softly. "Another day and no word."

Silvia picks up a tool and holds it a moment. Then she drops it back on the pile with a loud clang. "He'll come," she says, like a proclamation from God. It's the first time she's responded to any of my words about Giuliano.

"I hope so," I whisper.

"Oh, he'll come, all right. That's why he sent the grand cardinal with that message."

"But when?" I want to scream. "Piero's banished. Cardinal Giovanni's banished. But Giuliano isn't. He could come for me anytime. If he wanted to."

Silvia shakes her head. "Ain't we the pair—all disappointment. Dragging ourselves around." She grabs my wrist. "But you listen to me, Elisabetta. Listen hard. He's coming for you. There ain't nothing in the world I'm more sure of than that."

I sniffle back tears. "Without you, Silvia, I'd be ashes."

"Well, you ain't without me."

"Oh, Silvia. I'm so glad to have you back again. I've missed you. I don't deserve a friend as true as you."

"Well, then, you're lucky. 'Cause not much goes by who deserves it—and friendship ain't no exception."

I give a sad laugh. "Want the news?"

"You're going to recite it no matter what I say. And that's the truth. Get on with it already."

And so I tell Silvia what I've heard since our last installment. Several times a week a herald rides through the towns of the Republic of Florence announcing news. Papà goes to Greve on those occasions to learn everything. Then he comes home and tells us. And once every ten days or so Bartolomeo's father brings him out here for a night or two and fills us in on details the heralds leave out.

And I tell it to Silvia, leaving out nothing. It's become a ritual. Silvia says I'm really talking to myself and just forcing her to listen. And maybe that's true. It makes me feel less alone in this long wait for Giuliano. But I'm also hoping she'll pay attention and notice something I didn't recognize the importance of. Silvia figures things out.

So much has happened since the Medicis were banished from Florence. This is what I know; this is what I passed on to Silvia.

When the King of France heard Piero had been exiled, he feared Florence would back out of the agreement Piero had made with him, so he declared war. Florence quickly sent him a stream of obsequious ambassadors, and the king withdrew his declaration of war. The result was, when the French finally arrived, the city didn't know whether it was as enemy or friend.

So the people hung banners on buildings. They laid carpets in the roads. Church bells rang. But they also amassed weapons. Every city man had a firearm or sword close at hand. And the peasantry was ready, too, with bows and arrows and pitchforks. If the great bell should ring, more than thirty thousand armed men would rush to help.

Thirty thousand men were ready to fight!

Less than a week after I left Florence, King Charles VIII entered the city. The columns of infantry seemed never ending. Five thousand French and five thousand Swiss, with pikes and firearms and a train of artillery. Four thousand Breton archers, twenty thousand crossbowmen, three thousand armed cavalry. And, most spectacular of all, the king, in full armor under a richly decorated canopy carried by four knights, flanked by his marshalls and trailed by hundreds of French knights in splendid dresses and Swiss guards with plumed helmets.

I was told it in such detail that I felt I was seeing it myself. It made me cringe and shake. But King Charles VIII came in peace. The people cheered in relief.

After that wonderful news, Caterina and Old Sandra and Silvia and I prepared a feast for everyone who worked at Villa Vignamaggio.

The news didn't stay good, though. For eleven days the king negotiated with the heads of government. He wanted Florence to restore Piero de' Medici to power. But Florence wouldn't— Savonarola's preaching made sure of that. Men loyal to Piero were now outside the circle of power. Their homes had been sacked. Aunt Nanina and Uncle Bernardo had taken refuge in the house of Francesco—Bartolomeo's father.

In the end, the Florentine government paid the French a huge sum, and the king agreed to return the fortresses Piero had given him after his war with Naples. The King marched southward on his path to Naples. And Florence went back to figuring out what to do next. The government was a shambles.

But now it appears they have figured something out, finally. Under the guidance of Savonarola. Papà told Caterina and me about it last night. There will be a giant meeting in the city. Before dawn on the morrow, Papà and Caterina and I will travel to Florence. This is the news I give to Silvia now. She hears the name of Savonarola and squeezes my arm.

We separate for the midday meal, then come back together to attend to the worms. Rocco and Tomà work beside us, spinning the silk from the cocoons that are ready. The children in Valeria's family keep coming in with armloads of leaves. I set them to collecting whatever still clings to the mulberry trees. So there's no privacy anymore—no more talk between Silvia and me.

Evening comes. The supper meal is uneventful. I go to bed early and stare through the moonlight at the ceiling.

The eleventh of December. I haven't seen Giuliano for nearly seven weeks. I go over the words he said, the way his hands moved, the strength of his grip. How his hair curls at his temples and down his neck. How thick and soft his lips are. The smell of him. The sweetness. The pressure of his flesh. I curl into a ball and clamp my hands between my knees. I remember him as though he's here.

But then comes doubt, my regular companion now. I wonder if I'm remembering right. Or if each time I change something a little bit so that eventually all the little bits will accumulate and my memory will have nothing in common with what actually happened, nothing in common with the true man.

Sometimes I fear everything that happened between us was a fantasy, something my mind made up from wishes. Or a dream— a phantom of the night. No one knows we were on the verge of a marriage except Silvia, and she knows only because I told her. No one can offer independent confirmation of the events I keep telling myself I remember.

In the loneliest moments I am tempted to confide in Caterina. She treats me like a loved little sister now, and I love her back. But, despite her blood tie to Bernardo Rucellai, who stayed loyal to the Medici family till the bitter end, and despite her devotion to Aunt Nanina, her loyalty to Papà is even stronger. She sides with him. Together, they look forward to the new Florence.

I can't blame her. I side with Giuliano, now and forever, even though it means going against Papà. Love is more important than blood.

A smack comes from the shutter on my side window. I'm there in a flash. Could it be? I've been waiting so long for this. Please, let it be. I open wide the shutter and lean out into the chilling, glistening air. It has snowed. The rare snow—like on the day Cristiano left. The world is white as far as I can see. Uccio puts his front hooves on the sill and looks out with me.

Silvia waves from below. Finally.

I close the shutter and wrap myself in coat and boots. There's no way I can get Uccio to go down the stairs without a clatter. His hoofs simply can't be silenced. And I can't leave him in the room or he'll butt his head against the door till he wakes the dead.

I lift Uccio in my arms. It's no small feat; he's a mature billy. And he's going to make me stink of goat. But what else can I do? I trip off the bottom step. But I manage both not to fall and not to drop Uccio. And we're out the door, running across the snow.

Silvia takes my arm. Without a word we race, the three of us, to the old silk shed. We used to raise the worms here, before we built the new silking building. It has lain in disuse for years, serving only as storage space for old tools.

Silvia stops outside. "Go on, then."

Is Giuliano really in there? But . . . "What about Uccio?"

Silvia wrinkles her nose, but she's smiling. "All right. I'll take your goat for the night. But he's a smelly billy. Mamma will be angry with me. So then you owe me double."

"I'll owe you forever, anything you want."

"Good. Because I want something important."

"What?"

"Later." Silvia runs off, calling to Uccio.

"Go on, boy," I say. "Git." I go inside the shed.

CHAPTER *Twenty*

IN AN INSTANT Giuliano's arms enfold me. "You're here. At last."

My cheek presses against the ridge of his collarbone. After all these weeks of knowing him only as a phantom memory, I can hardly believe the physicality of him. His torso is hard within his jerkin. My fingers count ribs. He's lost weight. His left arm stays on my back but his right hand now caresses my hair. I feel the slight pressure as his palm moves down and cups my jaw line. He wants to lift my head toward his. My lips toward his. An unexpected shyness keeps me clinging where I am.

Something brushes the very top of my hair. I tilt my head the smallest bit, to feel his chin on my forehead. But what I feel is hair. And I realize he has a beard. He used to be clean-shaven. "You're the one who's been gone. In Bologna, I hear."

"Only briefly. We left there for Venice. Our grandfather, Cosimo, was exiled to Venice once. So Piero followed tradition. And the Venetians were good to us."

"Good to you?" I can't stop the edge in my voice. "You were happy away from me?"

"You're angry."

"Seven weeks, Giuliano."

"I would have come sooner if I could have. I swear. Do you believe me?"

And I do. All anger disappears. "Yes." Fragrant little clouds of warmth puff from his mouth in the chill of this shed. "You smell of hazelnuts."

"They're abundant in the Republic of Venice. I brought a sack to eat as we traveled."

"The last time we were this close together, you smelled of Malvasia wine. And the time before that, of apricot preserves."

He laughs. "I'll have to think about what I eat before each time I'm with you."

"I promised myself I'd eat apricots every day from then on. But I forgot. I haven't kept my promise at all."

"And I promised you I'd talk with your father at the end of that pavan we danced. These are times that strain promises."

"You're back now, Giuliano. Stay."

"We will. As soon as possible, we'll return to Florence. Piero is determined."

"Piero? Can he really? There's a decree."

"Yes. We are banished."

"No. Only your brothers, not you."

"If my brothers are, then I am."

"Loyalty again." My voice breaks.

"Without loyalty, what is a man?"

A tiny sound of pain escapes me.

"Please, Lisa. Understand me. Please. Piero has to stay a certain distance away. The cardinal can come closer, but even he isn't allowed to enter the city. Lucca is outside the boundaries of the decree, though."

"So that's where you're staying? Lucca?"

"Until Piero can organize a successful return."

"Do you really think he ever can?"

"His wife Alfonsina has been allowed to remain with her family in the city. She's doing her best to arrange things from the inside."

I pull away and look up at Giuliano's face. It's dark in here, but I can make out the fuzzy outline of a thin beard, the tip of his nose. "I don't think we can count on that."

"Indeed. It's hard to count on anything from one day to the next."

"You can count on me."

"I know, Monna Lisa. What I don't know is if you can count on me."

A shiver runs through me. "What do you mean?"

"At the moment I have nothing. Not even a home."

"Oh, Giuliano, that doesn't matter. Wherever we go, that's home." The words bubble out of me. "So long as we have each other, nothing can stop us."

"I cannot see your mouth, but I see the whites of your eyes. You're smiling. That smile can make me believe anything. It can almost make me believe what you just said."

"Almost?"

"You don't know what it's like—exile."

"You're thin."

He laughs. "That's not what I meant. We brothers haven't gone hungry. We could have stayed in Venice indefinitely if we wanted. The world is speckled with friends of the Medicis. And it's painted solid with people who may not be friends, but who owe us in one way or another. No, that's not it." He touches above his lip, where a mustache now sprouts. "There's no solidity to this life I've been leading since August."

"Is there solidity to any life?"

"You know there is, Lisa. There was a semblance of it at our palace on Via Lunga. There is an abundance of it here at Villa Vignamaggio."

"But without you largely pointless."

"I'd never rip you from your home unless I had something just as solid to offer."

"You are enough to offer. You."

"Exile, Lisa. Think about that. Please."

I lean against the wall behind me. I cannot afford to lie to myself. Piero's exile could be permanent. And Giuliano would not live where Piero was not allowed.

Exile. To live somewhere other than these exquisite hills, far from the church cemetery where Mamma lies. To see Papà and Caterina and Silvia only on visits. To raise children of my own in a foreign land. Deprivations that shatter the soul.

But it is a life with Giuliano. And though in so many ways, I hardly know this person, he has entered my heart permanently. In these seven weeks, he has been with me in spirit. Wherever I go, whatever I do, I am reasoning with him inside my head. I come across a fox den, and I want Giuliano to see the kits. I witness one of Bartolomeo's funny ways, and I want Giuliano to laugh with me. I want him to taste everything sublime that I taste, to smell everything I smell. When I cook, I'm cooking for him. He lives within me.

And now that we are here in more than spirit— now that we are two bodies with flesh and blood and bones—I want much more; I hunger for him.

I step toward him with decision. "I will always choose you."

He lets out a deep sigh, as though he's been holding his breath. "Hazelnuts are not the only thing I brought from Venice." Giuliano opens a pouch and hands me a small box made of paper all folded intricately into a perfect pentagon.

I open it and feel through the straw. Four spindly legs, a tail with a tassel at the end, a long long neck. "A glass giraffe?"

211

"The one we used to own, that we talked about at my father's funeral."

"How perfect."

"Far from it. I went to the finest glassblower of Murano. I had to draw him a picture because he'd never seen one, and my drawing skills are poor. But, still, the creature is rendered gracefully. You'll see in daylight."

"I treasure it already."

"When we are established again, I'll get you a real giraffe." Giuliano laughs happily. "I'll get you any animal you want." He strokes my hair, from my forehead, over the top, and down my neck. Like one might stroke a cat.

I dare to stroke him back. His forehead. His sparsely haired cheeks. My fingers run the line from between his brows, down his nose, to the valley in his top lip. This is the man I have pledged to marry. The love of my life.

Giuliano takes my hand and pulls me down. Fresh sweet hay covers the ground. Someone prepared it for us. Its pungent smell makes me woozy. And there's a heavy wool blanket to pull over us.

I set the box on the ground and carefully stand the tiny glass giraffe upright in it. "I stink of goat," I say quietly. "I had to carry Uccio down the stairs."

He gives a little laugh. "The turns of your conversation dizzy me. All right, till we meet again, you can remember hazelnuts and I'll remember goat."

We kiss slow and somehow sure. This is no dream. This is as true as mortality.

CHAPTER Twenty-one

Elisabetta!"

My eyes shoot open. It's dawn. Giuliano sits up straight like a bolt of lightning.

Papà towers over us in shock that turns quickly to rage. "What have you done!" His eyes that have been so tired for so long now would pop from his head. "Get up!"

But we're already up and putting ourselves in order.

"Scoundrel!" He lunges at Giuliano.

I throw myself between them. "Please, Papà. Listen. This is Giuliano . . ."

"I know exactly who he is." Papà grabs a shovel, the only thing within hand's reach. He throws me aside. I fall to my knees but quickly turn and clasp him around the legs. He swings that shovel and Giuliano ducks—slam!—it comes down on his back.

"Don't!" I scream.

Slam!

"No, Papà! No!"

Again and again.

"Stop, Antonio! You'll kill him!" Caterina pulls on Papà's arm and I hang from his legs, sobbing.

Papà swings again. Giuliano grabs the shovel blade and goes to butt Papà in the stomach with the handle, but he stops and stares, bent over and panting. Blood drips from his right temple. He uses the shovel like a cane to push himself upright. Then he throws it against the rear wall and staggers over to his boots and coat.

Papà lifts a weathered hand and sweeps it sideways with a grimace, as if to rid himself of something revolting. "Get out of here."

Giuliano pulls on his boots. He buttons his coat slowly. "We need to talk, Ser Antonio."

"Never. Get out of here now."

"I love her."

"You piece of filth. Not a one of you is worth anything."

Giuliano limps to the door. "I'll be back for her," he says. "Know this."

"I'll know nothing of the sort. You leave my family alone."

"She's my family, too. We are betrothed."

"Elisabetta is already betrothed."

"Already betrothed?" Giuliano looks at me, dazed.

"What are you talking about, Papà?"

"Go!" growls Papà at Giuliano. "Never let me set eyes on you again."

Giuliano leaves.

I run after him. But Papà clutches me around the waist from behind. He holds me while I kick. And I've been here before. Exactly in this position. Exactly as desperate. When Mamma died. But I won't lose Giuliano like I lost Mamma. I won't, I won't. I'll never stop kicking. "Let me go!"

"How?" shouts Papà, so loudly I think my head will split. "How could you do this?"

"I love him."

He claps his hand over my mouth. "Not another word! Tracks in the snow—we followed tracks in the snow. We thought some silly girlish whim had made you take that infernal goat out to this shed. And then this. Never, never in a million years did I expect this." He pushes me away so violently, I'm thrown to the ground again.

I jump to my feet and race for the door, but he blocks it. "You're coming to the house. You'll get dressed properly. We're going to Florence."

"I'm going after Giuliano."

"Don't speak that name around me."

"Giuliano Giuliano Giuliano."

He slaps me across the face.

I hug myself, stunned.

His face is as stunned as my own must be. Then it crumples. "My beloved daughter. How did such a thing happen? How did I ever allow this to happen?"

"You can't allow or disallow love."

"Love? Oh, little Betta, you've been too sheltered. This has nothing to do with love. You are never to see him again!"

"I don't have to do what you say. I'm betrothed. And he doesn't want a dowry, so it doesn't matter what you think. I'm betrothed."

"Indeed you are, my daughter. You are betrothed to Francesco del Giocondo."

"Who? Have you gone mad?"

"No. And I won't allow you to go mad. Have you no idea how dangerous the times are? You cannot have anything to do with a Medici."

"Politics don't rule my life the way they do yours. Can't you think for one moment of my happiness?"

"What?" Papà shakes his head dazedly. "Your happiness is all we've ever wanted."

"Francesco makes a good match." Caterina has been watching, clutching the folds of her bodice with both hands. Now she comes to Papà's side. She speaks softly, reasonably. "Please, Elisabetta. Think. You can take my dear departed sister's place. You can raise her son. You already love Bartolomeo. And he loves you."

"How can you say such a thing? You can't just dream up some crazy scheme on the spur of the moment."

"It's not spur of the moment at all," says Caterina. "We were going to announce it at your party in October."

"Announce it? Announce it?" And I'm screaming now. "How could you do that? Without consulting me?"

"We thought you had accepted the idea, embraced it." Caterina shakes her head helplessly.

"You knew I went to the kick ball game with Giuliano."

"The kick ball game? Yes, of course, I remember that. But Giuliano, well, he's just a boy still. I never guessed . . . And Francesco so clearly needs a wife. How could you not know that's what we all wanted? What we all thought you wanted? It was obvious. It went without saying."

"No, no no no! Nothing goes without saying. A woman's consent is required. I cannot believe this. I will not believe this. I never consented."

"In a way, you did," says Papà quietly. "Who do you think paid for all that splendor at your party? You know I don't have that kind of money."

I stare at him, stupid.

"Francesco di Bartolomeo di Zanobi del Giocondo."

I feel like I've been punched in the very center of my being. I see a halo around every object. "A never-ending name. He announced himself like that to me at Mamma's funeral. As some important thing. The pompous nitwit."

"Hush!" Caterina's hand goes to her throat. "Don't speak like that about Camilla's widower."

And I do feel mean to have said it, for Francesco is not a bad man. But right now that doesn't matter. I lower my voice. "Don't, Papà. Don't keep talking about him."

"Francesco," says Papà. "After all his generosity, you go and do this?"

"Giuliano," I say firmly. "Giuliano is my betrothed."

Papà's eyes flash. Pain distorts his face. He raises his hand as though to slap me again, but Caterina stays his wrist. "That's enough, Antonio. You cannot beat her into submission."

Papà looks at her. Then he pulls away and buries his hands in his pockets. "Francesco has agreed to a modest dowry," he says in a tired monotone. "One hundred and seventy gold florins and a small stretch of farmland. Now he'll ask for more, if he'll even take you at all."

"There's no reason he has to know," says Caterina.

I look at Caterina in fury. "Have you no backbone? You know this is wrong. I hate you!" Caterina winces. I have wounded her hideously, but I don't care. I whip around to face Papà. "I won't marry Francesco. I'll run away with Giuliano."

"To what? His family has nothing now. Not even access to whatever sums might be in the banks—if there are any at this point, which I doubt. He can't take care of you."

"We'll take care of each other."

"He's ruined, my Betta. And gone. He knows that himself, or he would have stayed and fought for you."

"He didn't fight because you're old. If he had slammed you with the shovel like you slammed him, you'd be dead."

"Look more closely, Betta. He's a coward. He slunk off with his tail between his legs. Good riddance to the lot of them." Papà brushes dust from his sleeves and straightens his clothing. His eyes meet mine and I see raw pity there. "You will marry

Francesco. It's a move up in the world for you. More than I ever hoped for."

"No."

"It's my right to marry you off. And it's already agreed upon."

"No and no and no."

"It's what your mother would have wanted."

This is much worse than a slap. This is a staggering blow. I will die.

"He's a silk merchant," says Caterina gently.

I will die.

"Just like your father. You know the business already—the most honorable and successful business of Florence. It will feel like home right away. With a child to love from the very start."

I will die.

"You'll be happy."

CHAPTER *Twenty-two*

I AM THERE, on 12 December 1494, in the cathedral of Santa Maria del Fiore, when Savonarola mounts the pulpit and makes his proclamation. Papà stands on one side of me, Caterina on the other. They press against me to hold me upright. I am their prisoner.

And I witness all of Florence become prisoner of rabid Savonarola. Oh, his words this morning are not insane. They are treacherously reasonable, even to me, whose mind can hardly focus, for it was just hours ago that Papà drove Giuliano away. My Giuliano.

Savonarola presents an outline of the government Florence should adopt. He must have been working on it for months, maybe years, for it is watertight. He says we should have a Grand Council, like that of the Republic of Venice. The will of the people should prevail, not that of the tyrant—the tyrant Piero, and the tyrant Lorenzo before him.

The church is packed. A rank smell rises from communal worry. Not a soul speaks against the monk. They sense their fate: already it is too dangerous. Already Savonarola has taken the role of tyrant as his own. He's been hell-bent from the start.

Leonardo da Vinci knew it. The first time I heard him speak about Savonarola, he talked of sanctimony. And Giuliano knew it. My heart turns to lead. The news of this town meeting was heralded all over the Republic. Giuliano must have foreseen what today would mean. He knew all of us would be locked away by this monk.

Could it be that the reason he came last night was to say good-bye to me before the key was turned in the lock? No. I won't believe that. That's the sort of thing Papà wants me to believe. He says Giuliano is done with me; it's over. But it can't be. Giuliano will return for me. Or he will send for me. We belong together.

Ten days pass, and we are still in the city. Guests of Francesco, to whom I do not speak. It turns me inside out that we should receive his generosity yet again. I play with Bartolomeo, but I will not even look at Francesco.

Aunt Nanina and Uncle Bernardo have left the shelter of Francesco's palace and returned to their own, even as workers repair it. That must be uncomfortable—but probably the idea of being in Papà's company was more uncomfortable. I'm sorry not to see Aunt Nanina; she loves Giuliano.

I am never left alone. If Papà is not by my side, Caterina is. And they always know where the other one is, so they can quickly pass me between them if they need to go off somewhere else. Even in bed I am not alone. Little Bartolomeo, confused but over-joyed by our presence in his father's home, insists on climbing in with me.

Another town meeting is called. The Council of the People and of the Comune have a government in place that Savonarola gives his blessings to. The monk becomes the virtual ruler of Florence. He was hell-bent to get his moral society, and now he has it—pious prisoners all.

And still we stay in Florence, though now I cannot imagine what Papà is waiting for. I have repeated to him that I will not marry Francesco. Yet we stay.

On Christmas Eve, I am shelling walnuts when a bang comes on the main door of Francesco's house. It's Silvia, accompanied by Alberto. Papà receives them in the hallway with alarm. "Has something gone wrong at Villa Vignamaggio?"

"No, no, Ser Antonio," says Alberto. "I just have a few decisions to make about the silkworms. It's tricky in cold weather, what with hibernation and all. And Silvia doesn't know everything."

"I do indeed know everything," snaps Silvia harshly.

"I wanted your counsel, Ser Antonio," says Alberto. "Just to be sure."

"Of course."

We go into the living room and Alberto and Papà talk about business. It's the most ordinary of things—nothing special about it. Papà tells Alberto what to do.

"Just like I said," snaps Silvia.

I'm surprised at her tone. But I'm annoyed for her, too. Of course Silvia knew what to do. I never realized what a blockhead Alberto is. And this is the man her father has betrothed her to.

Alberto frowns at Silvia. "There are other things I'd like to discuss as well. Maybe you two should leave us to talk alone." He turns to Papà. "If that's all right with you, Ser Antonio?"

Papà stands. "Caterina!" he calls. "Go, Betta, join Caterina in the music room. The three of you amuse yourselves for a while."

We walk through the hallway. Once out of sight of Papà, Silvia stops and hugs me close in the clumsiest way, one arm going up and over my shoulder. I feel her slide something quickly down the back of my bodice.

"Silvia," says Caterina, coming from the music room. "What a surprise."

I don't even know what is said after that. I cannot pay attention. I sense nothing but the object inside my dress.

Silvia and Alberto leave in a hurry. Tomorrow is Christmas, after all. They need to be with Silvia's family.

The day goes on and on, and I am never alone, never able to find out what Silvia delivered, until finally finally it is night and Bartolomeo is asleep beside me and I can be once again who I am, who I must be, Giuliano's Monna Lisa. By candlelight I find the parchment that I managed to slide into my sleeve as I undressed in Caterina's presence. I remove it now. A letter from my beloved. Folded in three parts. I break the seal and unfold. It is too brief.

Monna Lisa, you possess my heart. But I relinquish yours. For I cannot offer you what I know you deserve. And I will not offer you less. Forgive me. And then forget me. Giuliano.

I reach under my bed for the hidden paper box that Silvia, ever true, managed to sneak to me as Papà stuffed me into the coach that bitter morning we came here. I rip it apart and dash the glass giraffe against the wall. Graceful, delicate, beautiful, and gone. I drop backward onto the bed and fling my head from side to side, harder and faster and on and on. My brain scrambles and still I fling my head violently until there's nothing left of me. I lie spent. Yet tears continue to leak out my eyes and soak my hair. But then they, too, stop.

After a while I sit up. I touch my hands, my arms, my neck. I feel the beat of my heart. I hear my breath. I let a globule of hot wax drop on my wrist and it burns. I am alive. That doesn't make sense. For there's no reason to live.

I reread the letter, such as it is. Not really a letter. A message.

Delivered less than two weeks after we were together. He lost faith fast. Or maybe he just faced reality fast. Giuliano understands this world. Savonarola will never relent on this banishment.

But I could have gone with Giuliano somewhere else. Anywhere else. It's Mamma who wanted a noble life for me. I want love. I've always wanted love. It should be my right to choose whether or not to join Giuliano in exile. Giuliano shouldn't have made that decision for the two of us. He has betrayed me. For all his talk of loyalty, he has betrayed my heart. And his own.

I set the letter aflame, then blow it out before the fire gets too large. Then set it aflame. Then blow it out. Continuing like that until nothing remains but ashes.

The next two months are frozen. It's as though the weather emanates from my heart. No one can remember a cold like this, a blizzard like this, a freeze so hard you can walk on the Arno River. To me, though, it just seems natural. I slide over the icy days toward the end that I feel has been inexorable from the beginning—from when I was born a girl. I don't fight anyone. There is no reason to. There is no reason to do or not do anything. I agree to marry Francesco. I do not know if I am hostage to my love for my mother, Papà, and Caterina, or whether I simply have given up. I don't try to make sense out of it. Life has no sense.

My wedding feast is on 5 March 1495, a month short of two years after Papà and Caterina's, and a month short of the anniversary of Camilla's death, just as Papà and Caterina's wedding was a month short of the anniversary of Mamma's death. I wear Caterina's gown, which has been taken in considerably for me. It's funny, but white for weddings has become the rule. Savonarola says bright colors are to be eschewed, and what Savonarola says becomes the law of the day. The only color on me is from the yellow crocuses Caterina weaves through my hair, but we don't dare to add her pearls, for Savonarola decries jewelry. We have a short procession. Then a small and simple wedding feast at Francesco's home. That's the new word of the day in Savonarola's Florence. And it suits me fine. I have nothing to celebrate.

Silvia comes to the feast. This time Papà was the one to object to Silvia's presence. I drew on my one and only source of power: I simply answered that if she wasn't invited, I would tell Francesco about Giuliano. Silvia dares to wear the beautiful green dress that I wore to my party in October. She doesn't worry about being denounced, for who cares about a peasant girl, she reasons. And I cannot dispute her reasoning. For all Savonarola's talk about the people, his eye seems focused on the nobility.

This is the favor Silvia wanted of me. The favor that pays her back for helping Giuliano and me that night in the old silk shed, that night she took Uccio home with her. She wants nothing more than to be a guest at my wedding, dressed splendidly, looking for the last time upon a society she will never enter. In a month she weds Alberto.

At one point during the evening I stand beside her and she takes my arm with a small laugh. "You and me, it's happening to us just how they wanted," she says. "Ah, well. At least Alberto is decent."

That he is. I'm grateful for the little play he put on with Silvia when they delivered Giuliano's letter to me. Yes. It's happening just how they wanted.

So much of what Mamma and Papà and Caterina wanted for me turns out to be as irrelevant as I expected. But I learn that Caterina was right about one thing: my new life is better with a child to love from the start. I don't know where the well of delight resides in the human soul. I thought mine had dried up. But Bartolomeo manages to plumb it.

I remember when I sat on the bed and read Giuliano's letter and decided there was no reason to live anymore. I have changed in the months since then. Life may indeed have no meaning, but therein is the secret to it. For now I am free to watch it happen without rancor, without the least desire to change it.

And I am free to enjoy the pleasures that it offers. I give up cooking—for Jacobo, Francesco's cook, is a master, as I knew already. Instead, quite gradually, the pleasure of loving Bartolomeo becomes the focus of my life. And when my son, Piero, is born the next spring, I am grateful. I nurse him, pierced by the power of such tenderness. How can anyone turn over her child to a wet nurse?

Choosing the name Piero was the last dying ember of my old anger. A girl should name her firstborn son after her husband's father. But since my husband already had a son with Camilla, one might have expected I'd name this child after my own father. Instead, I chose the name Piero. Papà objected strenuously at first, thinking the naming was after the cursed Medici brother. I had the satisfaction of telling him it was after Leonardo da Vinci's father. He spluttered, like a giant procession candle going out. What tie did I have to Leonardo, that his father's name should be bestowed on my son? But he resisted asking. He still admires Leonardo. Perhaps he didn't dare know the answer.

It's just as well he didn't ask. I would have told him that sometimes fathers are chosen—and I'd have chosen a father who fostered freedom of thought and spirit in a child, as Leonardo's father had, rather than the father I was born to. It was a little speech he didn't need to hear, for all it would have done is wound him, not change him.

Rumors come often about Piero de' Medici, who now lives with his in-laws in Rome. They say he wakes at noon, in time for the big meal, then closes himself away in his room with a courtesan or a boy. He eats dinner up there alone with them, then goes out in the evening drinking and gambling, returning to his wife near dawn. He is hateful, and so he is hated. Some want him murdered.

But about Giuliano no news comes. I used to listen hard. I became excellent at discerning who might know about the Medici family and masterful at eavesdropping on their conversations. In those moments I was nothing but a receptacle, waiting breathlessly for their words to fill me. But it was as though the world conspired to erase Giuliano from my sphere of existence. Or perhaps my need cast a contrary spell on everyone, so that Giuliano disappeared from their spheres of existence when they were in my presence. Not once did I hear his name. And I never indulged myself in asking. I know Giuliano only at night; he is my dream lover.

We live right in the city, in Francesco's home. But it's not the Florence I was just beginning to know with Giuliano. It changes around us.

Women wear veils on the streets, if they go out at all. Many stay indoors almost all of the time, since God wants us home with our children, as He has told Savonarola, and as Savonarola has accordingly preached from the cathedral of Santa Maria del Fiore. The monk doesn't even allow women into his cathedral anymore.

This, actually, is fine with me. I prefer the company of my children. And when they sleep, I read. Caterina is only too happy to bring me a book whenever she visits, taking away the one that I have finished with. While I do not revel in books the way she does, finally I have learned to find solace in them. They hold reflections of struggles within myself, struggles I lacked any coherent method of dealing with. Right now I am working my way through a Latin translation of a book by the Greek scholar Plato about how people live together in a society. My old visiting tutor's eyes would pop from his head if he were to hear me say that. I admit to not understanding everything I read—oh, how I long for a Florentine translation—but I have no doubt that Plato would despise Savonarola, who I now think of as the enemy of true justice. For that reason alone, I persist in reading. Francesco expresses surprise at first. But then he leans over the book and gets engrossed. Soon we read together in the evenings, an act of quiet rebellion that makes partners of us at last. Perhaps all of Florence is filled with people reading steadily behind closed doors. Quietly ferocious.

And so we women stay sequestered mostly and, if we must emerge, we go veiled. But it isn't only women Savonarola wants covered. He closes communal public baths. Nudity must be guarded against for all. Nudity—that most natural of states.

Savonarola's war against colors results in an abundance of white, not just in bridal gowns. Everyone wears white, gray, or brown in public. His war is so successful that Papà, like other silk merchants, now leaves much of his cloth undyed.

Religious zealots stand on corners and shout, or, more and more frequently, cry.

There is no gambling in Florence, no tournaments, no parties, no chess games, for these things excite temporal interests. A curfew helps to ensure that, since nighttime makes man more susceptible to such temptations. The Florence whose continual noise I once marveled at is now silent after dark. There is no more art or scholarship, except that deemed proper by the myopic eye of the monk. Every breath of joy leaves the city.

This is no longer a place where passion can find purchase.

Boys dressed in white carry baskets through the streets. They sing hymns and knock on doors and accost people walking by. They collect what Savonarola calls "the vanities." Jewels, vases, extravagant clothing, money.

And then books. Alas, books! But of course books. Especially those by the ancients. Savonarola preaches it is dangerous to read pagan trash by Plato and Aristotle. The very writer who's befriended my soul is now outlawed. Francesco and I agree, for we are completely aligned in our views by now—Caterina's tome must be returned to her, rather than land in the hands of the monk. He will smuggle it back to her in the bottom of a toy chest. It is a small act, but in these days one full of risk. I am both proud and terrified as his coach rolls away. When he returns, our marriage experiences a rush of sensuality for the first time. It is an irony against the monk, one we both appreciate. And I cook for him such a magnificent meal that the children and servants, the only others we can invite safely to such an extravagant table, gasp in wonderment. After that, Francesco and I make clandestine visits to the library at the Santissima Annunziata monastery. We have a ready answer when anyone asks where we're going, for Francesco's family owns a chapel there. Another irony against the monk—a monastery offers sustenance to our hunger for reading.

But there are not many victories over Savonarola, and they are short-lived, indeed. The monk now turns his attention to paintings. His boys enter homes and bare the walls.

All of them—books and paintings—go up in flames, in a gigantic public bonfire in the piazza. Who knows what great pieces of art, what triumphs of the human spirit, turn to ashes and smoke under Savonarola's iron hand. The bonfire takes place during one of Caterina's visits. She stands beside me and emits a little shriek as the flame catches hold. She quickly claps her hand over her mouth and looks around in fear to see who has noticed. Francesco puts an arm around each of us and draws us close.

Inside my head I hear the keening wail of the writers and artists.

I watch it all. And I know Savonarola has lost his mind.

His only act of sanity is when he stops the people from burning the Medici library. I don't know why Savonarola saves that one library. Perhaps the hand of God rests on the monk's hand just long enough to keep it immobile at the crucial moment. Or maybe it is something prosaic—a lapse of evil due to a headache or gas.

All those things that go into animating a person, all those ineffables, they suffer under one assault after the other. The people of Florence suffer. Until they can no more. They rebel.

But it isn't as clean as that—it isn't as decent as that.

First, nature conspires; this, of course, is beyond the monk's doings. Plague returns. In 1497 it plucks a child here, a father there, all your brothers here, your niece there. Though it is brief, and the general memory, which is not memory at all but mere rumor, says it is not as virulent as it was in the last century, these deaths break our spirits.

And then Savonarola makes a mistake, the one mistake he has made from the beginning, but it finally catches up with him. He cannot contain his righteous indignation at human frailty. He points his finger at too many and makes enemies of the Franciscan monks and other holy men, including the Pope, who forbids him to preach.

But only God has the right to silence Savonarola.

Over and over, Savonarola offends a pope who has no real sense of shame, having brought his mistress into the Vatican to live and dispensing favors to his illegitimate offspring, even appointing them as cardinals. A competition between shameless men who consider themselves agents of the Lord is a terrible thing to behold. And when one of those men is Pope, the winner is predetermined. For the Pope can excommunicate.

Savonarola is accused of heresy and schism. At first his innocence and integrity are to be put to the ordeal by fire. But that is foiled in too many ways to recount. Then the monk is tortured, and confesses his crimes, then recants, and is tortured again, and confesses his crimes, and so it goes. It seems interminable.

Yet when the end actually comes, it feels swift: On 23 May 1498 Savonarola and two of his supporters are stripped of their monks' gowns and walk across the piazza in front of the Palazzo Vecchio, barefoot, in undertunics, with pinioned arms. People spit and shout vile words, but the clerics hold their chins high. Some say they look beatific, transported into a state of exaltation. One by one, they ascend the ladder of a scaffold erected just for them. One by one, they are garroted with a chain. Savonarola is last. He looks out over the crowd, then presents his neck to the hangman. Minutes later the wood under the scaffold is set aflame and the three bodies burn to ashes in front of the public.

Inexorably hell-bent.

Most of Florence's nobility witnesses the scene, Francesco among them, hence the details are known to all. I decline to attend, however. There have been too many burnings in the piazza. Instead, I close myself away with my wonderful Bartolomeo and Piero; I shut us off from the pervasive stench of rot that this city emits, and I cry. For everyone.

And I persuade dear Francesco to take us away from Florence.

PART *Three*

CHAPTER *Twenty-three*

SUMMER IN THE HILLS of Chianti wine country is a luscious blur—blue mist in morning, gold haze in afternoon. The month is August; the year, 1503. I lie in the grass and let insects crawl on me. When I was a girl, ambling around these hills, I brushed off insects with disgust. But Bartolomeo taught me better. He captures insects and studies them before freeing them again. So now the feel of these creatures' multiple feet simply tickles me gently. I would laugh—another thing Bartolomeo has taught me to do, since somewhere along the way I lost that ability—only I mustn't make noise right now.

Silvia lies beside me in a sleep so sound, she appears totally vulnerable. The sight of her almost frightens me.

"Mamma, close your eyes." Camilla, my precious daughter, skips over and showers us both with wildflower petals she has carefully plucked, one by one, from even the tiniest of flowers. Her four-year-old fingers are agile.

The petals fall on my face like poetry. I open my eyes and smile. Like me, Camilla was born on a Tuesday. Tuesday is the day of warriors. But not just infantry and cavalry. One can be a warrior in the name of science or humanities. Tuesday's child is generous and wise, self-reflecting, and susceptible, especially to passion. Tuesday's child has the capacity to love intensely, and to suffer from abandonment profoundly.

I believe Camilla will be a warrior for the highest of the humanities, the fine arts. She adores colors. In a literal sense. She makes piles of green things, piles of red things, piles of yellow things. She dances around them and sings her magic songs and waves her wispy arms. She is the definition of grace.

Her father thinks I named her after his previous wife, out of respect and deference, as a following wife will often do. But I am hardly a deferential sort. No, I named this daughter out of love for my stepmother Caterina—whose sister's name was Camilla. It just so happens that my husband's previous wife and my stepmother's sister are one and the same, so my husband need not be disabused of his belief. Besides, this misperception makes him happy, and he is a man who deserves happiness.

I think of how Caterina imbued Villa Vignamaggio with rainbow colors when she first came to live there. It's fitting that my Camilla should share this proclivity for colors.

Andrea, my eight-month-old, throws blades of grasses and mutilated flowers he wrests from the earth with his pudgy paws. He does everything Camilla does. Or he would, if he could. A most lovable and loving child. He is still a mystery to me, however. He hasn't yet begun to talk and reveal the inner workings of that brain. Neverthless, his eyes are already loquacious. He will never be a liar. Or not a successful one. In my more hopeful moments, I imagine him turning out thoughtful and steady, like his father.

My older boys—my stepson, Bartolomeo, and my firstborn, Piero—are with their father visiting relatives. I miss all three of them. It is not silly to miss my husband, for he is away on business often and too long. But to miss the boys is totally ridiculous. They have been gone but two days. And heaven knows, when they're here sometimes I close myself away from the noise for a moment's solitude. They are good-natured boys, but rough and tumble.

Four miracle children. And I will have more. These are things beyond the control of mere mortals, of course, but I know this family is not yet full size. I would love to have one more girl, for sisters are a beautiful thing. I never knew that until I had the fortune and privilege to love my father's young wife, Caterina. We are like sisters. She is at once aunt to my stepson and stepmother to me.

I love the complications of life. The weave.

It is sad that Caterina has never had children of her own. Since my mother also had difficulties becoming with child, I wonder if the problem might be Papà's, if such a thing is possible. But this is not an idea to voice. It helps no one.

And Caterina has found satisfaction in loving my brood.

Camilla skips away and Andrea crawls after her in a clumpity way. I am reminded of Uccio, the goat given to me by the love of my life. He skipped. And clumped. He died the day before Andrea was born—back in December. I suppose of old age. He was born the same year as Bartolomeo, after all. Eleven years ago.

Eleven years. Time is a gossamer filament, like a silk strand from a cocoon, flying just out of reach. No one can catch it and hold it firm.

Eleven years ago I met a man—a boy, then—who earned my heart. Nine years ago we promised to marry each other. More than eight years ago, I married another.

A woman's choices are limited. Particularly if she loves her father and her stepmother-sister. Particularly if she honors the memory of her mother.

I sit up and smell the world as deeply as I can. Then I brush the dirt and grass and flowers from Silvia's dress and arms. She gives a groan and goes on sleeping. She is spending a couple of weeks with me at our villa. She lost a baby. This is the third time. She carries them a few months, just long enough to be able to feel their kicks, to get a sense of their souls. A cruel amount of time. My heart breaks for her. After each loss she comes to stay with me. I care for her until she is strong again. Then she returns to Villa Vignamaggio, to her husband, Alberto.

Taking care of her like this gives me pleasure and makes me feel less guilty for living the life she so much wanted. Alberto is a peasant, like her father. The work is hard and the pay is low. They need children to help out. She is without luck.

In contrast, everything about my life is lucky, viewed from the right perspective.

Sometimes my determination flags and my perspective goes awry. In those times all I feel is searing loss.

A woman's choices are limited.

I suppose I could have joined a nunnery. But then I wouldn't be able to share my day with these children. And, I must admit, I wouldn't have the pleasures my constant husband offers.

Am I heartless? I wish I were.

"Aiii!" the scream comes.

I jump up and run. A fallen horse, a broken neck, a nightmare returned?

Camilla is tugging on Andrea, who has managed to fall, though he was only crawling, and smack his forehead on a stone. He rubs at the large red abrasion and refuses to sit up. He's a bit of a round fatty, and she's but a willow switch. His cry is primal, demanding that his pain be acknowledged by the world at large. I laugh in joy at such a reparable damage, kiss Camilla on the head, and sweep Andrea up into my arms. I carry him back to Silvia, who has woken and looks around groggily.

We talk as I nurse Andrea. He stopped crying the instant he took my breast. He's a simple boy. A mother's pearl.

"My milk came in this time," says Silvia.

I know that, of course. I cleaned her sheets. I won't let servants tend to her at these times; I do it myself. We have remained best friends. A most precious achievement—a right we asserted and won, against all odds.

"All three times my milk has come in." Her voice trails off. Then, "Oh! The next time it happens, I'll borrow a baby. I'll keep my milk flowing so I can be a wet nurse. That way I can hold babies all day whether God chooses to give me one or not."

"That's not a bad plan, Silvia." I believe in practical talk, though it tastes like vinegar splashed on cake. Lies between women are unforgivable. "But we are both only twenty-four. Too young to rule out possibilities."

"Twenty-four is old, Elisabetta."

"There are plenty of uncharted waters ahead. We must stay afloat."

"You're the one in a boat. I'm in the water. Swimming. And swallowing salt."

Andrea gulps as he swallows milk. He's a noisy, enthusiastic nurser. That's always been so gratifying to me. But for Silvia's sake, I wish this once he could be quiet.

"I was right," comes a familiar voice, one I never expected to hear again. He walks across the grass and lowers himself to sit facing us. "You are a vision of the Madonna. I knew you would be. I was absolutely right: Madonna Elisabetta."

"Ser Leonardo." I look up into a face that is aging rapidly—bulbous nose, long straggly hair and beard—but the same bold, burning eyes. I can hardly find my voice. "What brings you here?"

"You, Mona Lisa."

He's lived in Milan so long that he speaks now with a northern accent; he said "Mona" not "Monna," shortening the *n* sound. But the part that transfixes me is the second half of that address; my ears hear it greedily—they hear what they have longed to hear. Only one other person in the world has ever called me by that name. But I cannot believe Leonardo is still his friend. From what I have heard, Leonardo is an enemy to the Medici family these days. How did he come up with his address of me?

I caress Andrea's tiny ear. "Ser Leonardo, this is my friend . . ."

"Ah, yes." Leonardo reaches for Silvia's hand and kisses it. Sitting like that, I'm surprised at his flexibility, given his age. He's as flexible as my own sweet husband, who is only fourteen years my senior, while Leonardo must be older than me by close to double that amount. "Don't tell me your name. No, no. It will come to me."

"Leonardo the artist?" asks Silvia. "The one who does animals without skin?"

"I plead guilty. But of many more things than that. I sketch inventions, too."

"Flying boats," I say.

"Flying machines of various types, in my youth. But I've moved to the water now. I designed a device for breathing underwater and a shoe for walking on the surface and a floating ring to throw to someone drowning." He smiles at his own cleverness. "And a machine to calculate great sums. And this." He takes out an inexplicable drawing.

"Shallow bowls?" asks Silvia.

"Concave mirrors. It will be a machine that harnesses sunlight to heat water. I have much work to do on it yet." He tucks it back away. "For a future year. Ah!" He snaps his fingers. "Yes, there's your name. I knew it would come to me, Mona Silvia."

"Finally," says Silvia, turning to me.

Leonardo looks from Silvia to me quizzically; he cannot guess what she means. I know, though.

I try not to stare, but I must be sure. He has real hair, skin, nails, eyes, breath. Indeed, his breath is sour. He is not some vision. So he cannot know what he hasn't been told; he cannot pluck Silvia's name from thin air. And it was no coincidence that he shortened my name to Lisa. He's been talking with Giuliano.

I am ajangle. Unprepared. The girl I was at fifteen flames up inside me without warning.

CHAPTER Twenty-four

WE SIT at the dining table, though we finished our meal an hour ago. The children are in bed. Silvia has gone upstairs to rest. When I protested, she simply said, "You need to talk to each other." Leonardo and I need to talk to each other.

"I visited Milan," I say and listen to my voice with detached amusement. I sound rational. Ordinary. The matron everyone takes me for. I do not sound like a woman trying to smother an inner voice, a woman about to fly to pieces.

"When?"

"In spring of 1499. I saw your mural in the refectory of the monastery of Santa Maria delle Grazie. The last supper of Christ."

"The painting you were a perfect model for," says Leonardo, "a mistake, nevertheless."

"In what way?" I ask, truly surprised. "My husband called it a masterpiece."

"And you? What did you think of it?"

"I stood in front of it and cried. Everyone said it was because I was with child. With my Camilla. That wasn't why, though." I remember the painting clearly; it hurt that much. An ache comes to me even at this distance in time. "Christ is located beyond anger—calm as flat water. Not at all shining in wrath like you said he would be, but oh so much more heartrending for lack of it. And you can see the agitation in everyone else. You know they sense the torment ahead. It's nearly unbearable."

"Thank you, Mona Lisa. But it is also a mistake. My experiment with oil on dry plaster failed. By the time the Duke was driven out by the French, pieces were already flaking away from it, and I'd finished it only two years before. It will be completely gone by the time I die."

What really remains of any of us here on earth after we die? But I don't say that. Leonardo wants to live on forever through his work. He can't recognize how transient we are, how trivial. Were I to broach the topic, I might even harm his art. I wouldn't do that. Besides, I don't believe it: Leonardo has never belonged to just one time. My dear Francesco is right; Leonardo da Vinci is a master, even if perfidious.

"I looked for you," I say mildly. "But you happened to be out of the city, just when I was visiting."

"A pity."

"Then I was told you came back to Florence."

"You didn't come to find me in Florence, though?"

I had already decided never to enter the city again. Not after the reign and ruin of Savonarola. But I don't want to talk about that. "I heard that you divided your time between Florence and Rome, and that you were working for Cesare Borgia."

"I didn't work for Borgia until last year."

"He's a horrible man," I say, working to keep my tone level.

"I'm the first to agree. He has his enemies strangled or burned or cut to pieces. Whatever you have heard is wrong—he's far worse. He has an utter want of scruples. And on top of it, he's a morose bore."

"Yet you worked for him."

"As chief architect and engineer, on the fortresses in the central papal states. It wasn't a friendship. And I didn't do anything underhanded for him."

I won't back down. "He's an enemy to the Orsini family. Alfonsina's family."

"I don't work for him anymore. I am here in Florence."

He cannot placate me so easily. "An enemy of the Orsini family is an enemy of the Medici family. Have you no sense of loyalty?"

"Loyalty? I value nothing more highly. But not loyalty to man or God. I am loyal to truth. To science."

"You can rationalize all you want. But what you did was indefensible—for it hurt people you were supposed to be friends with. Alfonsina and Piero and their children have taken refuge with their Orsini relatives in Rome."

"As has Giuliano," says Leonardo.

A small cry bursts from my chest. I didn't mean it to. It's been so long. How can feelings last this long? All those years of never speaking, never hearing his name—they acted to seal me off, a kind of magic banishing. I was here, but I was gone. Now Leonardo has just spoken his name. The spell is broken. I do not want to talk of anything else now. Nothing else matters. Where do I begin?

And, no. No, no. The desire to ask, to know every detail of Giuliano's life, descriptions of his person, of how he spends his day, what his room looks like, what he talks about—that desire has no place in my present life. I am the third wife of Francesco di Bartolomeo di Zanobi del Giocondo. I am stepmother to Bartolomeo and mother to Piero, Camilla, and Andrea. The love that binds me to all of them, while so different from the passion of my youth, is essential. I will not be drawn off the true path. I will not even stumble. Loyalty. Not in the airy sense of Leonardo, but in the solid sense of Giuliano. It's his banner, after all. Loyalty.

I blow out the candles and stand. The very end of daylight comes weakly through the window. "What is your work now?" I ask.

"That's why I'm here. Come with me to Florence tomorrow. I'll show you."

"I'm busy."

"Out here in the country? What could keep you busy?"

I give a small laugh. Only city folk could say such a thing. And only a childless man. I could quote Plato to him; I could speak about how a strong family is the foundation of society, about the essential job of mothers. But I don't want to lean on others' words. All I say is, "I have children and a friend to care for here in this villa."

"And money enough to hire help to take your place for just two days."

My fingers run along the warm gold of the candelabra. Florence. The city has become like a creature to me. A living, breathing beast. Could I face the beast again? Over the twenty-four years of my lifetime, I saw the streets of Florence change drastically. When Lorenzo Il Magnifico was in charge, business flourished. Why, there must have been over a thousand shops in central Florence alone. Festivals lasted days, and people were sincerely happy, dancing and feasting and marveling at the tournaments. Then, in the brief two years that Piero was in charge, the finances of the city crumbled. Gangs terrorized passersby. Resentment at Piero's profligate ways turned into fury. So it was easy for Savonarola to take over. And inevitable that people who had known such extravagance would chafe under his rule and eventually destroy him. That's what has stayed with me these last few years—the deplorable end of that deplorable monk.

But now another image comes to mind: the east doors of the baptistery, and that head that protrudes from one of the smaller panels that frames the door, the head of the sculptor Ghiberti himself. His pate is shinier than the rest of the door, because everyone rubs their hand on it. My very earliest memory of the city is being in Papà's arms and rubbing that head. The other figures in the frame are from the Old Testament. It dawns on me now—the sculptor counted himself as equal to such heroes. That very act, that is Florence; that is the heartbeat of the city—art glorified to the point of being sacred, the artist as close to God. And I understand it now—Savonarola made us all understand it: without art the spirit withers.

Every corner of that city holds art. It is, even after everything that has happened, a glorious city. My eyes grow heavy. I'm fighting tears.

"Please." Leonardo's voice intrudes in its solidity. And it surprises me, for it holds a promise, though I cannot fathom what it might be.

"A woman traveling with a man, even a mother of four, is not above rumors."

He smiles. "A woman traveling with me would be cause for confusion among the rumor mongers." I blink in incomprehension. "Dearest Mona Lisa," he says gently, "I'm not known for fancying women."

"Oh." I flush. "Forgive my embarrassment. It is not for your behavior, but for my own isolation, which has necessitated your words."

"Will you accompany me then?"

There is a trustworthy woman I have called upon before. She could come to help Silvia and care for Camilla. And we still have a home in Florence, though only Francesco uses it. If Leonardo were in any way disagreeable, I could retreat immediately and then return the next day to this villa. "I'd have to bring baby Andrea."

"Agreed."

Late afternoon of the next day we arrive in Florence. I have been battling my misgivings the whole trip. What a fool I am. But now we are finally here; it is too late to turn back.

Andrea sits on my lap and looks out the coach window. Both my hands circle his middle. I hold on to him as desperately as a drowning wretch to one of Leonardo's floating rings. Yet the streets are oddly normal. Ordinary. People walk and talk. Commerce moves continually. Children kick balls. Cats skitter out of the way. I can almost believe Florence is a home of reason again. Perhaps coming here is not a mistake.

The coach stops. Leonardo gets out. He stands with his hand to me. I alight, Andrea on my hip. Near the corner of a building a young man talks with a young woman. He touches above his upper lip hesitantly. And memories flood.

The story of Savonarola exposes the corruption in everyone's heart. But it is not that aspect of it that has kept me out of Florence. Giuliano had called Savonarola self-righteous. He had talked of the tyranny of piety. His words were prophetic. Oh, yes, what has kept me out of Florence is the anguish of knowing how right Giuliano was about it all. How deeply decent he is. How much I lost when he left.

But I am different now. I can do this. It is important that I be able to do this. I accompany Leonardo into the quiet stone halls of the Santissima Annunziata.

CHAPTER Twenty-five

THE MONASTERY is a perfect place for me," says Leonardo. "It's close to the hospital of Santa Maria Nuova. I go there to dissect cadavers for my anatomy studies."

"Yes," I say vaguely.

"And the library has a collection of over five thousand codices."

"I know. I used to visit it often. My husband's family owns a chapel here."

"Yes, of course. I knew that. My father and your husband's father were friends for many years. Our city homes were practically around the corner from each other."

We go along a corridor to a staircase. I've never been in this section of the monastery, so I've never seen this particular staircase before. It's beautifully carved.

"The work of Michelozzo di Bartolomeo," says Leonardo, following my eyes. "A fine sculptor and architect in his day."

We ascend and my nose is assailed. I hold my hand in front of Andrea's face like a mask, but he pushes it away.

"Oil paints," says Leonardo. "The smell takes some getting used to."

He is attentive to me in an almost alarming way. Do I dare give him any more clues as to what is going on in my head?

"The monastic order of the Servants of Maria has set aside

rooms for rent," says Leonardo as we reach the top of the stairs. "These are all mine."

Three rooms burst with artwork in various stages of completion. One table holds drawings of birds in flight. There's that attention to the inner workings of the body. It's so obvious to me after Giuliano's words years ago. But what fascinates me most is that some of the drawings have words down the side, across the bottom, everywhere, in the strangest writing. I look closely. "You pen backward—from right to left."

"Shall I lend you a mirror to read it?"

I give a small laugh. "Why do you do that?"

He holds up his left hand and writes in the air. "The ink doesn't smudge that way. Unfortunately, most people have trouble deciphering. So for others, I write left to right."

I turn back to the drawings. "And you spell funny."

"Abbreviations. I know what they all mean."

"Some of these aren't abbreviations. They're just peculiar spellings."

"All right, you've caught me. I have a little trouble with orthography."

Remarkable. "I have some drawings by you, you know. A dragonfly, a dog, a goat, and a flying boat."

"So you kept them? Good."

"Not all. There was a horse, too. I gave it to Silvia." I don't tell him the drawings are still in my wedding chest, along with the secret presents Mamma put in. I will pass it all to my daughter, Camilla, when she marries. And I will have it painted for her with whatever scene she wants. Maybe I'll even ask Leonardo to do it, since that's what Giuliano had wanted once upon a time. But what a stupid thought. Leonardo will be dead by then. Or, if not, he'll be feeble.

Leonardo nods. "I've designed a much better flying machine now."

I go from easel to easel. "That's the Virgin. And little Jesus, around my Andrea's age." The baby is playing with a lamb. Andrea reaches out to touch it and I step back just in time to keep his hand from disturbing anything. A woman leans across Maria's lap, and the faces of all four—Maria, the unknown woman, Jesus, and the lamb—line up in a diagonal, two faces looking down, two looking up. The composition is perfect. The love in the faces massages my heart. I could be that mother; Caterina could be that unknown woman; Andrea could be that baby. "Who is the other woman?"

"Sant'Anna."

Should I be embarrassed not to have recognized her? Her red robe and green mantle should have given her away. And I was right to think of it as I did—for Santa Anna was Maria's mother. I walk to the next easel. Here's the Virgin and Jesus again. She's got a spindle and Jesus is playing with it. "Spinning. That's a theme I know well."

"I wish you'd served as my model for it."

I let that comment pass. Flattery means nothing to me.

The walls have quickly done froscoes—experiments with different methods, I would guess. And here the walls are covered with scribbled studies of animals. Birds again. Caterina would love to see this wall. "Your head must be full of birds."

"My head is full of everything."

An immodest, if true, remark. The next easel holds something I don't take to. The one after that is equally unmoving. Now there's a whole series of paintings I don't like. "The styles aren't uniform," I say, using a diplomacy motherhood has taught me.

"Most of these are by my pupils."

I laugh. This man really does think the world of himself.

One easel stands apart from the others. It's empty. But leaning against it on the floor is a poplar wood panel, about as tall as my leg is long. "A new project?"

"Exactly. Come." Leonardo leads me to a larger room that clearly serves as his bedroom. I stand in the doorway, unwilling to enter. "Please." He walks across the room and opens the door to an adjoining room that is not accessible from the central corridor.

What's the point in not seeing what he has to show me? I kiss the very top of Andrea's head for a boost of boldness. I cross the room and enter a smaller space full of wheels and gadgets and things I do not recognize and want to look at more closely when I come face to face with Giuliano. I sit. Right there on the floor, with Andrea in my arms. I don't know if I could have remained on my feet, but I wasn't willing to risk it. My bones seem to have turned to water. Andrea crawls away from me and picks up a wheel.

Giuliano is tall. It's as though someone took both ends of him and pulled. His neck is lengthened. Even his face seems longer. His mustache and beard are trimmed, but thick. His clothing hangs loose and floppy, but I can tell he is thin, though broad across the shoulders.

"Did you get my letter?" he asks.

I am burning it again in my head. "It came on Christmas Eve, like an unwanted present, an unbirth, if you will. You gave up on us quickly, don't you think?"

"It hasn't been the kind of life I wanted to give you."

"I didn't ask for any particular kind of life."

"It hasn't been the kind of life you deserved."

"Passionate love. A rare thing in this world. Did I not deserve that?"

He looks stricken.

Against my will, my heart goes out to him. What does it matter after all this time, anyway? And my life is filled with so many kinds of love. I look at Andrea and I know I wouldn't undo these last nine years even if I could.

Giuliano sits and closes me in his arms. At first I don't know what he's doing, why he's doing it. But then I feel the hot tears from my own eyes drop on my chest. I'm crying, and I didn't even know it. I'm sobbing. And he's rocking me, like a small child.

It is Andrea's tears that bring me to my senses. He's such a funny child. Whenever anyone else cries, he cries, too. Overly empathetic. Perhaps he won't be the even-keeled man his father is. No, I think he'll be an artist. Or a poet. I ease Giuliano away and take Andrea into my arms. I smother him with kisses, till he laughs. Then I wipe his face and mine with the hem of my skirt. And I look straight into Giuliano's black eyes. "So how have you been?"

Giuliano looks startled. Then he laughs. "Are we to try to have an ordinary conversation at this late point?"

I'm laughing, too. "Piero once said you think of laughing and naught else."

"He was wrong. But you do make me laugh. I'm grateful."

"I married a man named Giocondo—'jocular.' It should have been your name instead." I shake my head and start over. "You look well."

"And your beauty is abiding."

My beauty. My matronly beauty. But he's serious. To him I am still beautiful. I smile. "Tell me all about yourself."

"I will. But first—" Giuliano beckons to Leonardo, who's been standing nearby the whole time.

That artist witnessed our private encounter!

"That's it," says Giuliano. "That's the smile I want you to paint. The most beautiful smile in the world. Paint it so that no matter where I stand, she's smiling at me."

CHAPTER *Twenty-six*

IT TAKES FOUR YEARS, this painting. It starts with drawings. To me it feels like thousands of drawings. And then the sittings. I sit, while Leonardo just looks. I sit in morning light, in daylight, in moonlight. I sit in summer light, autumn light, winter light, spring light. And then the cycle of seasons all over again. And again. And again.

I agree to all this not for Giuliano's sake. No. Giuliano left me. And, no matter the reason for his act, my present life will not bend to his desires. I agree because Leonardo tells me he's been waiting to paint my portrait, waiting since that day at Lorenzo de' Medici's funeral, before my thirteenth birthday, waiting for me to be ready. He says he needs to do this. How he became seized with this idea, how he has decided I am now ready—these things I don't understand. But he is fierce in his declaration, and I am seduced. He has appealed to a vanity that runs deep: I could be important to the artistry of this incredible mind. I could persist in Leonardo's painting.

And so, I sit. With my hair down. Leonardo won't allow a headdress. Nor even a ribbon. He says he wants nothing to distract people from my face.

On and on I sit. Placid and resolute.

Thank the Lord for my children. Without their demands, Leonardo would have me in his studio for hours at a time.

Instead, I can come only briefly. But I come often. A couple of times a month. Year after year.

He never asks my opinion. But he always has me look at what he's done when we finish a session. And he studies my eyes to see what parts of the painting they linger on. He studies my lips, the setting of my jaw. He reads my face to discover my opinion.

It's just as well. I have never felt entirely comfortable talking about art. Not like Francesco and my stepmother. Let Leonardo glean my reactions in his own way.

Besides, I wouldn't want him to know exactly what I think. He is making a background from spinning together my answers to his questions about my childhood. But the image my words have created in his head, the image that he has painted on this poplar panel, has little to do with Villa Vignamaggio and the countryside around there. I would have preferred a familiar field with the hills I love beyond it.

No one knows Leonardo works on my portrait except Francesco and Silvia—he, because he needs to know in order not to have false worries, and she, because I need to tell her. No one asks what I do when I come to the monastery. If we do cause confusion among the rumormongers, I never hear of it. Leonardo seems beyond suspicion; besides, he stays busy with so many projects. And I am an unimpeachable mother. And, apparently, a particularly pious one, a regular visitor to the monastery chapels.

Many things change in these four years. Italy is besieged with wars. Milan and Venice and Ferrara and Naples and Lord only knows where else. On top of that, the bellicose French have caused more misery than all the Italian states put together.

The Republic of Florence has somehow managed not to be attacked, but more by luck than anything else. The government may be responsive to the will of the populace, but it is nonetheless inefficient and equivocal. It has been criticized openly by the rather haughty political thinker, the secretary of the government's inner circle, Niccolò Machiavelli. The only good thing that has happened is that Pisa is once more under Florentine control.

Oddly enough, though, the city of Florence is growing ever more beautiful. The artists whose work was so stunted during the reign of Savonarola have emerged again in full glory. But why should I be surprised? Ashes make fertile ground. Michelangelo's enormous statue of David, entirely stunning in his nude beauty, was completed in 1504. It stands in the piazza in front of the Palazzo Vecchio. I imagine Savonarola turning over in his grave every time an admiring eye falls on it.

Fra Bartolomeo has been working on a giant painting of the Virgin appearing to San Bernardo. It should be completed soon. And a new artist from Urbino, called Raffaello, has come to study with Leonardo. Leonardo likes to show me his drawings— he believes the young man has promise.

It's a torrent of art. And I'm part of it, whether anyone knows or not. Leonardo says I will be his best portrait, for he has studied me the same way he studies animals. From the inside out. He knows my loves: my passions and my solaces. He says I am the soul of the Republic—countryside and city all in one—and he will give the world that soul, in my portrait.

I don't respond to that kind of talk. The abstraction of it leaves me floating like the smallest dust mote. I know he believes it sincerely—I remember how he spoke to me at Lorenzo de' Medici's funeral, how he called me a scintillating point of light. But in a sense, I think he may be fooling himself. This portrait may be more about him than it is about me. For he is melancholy, unfulfilled. Despite his talk about being loyal to science, he is more like the rest of us than he will ever admit; he, too, has been helpless in the face of the powers that be.

But because Leonardo believes what he says, I have forgiven him the indiscretion of not leaving the room when Giuliano and I were together.

Today I climb the monastery stairs laboriously. My pregnancy slows me down. My thoughts are heavy, too. Lately I have dreamed of Giuliano.

Piero de' Medici joined the French army the winter after I last saw Giuliano, when Leonardo started my portrait. He was on a boat with French troops bound for a battle in Naples. It was overloaded, and it sank. He drowned in the Garigliano River, and was buried near there, at Montecassino in his brother Cardinal Giovanni's abbey.

I don't know how Giuliano took the news. I have received no communication from him since our meeting in this monastery in the presence of Leonardo. But I can imagine his grief.

As for Cardinal Giovanni, people say he lives a modest life for a Medici. He is consistently cheerful and reliably practical. He has managed to win the favor of important clergy. They say someday he'll be pope. I don't doubt it.

Of Giuliano I know nothing new. But I count on him to be who he has always been.

The fool, the wise one, and the good one.

Their father was right. Giuliano is good—the best of the three. Someday he will come back to Florence in victory. For if I am the Republic's soul, he is the Republic's will. Giuliano is destined to lead. Anything less would be a travesty.

I arrive at the top of the stairs and Leonardo greets me. He takes my hand and guides me to the studio where we work. But his paints are not scattered all over like usual. The room is clean. The only thing in it is the easel, with my painting.

"It's complete," he says. A declaration.

He told me it would be finished the next time I came, but I'm taken by surprise anyway. There have been so many times when I thought it was complete. But at the last moment he insisted on changing a fold of cloth here, a shaft of light there. Somehow I'd come to believe it would never end.

I'm almost sad.

"Do you see it?" asks Leonardo, rubbing his palms together.

I see what I have always seen on that panel.

"Look in the eyes. Giuliano wanted the portrait to smile at him, no matter where he stood. I made that happen through the eyes. They observe whoever passes. They see the truth. They are constant. This is my gift to him. To you." He shrugs. "Maybe even to myself."

And I no longer see anything for the blur of tears.

"What shall I call it?" He walks around behind me and looks at the painting from a distance. "Monna Lisa? Or La Gioconda?"

The first name came to me from Giuliano. The second name came via my marriage. Which is the woman in the painting? "Neither."

"What? Have you got a better name for it?"

I shake my head. "Don't put a name on it."

Leonardo seems taken aback. But then he nods. "As you wish. It's your choice."

A woman's choices are limited.

The baby inside me kicks. My child, my choice. Gratitude floods me.

I smile.

MANY BOOKS in both English and Italian, as well as muse-
ums in Italy, give reliable information on the time period of this
novel, from the fauna and flora (including the remarkable assem-
blage in nobles' gardens) to historical matters of politics, religion,
and culture. I have drawn on them for details about the death
of Lorenzo de' Medici, the developments leading to the exile of
Piero de' Medici, and the rise and fall of Girolamo Savonarola.

Likewise, much has been written about the painting by
Leonardo da Vinci known as *Mona Lisa* in America and as *La
Gioconda* in Italy. With regard to this material, however, there
are many points of confusion and ignorance. The books I con-
sulted disagree on the identity of the woman in the portrait and
disagree, as well, on things as basic as dates of birth and death of
less famous and/or more peripheral members of the Medici family and who did what when.

These confusions are understandable.

Leonardo did not sign, date, or title this famous portrait.

And many people in the nobility of Florence had the same first
name and same last name. If your brother died, you might well
name your next son after him. Boys were typically named after
grandfathers, so cousins wound up with the same names. It isn't
easy keeping track.

While I have done my best to untangle the information I

found, and while I have held true to undisputed historical data, I have looked at controversial points as offering freedom to make those choices that would move my tale in interesting directions. I have also taken liberties with shaping personal lives, always with an eye toward what was possible, and sometimes statistically probable, for the society as a whole.

Over and over, I returned to the portrait itself. Like the Leonardo of this story, I tried to glean information from the mysterious woman's eyes and her jawline and, most of all, her smile.